The Seventh Covenant

The Seventh Covenant

J. P. HANNAH

RESOURCE *Publications* · Eugene, Oregon

THE SEVENTH COVENANT

Resource Publications
An Imprint of Wipf and Stock Publishers
199 W. 8th Ave., Suite 3
Eugene, OR 97401

www.wipfandstock.com

PAPERBACK ISBN: 978-1-7252-9614-5
HARDCOVER ISBN: 978-1-7252-9615-2
EBOOK ISBN: 978-1-7252-9616-9

04/06/21

The spoken words of New Testament figures are based largely on the World English Bible (Public Domain).

Old Testament quotations (given in italics) are taken from the World English Bible (Public Domain) and New King James Version®. Copyright © 1982 by Thomas Nelson. Used by permission. All rights reserved.

Scripture quotations marked (RSV) are from the Revised Standard Version of the Bible, copyright © 1946, 1952, and 1971 the Division of Christian Education of the National Council of the Churches of Christ in the United States of America. Used by permission. All rights reserved.

Translations of Midrash Psalms are from https://www.matsati.com/index.php/midrash-tehillim/ with kind permission of the website creator. (Thank you, Duane!)

Babylonian Talmud quotations are from the translation by William Davidson.

Extracts from Josephus's *Antiquities of the Jews* (abbreviated as *Antiquities*) and *War of the Jews* are from the translations by William Whiston (Public Domain), courtesy of https://www.sacred-texts.com/.

Contents

Preface

THIS BOOK INVITES THE reader to plunge into Jesus's world, hear his teachings afresh, bask in his compassionate love, weep at his crucifixion, exalt in his resurrection as the conqueror of death, and celebrate his promised return, revealed to the Apostle John in the last vision of Judeo-Christian Scripture.

This scripture-based narrative was born from an earlier research project. As an agnostic mathematics lecturer with a passionate interest in the human condition, I spent many years investigating science and faith. This included exploration into quantum physics, cosmology, relativity theory, existentialism, idealism, Darwinism, theosophy, Buddhism, Islam, Hinduism, and various forms of mysticism. I initially ignored Christianity as an implausible story but finally decided that to be truly objective, I should at least develop an understanding of this teaching. So while negotiating traffic on the way to university, I listened skeptically to New Testament recordings.

I had deliberately set out to identify flaws in the Christian message, but the result was totally unexpected. I instead heard a consistent voice of authority and wisdom that was strikingly different from anything I had encountered. The outcome of that journey was my baptism into Christianity and the publication of my collected evidence in *A Skeptic's Investigation into Jesus* (Wipf and Stock).

But my research into Jewish life in first-century Palestine sparked a desire to write a faith-based account of the redeeming work of Jesus Christ, and this book is the result. I have found it inspiring to weave a narrative around the familiar gospel accounts, depicting what it might have been like to walk through Judea, Galilee, and Samaria with Jesus, listen to him teach on the Temple Mount, witness his miraculous healings, watch his ardent debates with fellow Jews who rejected his claims, and learn how his words and acts fulfilled messianic predictions made by the prophets of Judaism.

The story is firmly based on the four canonical gospels with minimal adaptations, compressing Jesus's work into a year between two spring times, from his gathering of the twelve to his Passover resurrection. In the epilogue, the revelation vision given to the Apostle John depicts how Jesus's return will bring to fruition God's cosmic plan for the redemption of His creation. Endnotes provide interesting relevant information from historical, biblical, and rabbinic works, which is best read separately so as not to interrupt the flow of the narrative.

I sincerely hope this book provides to each reader what I gained in writing it: an uplifting and immersive experience of our Lord's presence and his reassuring promises.

Historical Note

THE FOLLOWING CHARACTERS ARE fictitious: Tribune Lucius Ocella and his officer Stolo, Rabbi Hilkiah, his niece Rachel, and his students Daniel and Benjamin. The underground resistance movement led by Benjamin's brother Caleb is also a fictional device, based on historical reports of messianic uprisings around the turn of the era. The involvement in this plot of Jesus's disciples Judas Iscariot and Simon Zealotes is not taken from scripture but does suggest a motive for Judas's betrayal of Jesus.

The narrative also fleshes out other intriguing incidents in the Gospels. Why did Nathaniel declare that Jesus was the Son of God when the teacher said he saw him under a fig tree? After his miraculous catch of fish, why did Peter confess to being a sinful man? What was the basis of Pontius Pilate's offer to release a Jewish prisoner at Passover? This narrative provides possible explanations that are compatible with scripture.

Regarding personal names, the letter "J" was not in use at this time, so for example, Jesus would have been called Yeshua in Aramaic or Iēsous in Greek, and John would have been called Yochanan or Ioannes. But familiar anglicized names have been used here for ease of reading.

Some Hebrew/Aramaic Terms

Abba	Father
agunah	chained
am ha-aretz	people of the land
Baruch HaShem	Blessed be The Name
bar	son
bat	daughter
beth	house/place
Derech HaYam	Way of the Sea
El Elyon	Most High God
El Shaddai	Almighty God
goyim	non-Jewish nations
Hallelujah	Praise God
HaNotzri	the Nazorean
Hanukkah	Dedication
Hoshiana!	Save us now!
kohen	priest
Kohen HaGadol	the high priest
Maranatha!	Our Lord, come!
Pesach	Passover
Shalom/Shlama	Peace
Shavuot	Feast of Weeks/Pentecost
Sukkot	Feast of Booths/Tabernacles
Yom Kippur	Day of Atonement

Christological Significance of the Seven Judaic Feasts

THIS NARRATIVE ILLUSTRATES THE remarkable truth that Jesus's death, resurrection, and final return not only fulfil ancient prophecies and the promises of God but together provide a physical embodiment of the seven ancient feasts of Judaism.

	Feast	In the Old Testament	In relation to Jesus's work
Spring	Passover/ *Pesach* 14 Nisan	In Egypt, the blood of an unblemished lamb was daubed with hyssop on wooden doorposts to provide protection from death and liberation from slavery.	Jesus died on the cross. His blood sacrifice provides protection from God's wrath and liberation from our slavery to sin and guilt.
	Feast of Unleavened Bread 15–21 Nisan	Houses were purified by removing all leaven, a symbol of impurity.	Faith in Jesus provides purification and sanctification.
	Firstfruits First Sunday after Passover	One sheaf of the first spring bounty was waved before God as a promise of the coming harvest.	On this day, Jesus rose from death as the firstfruits of the future harvest for God.

	Feast	In the Old Testament	In relation to Jesus's work
Summer	Pentecost/ *Shavuot* Fifty days after Firstfruits	This greater summer harvest was celebrated using two wave loaves that were baked with leaven.	On this day, God's Holy Spirit fell upon the disciples and the great harvest of the church began, which came to include Gentiles.
Autumn	Day of Trumpets/ *Yom Teruah* 1 Tishri	Trumpets represented the presence and power of God.	Trumpets will announce Jesus's triumphant return.
	Day of Atonement/ *Yom Kippur* 10 Tishri	On this day of repentance and reconciliation, one goat was sacrificed and a scapegoat bore away the sins of the people.	Jesus's death fulfilled the roles of both ritual goats, and his return will usher in atonement and redemption.
	Tabernacles/ *Sukkot*/ Feast of Ingathering 15–21 Tishri	During this last feast of the year, God's people lived in *sukkot* (booths) to recall their dependence upon Him. The seventh day was the day of Great Salvation, and the eighth day of assembly represented a new beginning.	Jesus's promised return will inaugurate the final ingathering of God's people. There will be a pouring out of God's Spirit and all nations will dwell with Him. It will be the beginning of a new creation.

Maps and Images

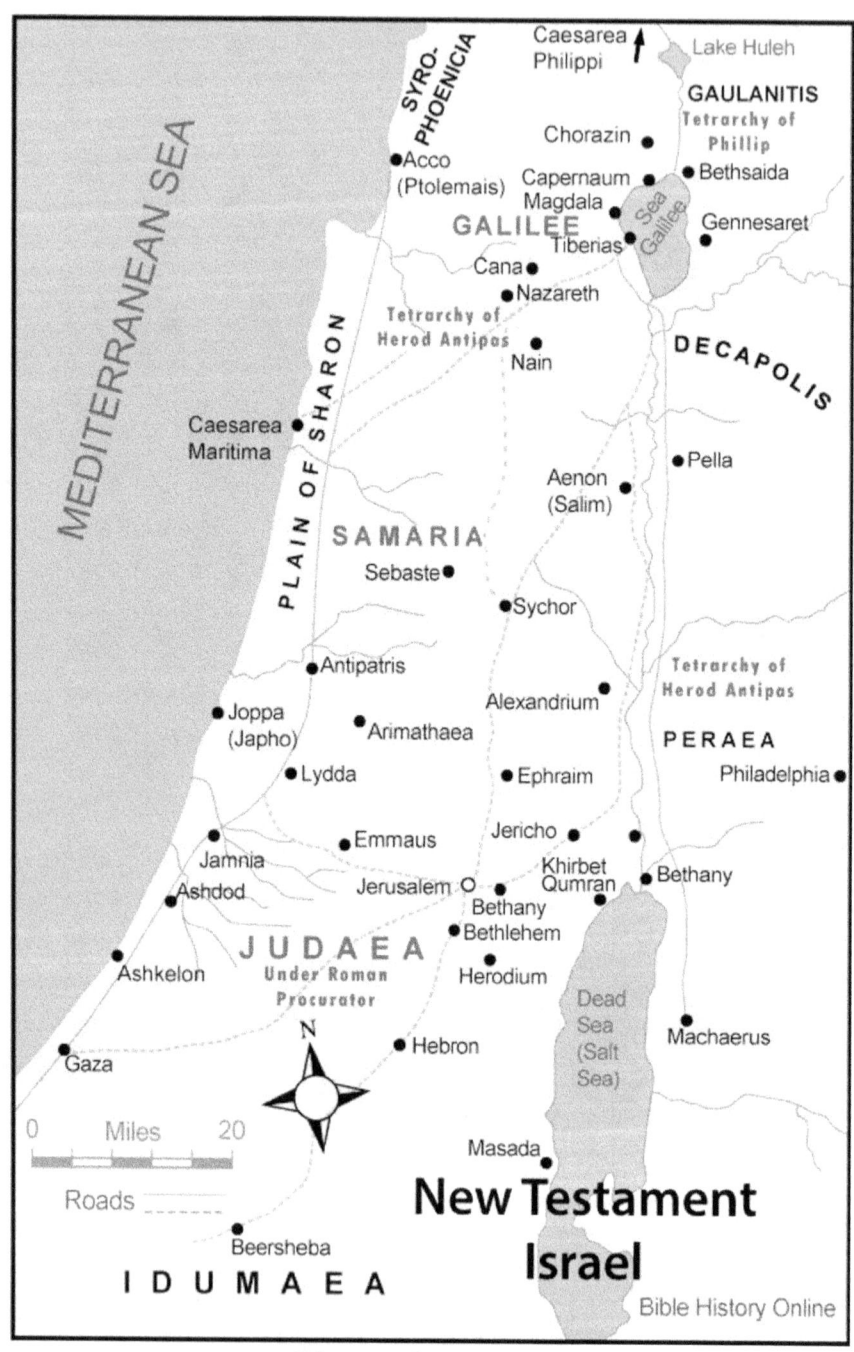

Palestine in the time of Jesus.
Image courtesy of bible-history.com.

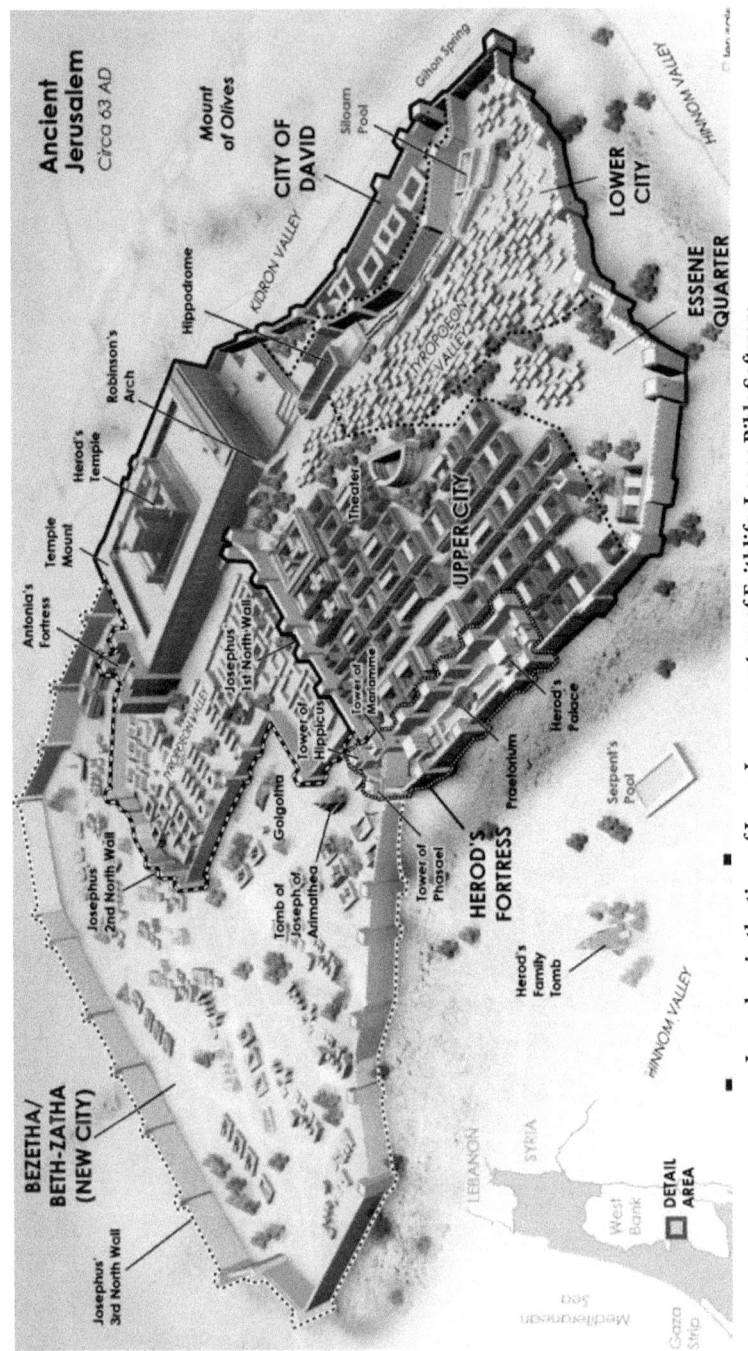

Jerusalem in the time of Jesus. Image courtesy of Faithlife, Logos Bible Software.

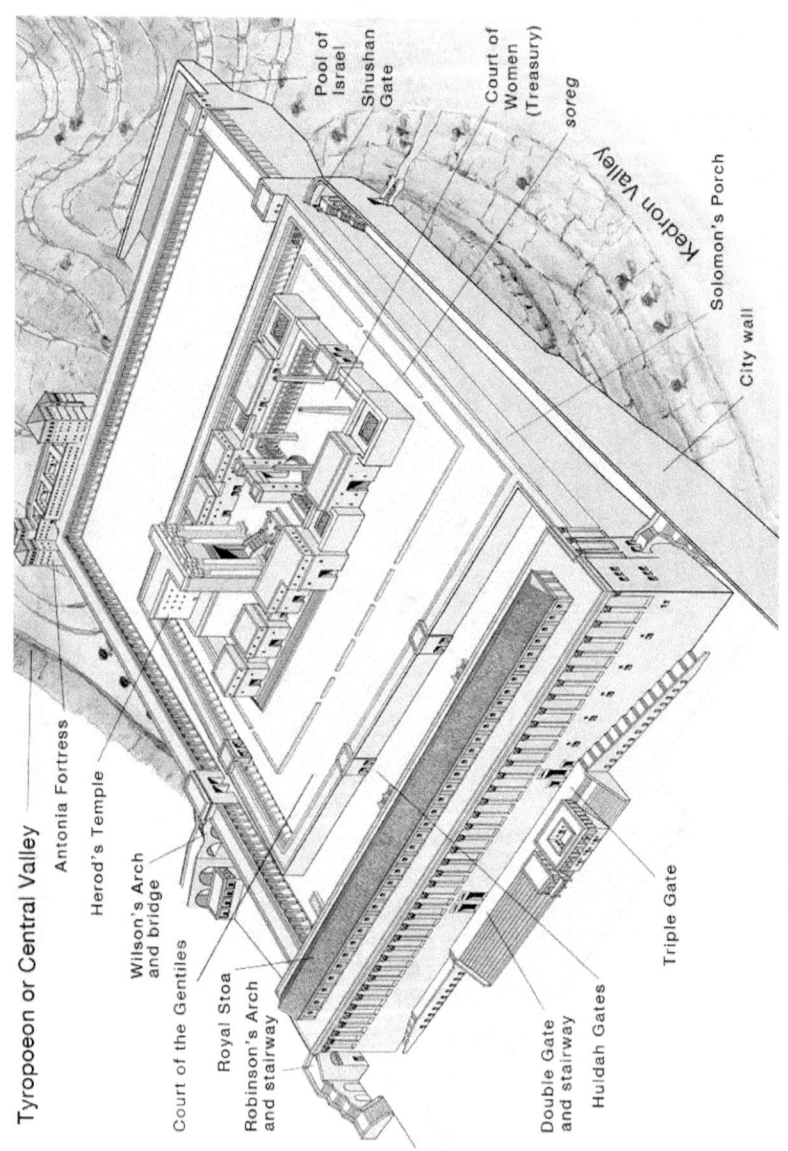

Tyropoeon or Central Valley

Antonia Fortress

Herod's Temple

Wilson's Arch
and bridge

Court of the Gentiles

Royal Stoa

Robinson's Arch
and stairway

Double Gate
and stairway

Huldah Gates

Triple Gate

Pool of
Israel

Shushan
Gate

Court of
Women
(Treasury)

soreg

Kedron Valley

Solomon's Porch

City wall

Herod's Temple. Image courtesy of Ritmeyer Archaeological Design.

Prologue

THE BLOOD-ORANGE SUN SWELLED over the horizon, daubing red and purple streaks across the canvas of sky as cool light spilled into the Jezreel Valley—the great battle-field of Israel. Tints of yellow and green started to appear among the dark foliage and the air gradually filled with bird-song and the fluttering of wings.

The growing brightness outlined an isolated figure on Mount Tabor, hands uplifted as he poured out prayer and praise to the One God. Then the man dropped his arms and surveyed the world that stretched around him, looking northeast to the snow-capped masses of Mount Hermon, west across the rich plains to Mount Carmel, and south to the highlands of Samaria. Below him, caravans were already making slow progress along *Derech HaYam*, the trade route known as the Way of the Sea that led to Damascus in one direction and along the sea coast to Egypt in the other. Any news that arose here in Galilee would be carried far beyond Palestine.

Camel drivers called out, their harsh cries resounding against flinty rocks as the man turned, pulled a shawl over his head, and started his descent toward the sleepy village of Nazareth. He must now be about his Father's business. And the world would be forever changed.

1

The Spirit of the Lord
Shall Rest upon Him

"HEAR THIS PROPHECY, RACHEL, and scribe it for me."

Rachel's mouth curved in a fond smile as her uncle stood even straighter and raised his trembling hands dramatically toward the low roof as he intoned memorized scripture:

> *In the former time, God brought into contempt the land of Zebulun and the land of Naphtali; but in the latter time, He has made it glorious, by the way of the sea, beyond the Jordan, Galilee of the nations!*

The deep voice reverberated off stark, whitewashed walls and Rachel's reed pen scratched laboriously across coarse papyrus, meticulously scribing the Hebrew letters from right to left as she took care to avoid smudging the dark ink. The aged Rabbi Hilkiah dropped his arms and adjusted his prayer shawl as he adopted a quieter tone.

"The ancient tribal lands of Jacob's sons Zebulun and Naphtali lay within Galilee to the north of us. Do you remember why these lands will be made glorious, Rachel? How does the prophecy continue?"

Rachel frowned briefly in concentration then answered confidently, "Isaiah wrote about a promised child." Her melodious voice quoted the well-known verses in a soothing rhythm:

> *The people who walked in darkness have seen a great light. For a child is born to us. A son is given to us, and the government will be on his shoulders. His name will be called*

Pele Jooz El-Gibbor-Ahi-Ad-Sar-Shalom: Wonderful, Counselor, Mighty God, Eternal Father, Prince of Peace.[1]

"Quite right, my little scholar!" Hilkiah dipped his head in approval. "Write it clearly. We know that Isaiah laid down this prophecy many hundreds of years ago, and he taught that this child who will bring a great light to Galilee will also be known as *Immanuel*—'God with us.'"

Drifting dust motes glinted in the shaft of light that streamed through the open shutters of the one small window. But despite the bright beam, Hilkiah's weak eyes could only make out a vague form as Rachel bent diligently over her scribing work, seated on the floor at the low wooden table. He blinked in concentration, using fond memory to fill in the details of the blurred figure of his niece. Smooth cheeks sloped down to a small pointed chin and two prominent top teeth. A vertical pucker sat permanently between strong eyebrows, sometimes deepening in a warning that could prompt even the revered rabbi to hastily retract his words. And the almond shape of Rachel's clear brown eyes illustrated perfectly the traditional connection between *shaqed,* the almond tree that blooms early in spring, and *shaqad,* meaning watchful and ready. Straying from his train of thought, the rabbi pondered over the association of almond, eye, and readiness as he murmured a verse from the prophet Jeremiah:

> *The word of the Lord came to me, saying, "Jeremiah, what do you see?" I said, "I see a branch of an almond tree." Then the Lord said to me, "You have seen well; for I watch over my word to perform it."*

Grey hairs trembled as Hilkiah closed his eyes and shook his head slightly in contemplation. "Aron's staff miraculously sprouted almond buds," he muttered. "And God instructed Moses to use an almond flower design for the Tabernacle lampstand, whose light signified God's faithful watching and the need for His people to remain alert . . . vigilant . . . ready . . ."

Rachel's hand hovered over the papyrus roll as she looked up quizzically.

"Abba?" she queried gently.

"Hmm?"

"We were at 'Immanuel.'"

"Ah, yes, yes, of course. 'God with us.' Now, let us see . . ."

Rachel waited patiently, long used to the abrupt turns and detours that were part of her beloved uncle's work. Hilkiah rose stiffly from the stone bench built into the wall, deep enough to hold his padded sleeping mat that was now rolled to one side. He shuffled slowly around the small room, collecting his thoughts. In recent years, there had been an upsurge of anticipation that the time was fast approaching when God would finally send forth the promised Messiah, His Anointed One who would . . . well there were many suggestions about what changes this significant figure might bring. Homes and inns throughout Palestine were humming with speculation about liberation from the Gentiles, healing for Israel, and a time of peace. The rabbi again felt the insistent pressure that had been building within him and which only eased when he dictated his thoughts, reaching into his sharp memory for the most relevant verses.

"You see, Rachel, the prophet Isaiah predicted the coming of the Messiah who will implement God's plan for His creation." Hilkiah stared up vaguely at the low roof and Rachel continued scribing as he resumed his quoting of scripture:

> *The Spirit of the Lord shall rest upon Him, the Spirit of wisdom and understanding, the Spirit of counsel and might. But with righteousness He shall judge the poor, and decide with equity for the meek of the earth. For the Gentiles shall seek Him, and His resting place shall be glorious.*[2]

Leaning heavily upon his staff, Hilkiah settled again on the bench, nodding confidently. "Yes. Yes. We are told that even the Gentiles will seek God's Messiah, Rachel. And the Spirit of the Lord will rest upon him! But when will this be? Hmm? And how can we ensure that we will be ready when he comes?"

Silence swelled in the small room and Rachel's hand poised again in expectation. Then she raised her head as a three-fold blast of silver trumpets sounded from the Jerusalem Temple Mount and echoed stridently across the Tyropoeon valley. It was time for the morning sacrifice.

"Here he is!"

Reaching out a lean, dark arm, the Baptist called John pointed toward the river bank as sunlight struck sparks off the dancing waters of the River Jordan. Its placid edges mirrored the blue spring sky, and a profusion of oleanders reflected a rich crimson garden onto its surface. Further out, the well-known figure of the baptizer stood knee-deep in the flowing stream, a leather girdle hitched around his coarse camel-hair tunic. Those waiting to confess their sins and be baptized turned their heads to watch as a small group of men made their way slowly down to the river, following a path that wound between boulders and rustling thorn bushes. John's enthusiastic voice boomed out again.

"I am the voice of one crying in the wilderness, '*Make straight the way for the Lord!*' as Isaiah prophesied. I have told you that I baptize with water but one is coming whose sandals I am not worthy to loosen. He will baptize you with the Holy Spirit and with fire!"

John had recently reported in great excitement that he had seen the Holy Spirit descend upon his cousin Jesus at his baptism,[3] which was a sign that the Nazarene was destined to baptize with God's Spirit. One of these approaching men must be he! Curious watchers peered through the shrubs that dotted the riverbank, their excited whispers intensifying as the strangers drew nearer with dust whipping around their sandaled feet.

Two of John the Baptist's disciples, Andrew and his friend also named John who had been helping with the purification ritual, clambered hastily from the water and pushed dripping through the crowd. Both had heard many inspiring speculations about the imminent arrival of the Messiah, and they continued to pray ardently for this event. They had been following the Baptist in the hopes that he was the Anointed One of God, but the teacher denied this and instead spoke of another who was to come. Could God's chosen implement of liberation really be coming toward them now? Hope made John's heart beat faster as he placed a hand on Andrew's shoulder and squinted earnestly against the bright sunlight. But no figure among the small band of newcomers seemed particularly impressive.

Then one of the approaching men lifted his head and looked directly at John with an intense gaze that seemed to swallow time and thought. A wordless illumination and certainty flooded him: the man standing before him was Jesus from Nazareth, and he, John, was completely known and unconditionally loved as he had never been before. John yielded to the glorious, liberating sensation, reveling in the deep joy that welled up powerfully within him.

Then light exploded behind his eyes and the Galilean teacher now appeared to have disheveled hair, cracked lips, and red-rimmed eyes. A sinister voice of temptation hissed in John's consciousness:

If you are the Son of God, turn this stone into bread!

Another voice, weary but firm, responded:

It is written: "Man shall not live on bread alone, but on every word that proceeds from the mouth of God."

Then in John's brightly lit mind, a naked couple faced each other in a lush garden, sharing bites of a ripe fruit while the same sibilant voice whispered seductively:

Eat . . . Eat . . . Then your eyes will be opened, and you will be like God, knowing good and evil!

The vision faded, and John again saw the lucid brown eyes before him, which seemed to pierce the very depths of his soul and share his thoughts as words rang clearly in his mind:

I am the living bread that came down from heaven. Whoever eats this bread will live forever.

An image of broken bread rose in John's consciousness as the two competing voices continued to echo:

Take, eat, this is my body . . .

Eat . . . Eat . . . Then you will be like God . . .

Suddenly, John felt a weight on his shoulder as he was spun around. "John! Are you all right? Don't you hear me?"

John stared blankly at Andrew's concerned frown. How could he explain what he had just experienced? He could not comprehend what had happened or what he now knew. Yet somehow, he knew that he knew it! Shaken by an overpowering impression of truth that was both profound and strangely elusive, John grabbed his friend's hand eagerly and turned his head as Jesus asked him gently, "Tell me, what do you seek?"

John hesitated. What *was* he seeking? He could not find adequate words to express his longing. But he felt irresistibly drawn to the Nazarene and blurted out an impulsive response.

"Lord, we would come with you wherever you are going!"

"Ah," Jesus replied cryptically, "but where am I going? Foxes have dens and birds have nests, but the Son of Man has no place to lay his head."[4]

John had no idea who the "son of man" might be, but he was certain that wherever Jesus went would be the place for him to lay his own head. He turned to say farewell to his former teacher, but the Baptist was already raising his hand and nodding in approval. His earlier words resounded in John's memory:

I am not the Messiah but I have been sent before him. The bride belongs to the bridegroom. But the friend of the bridegroom re-joices greatly when he hears the bridegroom's voice. This is my joy, and it is now complete.

Oblivious to Andrew's hand still clutched in his grasp, John pressed closer to the intriguing figure of Jesus who was slowly moving off, followed by curious men and women.

For the remainder of the day, the small group immersed themselves in the words of the teacher from Nazareth. They watched enthralled as his large, eloquent hands made expressive sweeps, cupped the air in emphasis, pointed to flowers and birds to illustrate his points, and most wonderful of all, touched each one of them: a hand on a shoulder or head as he passed, a firm clasp of hands between his, a child pulled gently onto his lap. Each gesture saying, *you are welcome, you are accepted just as you are—you are loved.* His teachings seemed to permeate not only their mind and spirit but even blood, sinew, and bone. John was entranced, challenged, reassured—finally home.

But not everyone shared this response. Scattered scowls and disapproving mutters were not noticed in the general mood of elation. And only one person in the group was aware of how menacing that antagonism was to become.

2

You Will See the Angels of God Ascending and Descending on the Son of Man

Then Manoah said to his wife, "We are doomed to die because we have seen God!"

WISPS OF STEAM ROSE from Hilkiah's honey-sweetened breakfast curds as they slowly cooled on the low table, barely touched in the rabbi's impatience to explore messianic promises. Shifting her position on the rush mat, Rachel dutifully finished scribing the dictated verse as her uncle explained eagerly.

"You see, Rachel, when the Angel of the Lord appeared before Manoah and his wife to promise the birth of Samson, they understood that they had been visited by God Himself! But how could this angelic figure be the very Presence of God? This must be important for us to understand . . ."

But Rachel's mind was not on scripture today. As Hilkiah mumbled to himself, she sighed and gazed longingly through the small window. It was her favorite month of Lyar, when the last rains of the season had generously sprinkled the land with blood-red poppies and clusters of pink almond blossoms. A secret promise seemed to hang heavily in the sweet air, and she longed to walk down the busy main road, past the Pool of Siloam, out through the Fountain Gate, and east across the Brook Kidron to wander among the peaceful groves that graced the Mount of Olives.

She knew the hillsides well and smiled fondly as she pictured the feathery canopies of silvery-green olive trees mingling with darker cypress, the huge fig trees writhing up out of rocky soil, and knotty palm stems reaching high up to tufts that waved in breezes laden with the scents of pomegranate and orange buds. A messianic prophecy sprang unbidden into Rachel's mind, and she murmured to herself, "*On that day, His feet will stand on Har HaZeitim, the Mount of Olives—*"

"And what did he say, Rachel? Rachel?"

She whipped her head round as her Abba urgently inquired again.

"When Manoah asked for his name, what did the Angel of the Lord say?"

"Uhm," Rachel quickly refocused her attention. "The Angel said, '*Why do you ask my name? For it is wonderful!*'"

"This is correct!" The rabbi beamed proudly. "Write it down, my little scribe. But why is this important, you may ask? How does this Angel link to our investigation into the Messiah? I will tell you. Remember, Isaiah prophesied that the Messiah will be called 'Wonderful.' *Wonderful*, Rachel! So what are we to understand about this Angel of the Lord whose name is also 'wonderful'? Hmm? Could the promised Messiah somehow be linked to the Lord's special Angel who was also His own Presence? What are we to make of these connections?"

Frowning in contemplation, Hilkiah wandered absently to the window with his hands clasped behind his back, but Rachel doubted that he noticed any of the beauty outside. And despite the lime tamped firmly onto the smooth floor of clay and ash, a fine dust in the air tickled her throat and made her stifle a cough. Sighing again, she dipped her pen into the clay inkpot and forced herself to concentrate as her Abba gestured with a knobbly finger in emphasis.

"And there is yet another significant nameless figure in the Torah, Rachel. This mysterious man wrestled in the night with the young patriarch Jacob, and like the Angel of the Lord, this stranger also refused to provide his name. But Jacob called the place *Peniel*—Face of God—because he knew that in this encounter he had seen God face to face! Here is another experience of God Himself, Rachel!"

Hilkiah shook his head in wonderment, pondering the significance of these events recorded in sacred scripture. And in spite of her reluctance, Rachel was intrigued by the discussion. "Abba," she said softly, laying down her pen, "didn't Father Jacob also dream he saw God at the top of a ladder that reached up to heaven? With angels ascending and descending on it?"

"He did, Rachel, he did! Jacob's ladder symbolizes the connection between heaven and earth, with God conveying His thoughts to us and receiving our prayers. Unlike pagan religions that build towers to ascend to their gods, we wait in faith for God to reach down to us. When Jacob awoke from his dream about this divine ladder, he set up a stone pillar and renamed the place *Beth-el*: House of God."

"But Abba . . ." Rachel said hesitantly, raising two fingers to her mouth in thought.

"Yes, my child?"

"I seem to recall that in a later dream, the Angel of the Lord appeared to Jacob and said, '*I am the God of Bethel, where you anointed the pillar.*'"[5]

"This is again correct!" Hilkiah rubbed his hands in excitement. "This mysterious, unnamed Angel claimed to be the very same God who appeared to Jacob in a dream!"

"Does this mean . . . Could it be . . . ?" The young woman's face fell into solemn lines as she grappled with the enormity of the implication.

"Yes, Rachel." Hilkiah walked slowly toward his niece and bent over slightly to lay both hands on her shoulders as he looked down intently. "According to scripture, the Angel of the Lord—*Malak YHWH*—was also Almighty God Himself!"

Rachel's eyes widened as her Abba straightened up, nodding gravely. "And this is not the only time this Angel is identified with God," he added. "God and the Angel both spoke to Moses from within the flaming bush that was not consumed. And the Angel spoke with absolute authority about *his* covenant with Israel! Write down what the Angel of the Lord said, Rachel: '*I led you up from Egypt and brought you to the land of which I swore to your fathers; and I said, I will never break My covenant with you.*'"

Hilkiah sighed deeply and raised his milky eyes toward the ceiling. "I ask myself, Rachel, how could the Angel speak of establishing his covenant with Israel, when this was God's work? And we are also told that God appeared in human form to Abraham at Mamre, accompanied by two angels.[6] Was this perhaps another appearance of the Angel of the Lord? But how is it possible that this Angel could have direct encounters with people but also claim to be God? Who was this mysterious being who was other than God and yet expressed His very Presence on earth?"[7]

Hilkiah slowly shook his head in bemusement as Rachel waited without responding, overwhelmed by the profound question. Gradually, the room filled with a deep silence, broken only by cries and calls drifting in from the dusty street.

Shouts of encouragement bounced off the eddying waters and echoed across the surrounding hills as men and women hefted packs onto their shoulders and edged cautiously into the weeds and sand in preparation to ford the Jordan.

This river arose in the north, flowing from fresh springs at the base of snowy Mount Hermon almost two thousand feet above sea level. Its waters then leaped and tumbled, merged with other tributaries, and coursed through the enormous rift valley that stretched from Syria through to Africa. On its way south, the Jordan River filled the mountain-ringed Sea of Galilee, rushing out to cut into the soft wide plain, then it slowed down to wind a tortuous path of sharp curves, bubbling over rapids to drop down to its final resting place in the Dead Sea, far below sea level.

One of the busiest river fords lay on the main road that led east from Jerusalem to Jericho, then across the Jordan River, through the terraced hillsides, and into the highlands of Perea and the arid semi-desert. From their elevated position on a rocky trail, two of Jesus's disciples looked down with interest as men now steadied themselves with stout walking staves, forming a chain to guide children, women, and goats, hand-over-hand through the churning shallow waters while blue-headed kingfishers hovered and dived without concern.

"They'd better watch out for flash flooding," John remarked sagely, as travelers stepped carefully into the tugging zigzag currents of muddy water. "The hilltop snows are still melting and it only takes one cloudburst somewhere upstream."

His brother James nodded. "You're right. And a sudden flood would drive out the creatures that live in those thickets. No one wants to tackle an angry boar." The riverine boar was notoriously dangerous, its lethal, dagger-like tusks able to be driven deep into muscle and even bone by the bunched power of brawny shoulders. "A leopard once killed a man at that bend up there," James continued, pointing with the staff he was whittling. "And I've even seen lion along this stretch—"

"Is that Philip I see on the path?" John interrupted, looking up. "And who is that with him? Maybe he's brought someone else to meet the master."

James scrambled up from his boulder seat and they both walked briskly toward the arriving men as they heard Philip's excited call.

"Master! Master! I have brought Nathaniel to you!"

Philip was eagerly pushing a young man through the group of disciples. Under the dappled shade of a spreading umbrella of prickly oaks, Jesus rose to his feet and lifted an arm in welcome. "So, this is Nathaniel: 'gift of God,'" he said in greeting. "Perhaps God has truly given you. What do you think, Nathaniel from Cana?"

But the newcomer merely averted his eyes. Philip nudged him forward and laughed teasingly. "Answer, simpleton," he said. "The teacher asks you a question. Are you given by God as your name suggests? Be sure to speak truly now, for I have told you this is the one of whom Moses and the prophets wrote." Philip turned in mock seriousness to Jesus. "Do you know, Lord, this one had the impudence to ask, 'Can anything good come out of Nazareth?'"

The mortified Nathaniel flushed darkly, but Jesus smiled and spoke gently. "Nathaniel, do not be troubled. I tell you, you are indeed a gift from God. Sit with us in the shade. Come, do not be concerned. Philip, your friend is parched from the walk—bring him something to drink."

Jesus sat down and leaned against a broad trunk as his followers settled around him. "Nathaniel," he said, gesturing to a place beside him for the reluctant visitor. "You know about our patriarch Jacob, yes? What do you suppose is the significance of his name?"

Nathaniel puckered his forehead in thought but merely shrugged his shoulders as he squatted in the shade.

"I know, Lord!" John exclaimed. "It means 'he who supplants,' from *aqeb*: heel."

"Yes indeed, John. We are told that Jacob, who was renamed Israel by the Angel of the Lord, was born holding the heel of his twin Esau as if to trip him up. And he would later trick his brother out of the firstborn birthright in exchange for a bowl of stew. But here before us in this place, we now have—Nathaniel." Jesus turned to face his uneasy guest and smiled broadly. "To everyone who will hear, I say that this is an Israelite in whom there is no deceit!"

Some disciples laughed politely. But Nathaniel shrugged again and responded tersely, "You may say what you wish, learned teacher, but you know nothing about me. You have not even seen me before this day."

"Ah, Nathaniel, and yet," Jesus said quietly as he leaned forward, "I have seen you. Before Philip called you, when you were under the fig tree yesterday—I saw you." Then he raised his head slightly and fixed Nathaniel with a piercing gaze that seemed to swallow time and thought.

Nathaniel's square features set like rock as the disciples looked at each other in surprise. Had their master already met this stranger? But for Nathaniel, the men and women had disappeared. In their place, a massive fig tree towered before him, stretching its swollen, gnarled limbs into the blue sky. And he saw himself sitting alone in its shade, gesturing and muttering intensely to himself. Then a branch crashed through the greenery with a tearing sound, raising a puff of sand near him as he gave a startled jump, and a bird raced past with a whirring of wings. Nathaniel recognized these events from the day before, and recollections welled up afresh within him.

Again, he heard the soporific drone of fig wasps and the cooing of doves. Again, he felt the silky spring air on his skin, carrying the fragrance of blossoms in the canopy above. Interwoven with these sensations were the thoughts that had assailed him yesterday—thoughts about God's assurance through the prophet Micah that in the last days, every man would rest in peace beneath his fig tree. But Nathaniel felt a sharp pricking behind his eyes as the devastating sense of loss flooded him anew. His young wife and son were gone. Torn from him by the cruel ordeal of childbirth. He had insisted that his beloved Tamar wear an amulet as protection against miscarriage, and he had excitedly planted the traditional cedar tree, which in time would have provided branches for their child's wedding canopy in the continuing cycle of life. But all his jubilant plans and hopes now lay in bitter ashes. Why did God promise peace and yet permit this dreadful anguish? As Nathaniel wrestled with his pain and fierce anger, words of despair from the scroll of Job, which had haunted him before, rose again in his mind:

> I cry out to you, God, but you do not answer. The churning inside me never stops; days of suffering confront me.

> Why do the wicked live on, growing old and increasing in power?

> If only I knew where to find God; if only I could go to his dwelling! I would state my case before Him and fill my mouth with arguments!

> But He is not a mere mortal like me that I might answer Him, that we might confront each other in court. If only there was someone to mediate between us, someone to bring us together.

Nathaniel keenly shared Job's desperate yearning for a mediator who could intercede for them with God. Then a second bird fluttered past. But Nathaniel drew in a sharp breath, suddenly aware that this vision of yesterday's events could not be from his memories because he was watching the scene unfold from a viewpoint *behind* himself! He could see the back of his head as it angled up to check for more plummeting branches.

The image slowly faded, and Nathaniel was once again aware of Jesus's affectionate smile. Then a realization struck him with a force that made him giddy: the lucid vision of himself under the fig tree was this teacher's view! Somehow Nathaniel knew that when he had been experiencing the most acute sense of loneliness and loss, feeling totally desolate and abandoned by God, he had not been on his own after all—Jesus had been with him all the time, watching and caring about his suffering. Although the jagged loss still burned within him, it was made more endurable by his new comprehension that he did not bear the sorrow alone, and an urgent desire surged within him to remain close to this enigmatic teacher. Staring at Jesus in wonder, he whispered in muted tones of reverence, "Rabbi, you are the King of Israel! And the Son of God!"

Jesus laid a firm hand on Nathaniel's knee as he replied, "Because I said to you, 'I saw you beneath the fig tree,' do you believe? Be sure that you will see greater things than these! Truly, truly," he said, turning to address those around him, "I tell you all, hereafter you will see heaven open and the angels of God ascending and descending on the Son of Man."

This was another of Jesus's mysterious references to a "son of man," and his puzzled disciples could perceive no link to the opening of heaven or this visitor beneath a fig tree. But in Nathaniel's mind, a vivid image arose of the celestial ladder of angels in the patriarch Jacob's dream. His awe-struck gaze remained fixed on the teacher and he held his breath as a powerful knowledge flooded him—the certainty that Jesus of Nazareth was somehow destined to become this divine connection between heaven and earth.

3

You Shall Love the Lord Your God with All Your Heart

RACHEL AVERTED HER EYES and the furrow between her eyebrows deepened. Pretending to check for something in her basket, she walked stiffly past the small knot of women who waited patiently for the baker to place their risen dough in his oven. As their animated chattering dropped to a murmur, a prickling discomfort crawled along Rachel's arms. Still frowning into the basket, she urged her feet to plant themselves firmly, one ahead of the other.

After Zebediah had failed to return almost two years ago, Rachel had become *agunah*—a "chained" woman. Although there was no longer a husband in her home, she could not be declared divorced because only a man could initiate this procedure. Whether Zebediah was dead or had deserted her made no difference to Rachel's status: she was in limbo, neither single nor a wife, and women seemed awkward in her presence. They would lavish sympathy and support on a widow, but Rachel felt shrouded by a dark cloud of ill-omen. Conversations seemed to peter out as she approached and only pick up when she moved away. Her marriage had been arranged for financial reasons, and she did not pray for Zebediah's return, but she did resent the unspoken reproach of other women that had led to a mounting sense of isolation. She was also tortured by the harsh truth that she would probably never experience the love of a son or daughter. Never feel soft arms reaching around her neck or a warm cheek against hers. And dreams of a male presence sometimes disturbed her sleep, although she would not admit this to herself.

As Rachel walked on, sibilant female whispers intensified behind her, and she suspected she heard suppressed tittering. A familiar dark, gritty emotion surged within her, powerful and threatening. The world went slightly out of focus and a metallic taste flooded her mouth. Tears burned behind her eyes as panic gripped her—she must not, she could not, fall down here. Biting her tongue, she forced her shoulders back and hefted the basket onto her other arm as she stalked proudly down the dusty Jerusalem street, reaching out silently to God for support:

> *El Shaddai, I pray for your mercy. Please, Lord, support me. Do not let me fall.*

As soon as she rounded the next corner, Rachel leaned heavily against a crumbling clay wall, watched impassively by a mangy stray dog. She felt weak and dizzy. Her chest heaved and she struggled to catch her breath.

Since her youth, she had suffered these fierce irrational attacks—a confused turmoil of anxiety, rage, and despair, often followed by blackouts or outbursts of violence that only her mother had been able to calm. The two had forged a close bond after her Abba Maoz had unexpectedly handed her mother a document of divorcement before leaving Palestine, callously abandoning them to struggle on without a husband and father. But not many years later, a merciless fever had struck her mother, leaving the young Rachel orphaned and completely bereft of comfort. She had learnt to seek solace in familiar scripture, and she now whispered her mother's beloved verses of Job, grasping desperately for a sense of calm between sobbing pants:

> *Naked I came . . . from my mother's womb and . . . naked shall I*
> *. . . return . . . The Lord gave . . . and the Lord has . . . taken away*
> *. . . Blessed be the . . . name of the Lord . . . Baruch HaShem.*

God had taken much from Rachel, but she tried to breathe more deeply as she summoned up her mother's soothing voice: "*Remember to always count your blessings, Rachel, and leave all else in the hands of the Lord.*" Rachel was certainly grateful for her mother's aged brother Hilkiah who had taken her into his home as a young orphan. The widowed rabbi had allowed her to call him Abba, taught her to read and write, and even provided a small dowry that enabled her to be respectably married. And Rachel knew no other women who were privileged to study Torah as she was because most religious leaders took literally Moses's injunction to teach their sons and their sons' sons. Rachel's heart swelled with pride that she was born into such a rich heritage and that as a woman she was learning so much about the history and beliefs of their people. Her self-pity and bitterness gradually subsided, and she quietly murmured God's reassuring words:

> *Fear not, for I am with you; be not dismayed, for I am your God. I will strengthen you. I will uphold you with My righteous right hand.*

Her heartache eased, and the dog stopped licking itself to look on as she straightened up and grasped her basket. When she reached Abba's house she would cook his favorite broth of lentils, garlic, and wild onions, and today there were fresh dates and small dried fishes among her purchases. Yes, she should of course count each blessing from the Lord.

Rachel felt restored to peace by the time she walked down the narrow alleyway and lifted the hanging mat, bleached pale by the sun, to enter the small courtyard of her Abba's modest home. As always, she reached out to the small *mezuzah* case on the doorpost of the house and touched the engraved letter *shin* that represented God's holy name: *Shaddai*. Rachel always felt moved by this powerful symbol—a fiery crown of three flames in one. As she gently traced the letter, she recalled her mother's teaching that the base of the pictogram represented the changeless essence of God, which was dark to the world, while the outer flames depicted God's revelation of Himself in an ever-dancing flame of Creation.

The parchment inside the case was inscribed with precious Torah verses according to God's commandment: "*You shall write them on the doorposts of your house and on your gates.*" Kissing her fingers, Rachel closed her eyes and reverently whispered the first verses: "*Shema, Israel, YHWH Eloheinu, YHWH echad. Hear, Israel, The Lord our God, the Lord is one!*[8] *You shall love the Lord your God with all your heart, with all your soul, and with all your might.*"

But as she stepped over the threshold block of limestone, Rachel quickly discovered that any preparation of food would have to wait. Interrupting his restless pacing, her Abba grasped her elbow and hastily pulled her in.

"Rachel! Rachel! Come sit, my little scribe, and write!"

Jesus's work had only recently begun, but fierce antagonism was already mounting. And ominous news was now spreading rapidly: John the Baptist had been seized by the soldiers of Herod Antipas.

As the son of Herod the Great by a Samaritan woman, Antipas controlled the regions of Galilee and Perea. He seemed to feel threatened by the growing popularity and uncompromising teachings of the Baptist, who had condemned the tetrarch's recent marriage to his sister-in-law, Herodias. And as a result of Antipas's suspicion and resentment, John now lay imprisoned in the fortified citadel of Machaerus on the eastern side of the Dead Sea.

Alerted by the arrest, Jesus set his face toward Galilee, traveling north with his disciples from Judea through Samaria. For two days, their feet pushed the world around beneath them. They trudged patiently across grasses strewn with gay wildflowers, between patchworks of vineyards and orchards fenced off by stone walls and thorn branches, through valleys with fold upon fold of gently undulating mountains that shaded off into the distance, and along riverbanks where the sun-cracked mud formed haphazard patterns across forked prints of water birds.

Their first overnight stop was an inn near Bethel. Pilgrims and merchants lolled on the ground in unfurnished rooms around a large open courtyard where beasts of burden stood patiently beside carts and unpacked loads. The honeyed locusts were a welcome treat, washed down with sweet cider. But the air was pungent with the reek of sweat and wood smoke, and noisy games of dice went on through most of the night, so that daylight arrived far too soon for heavy, blinking eyes. The group spent the second night more peacefully on the edge of a field, rolled up in their cloaks beneath gently waving trees while the panorama of stars wheeled slowly overhead.

On this third morning, the pale sky of early summer was a featureless expanse that stretched unbroken to the horizon. The disciples sprawled beneath a clump of terebinth trees, nibbling the last of their supplies while industrious insects worked feverishly among the drooping purple flowers, filling the perfumed air with high-pitched zinging and buzzing.

Jesus sat alone with a heavy heart, praying ardently as he pictured his indomitable cousin lifting his hands in the menacing darkness of a prison cell. He knew that whatever Antipas's intentions might be, John would remain firm in his commitment to the message of truth—that

God's kingdom had come upon them. But the storm was definitely gathering. Then a voice interrupted his thoughts.

"Teacher!"

A young man wiped his mouth and turned toward Jesus, leaning on one elbow as he drew the last piece of fruit from a string of dried dates. "Teacher, which is the greatest commandment in the Law?"

Jesus's answer came without hesitation. "'*You will love the Lord your God with all your heart and with all your soul and with all your mind.*' This is the first and greatest commandment. And the second is like it: '*Love your neighbor as yourself.*' All the Law and the Prophets hang upon these two commandments."

The disciple opened his mouth to respond but closed it as voices floated up. Heads turned to watch as John and James, the sons of Zebedee, approached and collapsed wearily in the shade. Scratching his sweating head under the cord of a striped kerchief, John blurted out his report, glowering and waving a fist in disappointed frustration.

"We could not find one helpful hand anywhere in that God-forsaken village!"

"These Samaritans say they have no supplies for us Jews!" James chipped in, equally furious. "And you can forget about finding any rooms to sleep in!" He spat on the ground in disgust.

The other lounging disciples sat up, muttering angrily. The mutual suspicion and hatred between Jews and Samaritans had a long history. After the death of King Solomon, the Jewish nation had split into northern Israel, centered on Samaria, and southern Judah, centered on Jerusalem. When the Assyrians conquered Israel, they took most of the population into exile, and the remainder interbred with imported Gentiles to form the mixed-heritage people known as the Samaritans. The Babylonians later defeated Judah, destroying the Jerusalem Temple and deporting many inhabitants to Babylon.[9] When these exiles were released by the conquering Persian King Cyrus, some had returned to rebuild a modest Second Temple in Jerusalem. But they had bluntly snubbed the offer of assistance from the Samaritans, who they considered to be impure, and the northern group had finally built their own temple to God on Mount Gerizim.[10]

John's simmering fury overrode his weariness, and he leaped to his feet. "These half-breed Samaritans are surely cursed by God!" he spluttered angrily. "Not only do they love to sell us into slavery, they also murder Jewish pilgrims who pass through this region!"

"They do, the miserable swine!" added Judas Iscariot, glowering darkly as he stood to offer his bitter contribution. "And we all remember that when King Antiochus violently tried to eradicate our faith and our people, the spineless Samaritans avoided persecution by renouncing any Jewish connection. Yes, they were only too happy to claim their gentile heritage! The cowardly sellouts even offered to dedicate their Gerizim temple to the pagan god Jupiter to save their worthless skins![11] They can't be surprised that we finally destroyed that blasphemous structure and declared the day to be an annual celebration!"

"Lord!" John cried out impetuously, seething under their recent rejection. "Do you wish us to call down fire from heaven to consume them?"

"Yes, Lord, let us do that!" his brother shouted, nodding in hearty agreement.

But Jesus rose and placed his hands firmly on John's shoulders, his touch muting the disciple's anger as he issued a gentle rebuke. "John, James, I shall have to call you *Boanerges*: Sons of Thunder! What have I been teaching you all this time?"

Opening his arms to encompass the group, Jesus spoke clearly, his voice ringing out in the dry air. "To those who have ears to hear, I say this: love your enemies and pray for those who mistreat you. Even if someone strikes you on one cheek, turn to them the other also. For then you will be children of the Most High, who is kind even to the ungrateful and the wicked. After all, does He not cause His sun to rise on both the evil and the good, and send down rain on the just and the unjust alike? Be therefore merciful, as your Father in heaven is merciful."

Some raised eyebrows suggested that Jesus's words were not being particularly well received. Nevertheless, as he took up his staff in preparation to continue the journey, his disciples labored reluctantly to their feet, keen to find water, fresh food, and a cool place to rest.

4

The Fields Are Ripe for Harvest

As soon as Hilkiah had spotted Rachel in the doorway, he had grabbed her arm, dumped her basket on the ground, and guided her urgently to the low table where her reed pen was laid ready. Verse after verse of scripture had tumbled out of him. Prophecy after prophecy about the coming of the Messiah who would usher in God's kingdom.

But Rachel's head now bowed wearily. She usually enjoyed writing down her Abba's musings and snippets of precious scripture, but today the summer warmth sapped her energy and frayed her concentration. Hot air funneled down the haphazard alleyways, permeating the room with smells of burnt cooking oil, dusty dung, and overripe fruit, and carrying the distracting shouts of exuberant children and monotonous grating as women turned flat stones to grind corn. The drone of a large glossy blowfly seemed to drill into Rachel's skull and blur her uncle's mumbled words. What was he saying about harvests? She was reluctant to interrupt, but it would be distressing if he asked her to read what he had dictated.

"Abba, I am sorry. What was that about a harvest?"

"What?" Hilkiah gazed around vaguely as if surprised to find he was not alone. "Harvest? Oh, yes, yes. God is Lord of the harvest. It is almost fifty days since the *Pesach* celebration of Firstfruits, so it will soon be the harvest festival of *Shavuot* or Pentecost.[12] And this is what I find interesting, Rachel: you will recall that in the spring celebration of Firstfruits, the priests waved one sheaf of ripe barley before God. But during the larger wheat harvest of *Shavuot*, they will use two loaves that are made with leaven. But I am asking myself, little one, why *two* loaves? And why *with* leaven, when leaven is a symbol of impurity that cannot be used during

Pesach? You see, we first have a single offering for the spring harvest and then a double offering for the summer harvest, but what do these symbols mean? I am sure they are significant, Rachel. Write! Write!"

Rachel wished she could even feel slightly interested in the symbolism, but the air was so stifling. Suppressing a sigh, she flexed her stiff shoulders, blinked to refocus her vision, and pushed the reed pen across the papyrus as her Abba raised his eyes to the roof and spoke in deep reflection.

"Jeremiah taught us that the nation of Israel is holiness to the Lord and the firstfruits of His increase. And the prophet linked the summer harvest with God's promise of salvation. Write what Jeremiah said about the people in exile:

> Listen! The cry of the daughter of my people from a far country:
> 'The harvest is past, the summer is ended, and we are not saved.'

There must be an important lesson for us here." Hilkiah smoothed his beard absentmindedly as he wrestled with his thoughts. "As the nation of Israel, we are God's firstfruits and the promise of a greater ingathering for God. And yet," the rabbi tilted his head, frowning as he raised a crooked finger, "not all will be saved. And like a field of wheat, God's harvest needs water to grow ripe for the sickle. God's Holy Spirit is often described as living water, and Jeremiah warned the people about forsaking the Lord, who is the only fountain of living water, and relying mistakenly on their own cracked cisterns. But despite our stiff-necked disloyalty, God has mercifully provided hope for our future:

> When the poor and needy seek water, and there is none, and their
> tongue is parched with thirst, I the Lord will answer them.

This is a wonderful promise indeed, Rachel!"

A harsh braying erupted outside. Rachel looked up with a smile as a donkey trotted past, its ears flashing briefly across the high window, followed by shrill scolding that slowly faded away. Oblivious to the distraction, Hilkiah rubbed his hands and puckered his lips in meditation.

"I must understand this. There is a promised future harvest for God, nurtured by the living water of His Holy Spirit. But when? And how will God's Spirit be brought to us?"

The sun was still shining fiercely when Jesus and his followers reached the picturesque, olive-clad Vale of Shechem in Samaria, which had played a central role in the lives of the patriarchs. It was here that Abraham first built an altar in the Promised Land and received God's pledge to His chosen people. The narrow valley ran between Mount Ebal in the north and Mount Gerizim in the south, which were only five hundred yards apart at their base. In obedience to God's command, the people of Israel had gathered here under Moses, half on each mountain, to call out His potential blessings and curses on the nation.

Now Jesus's group plodded wearily into the valley, their path leading alongside a field of wheat that was ripe for harvesting. The wind buffeted the stalks into pale surging waves while men and women made slow progress through the crop, methodically wielded scythes and tying bundles, and children gleaned behind or ran to and fro with skins of water. The disciples straggled up to the outskirts of Sychar, gratefully ate nuts from a clump of wild pistachio trees, and agreed to continue into the town in the hope of buying supplies. But Jesus declined and waved them off as he settled on the ground, leaning his back against the stone wall of the famous well that was dug in the time of the patriarch Jacob.

The voices of his followers slowly faded. Birds resumed their chirping. A lizard scuttled onto the parapet of the well and confidently cocked its head as it raised and lowered each foot in turn. Jesus lifted his face to the sun, closing his eyes as he allowed the rare peace to seep into his soul. Waiting.

A while later, a humming sound rose above the rustle of branches. Then a woman swayed into sight, balancing an earthenware jar on her right shoulder and dangling a flat leather bucket from a rope. When she noticed a man alone at the well, she flinched and stopped in her tracks, glancing around nervously as she wiped sweat from a nut-brown forehead. Jesus raised a hand, palm open, and beckoned her forward.

"I am thirsty," he said simply. "Please draw me water."

The woman frowned at the Galilean accent and again anxiously scanned the shadows of the trees as a breeze whirled dust across the path. Seeing no other strangers, she decided to take the offensive. Jutting her chin forward, she settled her stance and rested the jar on a hip thrust out to one side.

"How can you, a Jewish man, speak to me? You have no dealings with us Samaritans—you look down upon us and shun us. Why do you now ask a despised Samaritan woman for a drink?"

The stranger did not respond or move from his place but gazed at her steadily until she shifted uncomfortably in the growing stillness. Then he spoke quietly.

"If you knew the gift of God and who it is that asks you for a drink, you would have asked and received living water—a spring of water welling up to everlasting life. Whoever drinks this water will never thirst again."

The woman widened her eyes in scornful disbelief and snorted with derision.

"Kind sir," she said sarcastically, "what 'living water'? I notice that you do not carry anything to draw any kind of water with. But please—do give me some of this wondrous water so I will never again be thirsty or have to lug around this heavy pitcher. Let us see this magical water!"

Birds twittered and chirruped as Jesus stared intently at the lone woman. Water was usually drawn in the coolth of the morning or evening, not at the hottest time of the day.

"I have much to say," he said firmly. "Return home and bring your husband to hear my words."

The woman flushed, resentful of the foreigner's commanding manner. "I have no husband," she snapped, looking down at the ground.

"You speak truly. For you have had five husbands, but the man you are now with is not your husband."

Startled, the woman jerked up her head and peered earnestly at the Galilean. Had she heard correctly? How did he know such details about her life? She had not seen him before, and he looked like a traveler who was merely passing through. For a moment even the birdsong fell silent. Then she responded with a more respectful tone.

"Are you some kind of seer, sir? A prophet, perhaps?"

But Jesus merely closed his eyes and again raised his face to the sun. Feeling drawn to the intriguing figure, the woman placed her jug on the rough wall and stepped toward him.

"Sir," she asked politely, "what can you teach me about the correct worship of God? We have worshiped on this mountain for many centuries." Bangles chimed as a dark arm pointed to the craggy, sparsely vegetated slopes of Mount Gerizim. "But you Jews claim that we should only worship in your temple."

"Woman," Jesus replied softly, turning his head to look at her, "believe me, a time is coming when you will worship the Father neither on this mountain nor in Jerusalem. A time is coming and has now come when true worshipers will worship the Father in Spirit and in Truth."

The Samaritan's eyebrows drew together in a puzzled expression. The conflict about whether to worship at Jerusalem or Gerizim was well known, but it made no sense to serve God in *neither* place! And yet she was reluctant to end the conversation, sensing that this stranger might hold keys to some truths.

"Well," she said, settling on the ground. "I know that when the Messiah comes, he will explain everything to us."

Then the stranger held her eyes with a penetrating stare, and she heard his clear words.

"I am he. And whoever believes in me will never thirst."

The woman remained in place, fixed by Jesus's forceful gaze. Then approaching voices broke the spell as the returning disciples shambled up to the well with bulging leather pouches. John held up some fruit and called out cheerfully, "Now we have plenty of food, Lord! Grapes bigger than a man's thumb and the sweetest—"

But he broke off as he noticed the woman seated near their master. Was he seeing correctly? How could this audacious Samaritan female publicly attach herself to a respected Jewish teacher? Staring into his face like that—it was brazenly impertinent! Why did Jesus allow her to sit so close to him? John opened one hand and looked around at his companions with eyebrows raised, seeking confirmation of this offensive sight. They wanted to blurt out questions and challenge the woman. But Jesus merely smiled up at them, and all thought of protest evaporated. While the fatigued group settled in the shade to share out their new supplies, the woman walked briskly back down the dusty track, her empty water jar still on the wall.

John approached their teacher, holding out bread and dates. "Lord, you should eat something."

Jesus nodded and opened his hands. But the plump fruit and still-warm barley bread remained in his palms as he turned to address the scattered disciples. "I have food, my friends. I have food to eat that you do not know about."

His followers looked puzzled and Judas mumbled, "Who could have brought him food?"

"Perhaps the Samaritan woman gave him something to eat," James suggested softly.

Then Jesus's voice sounded across the open space. "My food is to do the will of him who sent me," he explained, "and to finish his work."

Drained by their long walk and the relentless sun, no one questioned their teacher's perplexing words as the group relaxed gratefully, massaging tired feet and swatting flies. At least in Samaria they did not have to talk to many people because no one here was interested in a Jewish prophet. But a short while later, Jesus's raised voice penetrated their well-fed stupor.

"Do you not have a saying, 'It is still four months until harvest'? I tell you, lift up your eyes and look at the fields!" Heads turned as Jesus pointed. "The harvest is plentiful, although the workers are few."

As they watched, the Samaritan woman appeared over the slight rise, followed by a string of men and women. As the surprised disciples scrambled to their feet, almost a dozen people gathered a short distance away. After a brief discussion among themselves, a Samaritan stepped forward, holding a hand over his heart in a gesture of deference.

"Teacher," he said, dipping his head respectfully, "our daughter has informed us of your powers. We would hear your words, and we invite you into our town to preach." Then he turned to Jesus's followers. "You are all most welcome in our homes," he said courteously.

As the disciples smiled in pleased surprise, John murmured thoughtfully to himself, "Yes. The fields are indeed ripe for harvest."

5

The Lord Has Anointed Me to Preach Good Tidings to the Poor

RACHEL LOVED BEING ON the flat rooftop of her Abba's house with the world lying open around her. From here she could enjoy the dramatic buildup of rain clouds across the wide expanse of sky, or if she left her nearby home early enough, delight in the violet and golden glory of dawn. This morning she sat comfortably in a shaded corner, holding her weaving at arm's length to check the new pattern. Her willow baskets were always popular, and this one would fetch a good price. Then she listened carefully as a familiar voice rang out below.

"'Lift up your eyes and look about you! Then you will know that I, the Lord, am your Savior, your Redeemer!' Rabbi, are these not wonderful words of God that we hear through His prophet Isaiah?"

Drawn by the fervent voice, Rachel stood up and peered over the low parapet. Five young students lingered in the small courtyard below, clearly reluctant to take leave of their rabbi as they stood around him, competing for his approval. It was Benjamin's familiar voice she had heard, and as the animated conversation continued, she shaded her eyes against the bright sunlight and allowed her gaze to wander leisurely over his lithe figure. His reputation as a scholar was growing, and she respected his skill. His open admiration of her Abba also touched her heart, and she knew he aspired to the same status of revered teacher.

Yes, Benjamin was a kindred spirit. Like her, he was enthralled by God's word and had no interest in mundane pursuits and trivial prattle. Other women might look down on her for being *agunah*, but why should she care? Which of them had her learning and insight into the precious treasures of their culture? They might be satisfied with wiping wet noses and sharing household advice, but she was like the young men below her—filled with the glory of God's word! Rachel flushed with hot pride. She could share so much with a man like Benjamin. But what could he discuss with his ignorant, pretty wife? How could such a woman understand his passion for scripture that is like a lamp for one's feet?

Rachel held her breath as Benjamin raised his hand and the sunlight dusted gold flecks across the soft hairs of his arm. He briefly adjusted his head scarf, idly running a hand through sleek, dark curls before replacing it. Then he noticed a shadow on the bare ground and raised his head curiously. Rachel hastily ducked away to sit in her corner, leaning her head against the wall and closing her eyes as warm gusts of air flapped the pegged shade cloth above her. These students were notoriously arrogant about their learning, but she could surprise them all with her knowledge. She would dearly love to surprise Benjamin. Then her Abba's voice caught her attention.

"Indeed, young Benjamin, indeed! Isaiah assures us of God's holy promise that He will bless Israel and redeem His people from suffering. And remember Isaiah's prophetic words about the great Day of the Lord:

> *The Spirit of the Lord God is upon me*
> *because the Lord has anointed me to preach good tidings to the poor.*
> *He has sent me to heal the brokenhearted,*
> *to proclaim liberty to the captives,*
> *and the opening of the prison to those who are bound.*
> *To proclaim the acceptable year of the Lord,*
> *and the day of vengeance of our God;*
> *to comfort all who mourn.*

Truly, this is a divine promise for us to treasure!"

Rachel pressed her back against the cool clay wall, her body thrilling at the timbre of Benjamin's reverent echo that rose from the courtyard.

"To proclaim the acceptable year of the Lord. To comfort all who mourn."

For two days, Jesus and his followers had traveled from the Samaritan town of Sychar, pacing evenly through morning mist and the searing sun of midday. They had tramped across glorious fields of sky-blue flax, through groves of figs and almonds, around hills swathed with carob trees and dark oaks, and among green thickets vibrant with the calls of partridges and the sudden crash of startled hare and gazelle. Finally they had crossed into Galilee, and Nazareth had come into sight, nestling within the mountains that curved around it like a scalloped seashell.

Now a hush fell over the Nazareth synagogue as the custodian ceremoniously removed a scroll from its storage case, slowly unwound its protective cloth, and solemnly handed it over to Jesus. The seated men and women watched every move, some with creased brows and pursed lips that expressed skepticism and resentment. Wasn't this the carpenter son of Mary who had lived for years in this town with his sisters and brothers? And yet he had recently been traveling throughout Galilee, preaching repentance and the arrival of the kingdom of God. What did he know of such things? Who was he to preach to anyone? But there was silence as Jesus unrolled the scroll of Isaiah and his strong voice filled the room, quoting from the ancient prophet:

> *The Spirit of the Lord is upon me*
> *Because he has anointed me to preach good news to the poor.*
> *He has sent me to heal the brokenhearted,*
> *To proclaim release to the captives,*
> *Recovering of sight to the blind,*
> *To deliver those who are crushed*
> *And to proclaim the acceptable year of the Lord.*

No one spoke as Jesus rolled up the scroll, handed it back, and took his seat, assuming the traditional position for teaching. All eyes focused on him. He began by saying, "Today, this scripture is fulfilled in your hearing."

A few heads nodded tentatively. So far, this sounded acceptable. Perhaps Jesus would proclaim the imminence of God's blessings for their nation. Most of the congregation knew the next few verses of this scripture: the prophet Isaiah taught that God would wreak vengeance on His people's oppressors; He would comfort those who mourn in Zion; Israel would triumph over their enemies; they would eat the riches of the Gentiles, and foreign sons would be their laborers. Yes, this was all very good news indeed, and they were willing to hear it. However, Jesus did not continue along these expected lines. Instead, his next words slowly etched deepening scowls on the faces around him.

"Truly I tell you, no prophet is accepted in his hometown. You think you are the only recipient of God's favor. But when the rains did not fall for three and a half years and there was severe famine in the land, the prophet Elijah was not sent to help Israel but to bless a widow in Sidon. And did the next great prophet Elisha cleanse any Israelite of leprosy? No! But he did heal Naaman, the leprous Syrian . . ."

As the meaning of Jesus's words began to sink in, the restless muttering quickly swelled to a furious uproar. What insult was this? Everyone knew that God would crush their heathen enemies. How dare this upstart ignore His promises through Isaiah and imply that God's favor was with the *goyim* rather than the Jews! He deserved to be disciplined for such impiety! Men leaped to their feet, jostling each other in their indignant determination to seize and punish the arrogant young man. Filled with righteous anger, the crowd bustled Jesus out of the synagogue and along the street. In growing panic, his disciples frantically tried to reach him at the center of the swirling vortex, terrified that the throng meant to cast him down from a neighboring clifftop.[13] But in the noisy confusion, the teacher was gone.

Jesus had left Judea to preach in the relative safety of Galilee, but his home town was proving to be as threatening as the Judean synagogues. There were so many who took offense to his teachings and his interpretation of scripture. Yes, trouble was definitely brewing.

6

We Have Found the Messiah!

KEE-WICK! KEE-WICK! TRIBUNE LUCIUS Ocella looked up as a sparrowhawk burst from the billowing clouds and cut across the burnished sky, powering forward in its characteristic flap-flap-glide, flap-flap-glide. Then another appeared, and the two joined in a graceful display, slowly spiraling back up into the brilliant white mass.

The tribune scanned the skies for signs of their return then looked down to survey Jerusalem from his commanding height on a tower of the palatial Antonia fortress that rose forbiddingly on the northwest corner of the Temple Mount.[14] This flattened Mount covered the northern end of a narrow spur of land that sloped sharply down into the Kidron valley on the east and the Tyropoeon valley on the west. Its thirty-five-acre extent was the result of ambitious expansion work by the Jewish King Herod, and Lucius was impressed by the engineering feat. Massive retaining walls towered a hundred feet above the two precipitous valleys, almost fifteen feet thick in places and incorporating some of the largest building blocks ever used. Large structures and colonnades covered the vast area and in the middle stood the famous Temple dedicated to the Jewish god.

To the south and west of the Mount sprawled the city of Jerusalem, with palatial homes on the upper western slopes, busy streets and bazaars, and tiny houses that spilled haphazardly into the deep cleft of the Tyropoeon valley. A thick stone wall of approximately four miles encompassed the entire city, punctuated by large gateways where publicans levied taxes on all goods.

Squinting against the brilliant sunlight and a whipping breeze, the tribune made his habitual inspection of the main roads out of the city. The northern road led through Samaria to Galilee, the western road reached Joppa on the seacoast of the vast blue *Mare Nostrum*, the southwestern road led to Gaza, also on the coast, a southern road passed through Bethlehem and Hebron, and looking eastward, Lucius could see the road that crossed the deep ravine of the Kidron valley, rising along the Mount of Olives on its way toward Jericho. As Lucius watched, a priest exited from the Eastern Gate of the Mount and paced along the arched causeway that led directly over the valley to avoid contamination from the graves of Jews buried in the shadow of the Temple Mount.

"Morning report is an all clear, sir," said a gruff voice at his shoulder.

"Good to hear, Stolo." Lucius turned his head and nodded briefly at his heavy-jawed officer. Then he gestured across the vista before them. "Quite impressive for a province, don't you think? The client king, called Herod the Great by his people, clearly learned a lot from our culture. I've seen the impressive palaces he built at Herodium and Jericho, and he constructed the entire Sebastos harbor from scratch."

"So I've heard, sir," was the polite response. The expressionless Stolo stared out across the city, shoulders drawn up stiffly. After a pause, he added, "Not very popular with his people, though."

"Really?" Lucius raised one eyebrow.

"Apparently not, sir. Herod was the son of an Idumean, you see. Technically not Jewish. And his promotion of non-Jewish practices raised quite a stir, sir."

Stolo fell respectfully silent until Lucius waved a hand and said brusquely, "Go on. Explain."

"Well, sir, Herod erected temples and statues in honor of Emperor Augustus, and he constructed that enormous amphitheater you see over there for Roman-style games. All against Jewish tradition, of course. He even placed a golden eagle—symbol of our imperial power—over the gate of their Temple. And when a group of Jews tried to destroy it, he had them killed."

"Ah, I suppose those actions would not have been well received."

"Indeed not, sir. And I've been told that the Jews resented paying heavy taxes for Herod's ambitious building projects. In fact, there were many plots against the king's life."

"Yes, I have heard that. None were successful though."

"No, sir. But the plots did make him paranoid enough to murder his beloved wife and some of his sons. He also surrounded himself with foreign mercenaries and built strongholds like this Antonia fortress."

Lucius gave a short laugh. "Yes, the wily Herod named it after Marc Antony, but he was certainly quick to switch allegiance to the victorious Augustus Caesar after the Battle of Actium! Apparently Herod finally died from some excruciatingly painful disease. Probably deserved it."

The tribune's brow creased as he recalled the chaos that had arisen after Herod's death approximately thirty years ago. According to Lucius's senatorial father, the king's sons had immediately vied for the royal position, becoming embroiled in claims and accusations that fostered an atmosphere of rebellion and sparked a string of messianic revolts. During a period when the two main contenders, Antipas and Archelaus, were away in Rome lobbying support for their competing political ambitions, Palestine had fallen into a widespread state of turmoil and violence.[15]

"Caused enormous trouble, that death," the tribune murmured. "Especially in Galilee, a real hotbed of messianic preaching and anti-Roman defiance."

"Was that when the rebel Judas spearheaded a major uprising, sir?" Stolo asked, still looking sternly ahead. "Didn't he and his rabble attack the palace in the Galilean capital Sepphoris? And loot weapons from the royal armory?"

"There was a brief revolt, yes. But Quinctilius Varus, governor of Syria, launched a swift and decisive response." The tribune's voice took on a rare note of enthusiasm as his finger traced the short history in a jagged line on the parapet. "His highly trained troops first moved into Galilee, burned Sepphoris to the ground, and sold the inhabitants into slavery. Then they marched on Emmaus in Judea and burned that down too, and they finally entered Jerusalem where rebels were besieging Roman soldiers in Herod's Palace over there."

Lucius briefly raised a bronzed arm to indicate a magnificent palace in the wealthy Upper City.

"Thousands of Jewish pilgrims were here for their feast of Pentecost," he explained. "But Varus's legion was far more than a match for any opposition. They took control without a pitched battle, and soldiers then scoured the countryside to round up any rebels. I'm told they crucified almost two thousand Jews in just a few days." The tribune nodded, his mouth forming a thin line of grim approval. "Since then, of course, our forces have been permanently quartered here at the Antonia and behind Herod's Palace."

While he spoke, Lucius instinctively continued to scrutinize the teeming crowd on the Temple grounds below, alert for any suspicious behavior that might hint at a potential explosion of the fanatical hostility that always simmered beneath the surface of this city. He mentally marked the positions where he would place additional soldiers during the next Jewish festival when the population of Jerusalem would increase by hundreds of thousands. Then he pointed to two aerial bridges connecting the Antonia fortress to the nearest roofs of the Temple.

"Remember the strategic importance of those bridges, Stolo. At the slightest sign of a challenge to our authority, you must use that access. Within seconds, I want soldiers raining down arrows and pouring into the plaza to engage the rebels."

Stolo nodded solemnly as the wind ruffled the horsehair plume of his helmet. Lucius continued to observe the vast Temple complex below, noting the different sections that were said to represent increasing holiness and proximity to God. The enormous outer Court of Gentiles was open to all people but was barred by a low wall with warnings in Latin and Greek that Gentiles who ventured any further would be killed. The next enclosed area was the women's court for all Jews, beyond which was the court for Jewish men, divided by another low wall from the section for priests and sacrifices. Only this area had access into the actual Temple, which consisted of the Holy Place and then the very inner Holy of Holies, hidden behind a thick curtain, in which you finally found—nothing![16]

Lucius snorted involuntarily, drawing a surprised sideways glance from his officer. The tribune's expression soured as he brooded over the ludicrous notion of an enormous religious center that focused on an empty room! And yet these Jews had the audacity to entertain an offensive and blatant contempt for Roman civilization. Their disdainful pride as a people favored by their "One God" was insufferable. In the tribune's opinion, it was unfortunate that Rome chose to placate these people rather than crushing their deluded arrogance. Why should Jews not assimilate Roman imperial gods as other client states did? Allowing religious privileges to this prickly, antagonistic nation only encouraged their separatist nonsense. A bitter resentment burned in Lucius's chest.

"Why do these people deserve special treatment, Stolo?" he burst out in frustration, thumping a fist on the parapet wall. "Thousands of Jews in our provinces profit on the back of *Pax Romana*, yet we allow them to hoard their money and send it to this center of their primitive superstition. Yes, they are only too happy to claim Roman civic rights, but at the same time they insist on being exempt from its responsibilities, particularly on their precious sabbath day. We allow them to settle legal disputes according to their own laws and even permit them to jeopardize the stability of the empire by refusing to worship the emperor and our state gods!" Lucius shook his head in frustration, one hand cradling an elbow while the other absentmindedly traced a long, jagged scar on his left cheek.

"Quite so, sir," Stolo responded diplomatically. "As always, we're not called upon to form policy, just enforce it. But at least we keep their high priest's ceremonial garb here in the fortress. They always need our permission for their primitive rituals."

Lucius nodded firmly and grunted in approval. It was crucial to maintain control of Jewish holy objects because nothing raised their rebellious spirit like a religious feast.

"And the worst stoking of this people's national pride," he muttered scornfully, "comes from their absurd and dangerous expectation of some liberating messiah. Thank Jupiter they at least aren't a drinking tribe!"

Lucius narrowed his eyes against the glare as he looked up for any sign of the sparrowhawks. Then he indicated for the officer to continue with his duties and paced swiftly back to his rooms.

Bracing himself against the rocking of the boat, Simon grasped the rough wet rope and again skillfully hauled in his throw net with calloused hands. But experienced fingers quickly communicated bitter disappointment to his heart. Yet another useless catch of seaweed and dross. Snorting in disgust, the frustrated fisherman tossed the dripping, shell-stippled net onto the deck and sat down heavily. He was done trying. He flicked his head to discourage a pesky fly from settling on his salty brow, his bulky shoulders twitching irritably under a tunic now stiff with dried sweat.

Simon was dissatisfied and tense. In fact, he had been on edge since the incident in Judea when his brother Andrew had grasped him by the shoulders, crying out enthusiastically, "We have found the Messiah!" Andrew had insisted on dragging him from his business commitments, and barely an hour later Simon had found himself being reluctantly pushed toward the teacher from Nazareth.

"Lord, Lord, this is my brother Simon!" Andrew had called out eagerly. "I have told him that you are the one we have all been waiting for!"

Jesus had greeted the brothers warmly in Aramaic. "*Shlama.* Welcome to you Andrew, and also to you, Simon bar-Jonah."

But Simon had been decidedly unimpressed by this teacher from the obscure town of Nazareth. He had heard many messianic rumors about a powerful Jewish leader who would rally Israel and liberate them from Roman rule, but this mild-looking man was surely no warrior-king. Glancing sideways, he had briefly given Andrew a wry expression of amusement. What kind of messiah was this?

Batting away the persistent fly, Simon spread out the net to dry and shook his head again, this time in impatience. When he and Andrew had returned to Capernaum where Jesus also resided, everyone was talking ardently about the man and his teachings.[17] But Simon did not share their fervor. Sure, the Nazarene had apparently cast out an impure spirit from some poor fellow in the synagogue, but such things were not unheard of. Why were Andrew and the others so *besotted* with this teacher? Their obsessive adoration infuriated Simon. And had they forgotten that there were nets to mend and accounts to check? Repentance was all fine and well, but it would not locate fish, net fish, or salt fish! He and Andrew had made useful contacts in Judea, but promised consignments now had to be caught, processed, and transported to pay for the never-ending burden of expenses, taxes, and fishing leases. And Simon was not alone in his concern: their partner Zebedee frequently complained that his sons James and John were being distracted from their fishing duties, instead conducting long debates with Jesus that often extended late into the night. Some of the man's teachings might make sense, but this was no time to be lolling around pondering how nigh the kingdom of God was! What were *really* nigh were contractual commitments, and Simon needed his coworkers to focus on the tasks at hand.

And so what if Jesus had laid his hands on Simon's ill mother-in-law? Her fever would probably have broken anyway. His easily impressed wife might be infatuated with the man, and all manner of people might flock to him as a healer, but a powerful resistance had been building up within Simon. He just wanted life to be the same, not to be turned upside down by Andrew's insistence that they give up their work and "follow the Lord." No religious teacher would put food on the table for their families, and Simon wished that Andrew would remember their father's philosophy that God helped those who helped themselves . . .

"Kefa . . . Kefa!"

It took a while for the call to penetrate Simon's exasperated musing. Furrows of irritation lined his forehead. Who had given Jesus permission to provide him with this new name? The Aramaic *Kefa*, or Greek *Petra*, meant rock, but this held no significance for Simon. He answered curtly, without looking round.

"What?"

"Put out into the deeper waters and cast again," came the firm instruction from the prow of the boat.

Simon felt a familiar prickle of heat rising up the back of his neck. He and Andrew had fished all through the night, particularly in the deeper waters. Their three long trammel nets formed an effective trapping system for night fishing, hanging vertically between a shared floating line and a weighted sinking line. But the two of them had lowered and hauled in the heavy nets again and again and yet again, toiling under scudding moonlit clouds until their wet hands were stiff with cold and their muscles were bunched and sore, with almost no reward for their efforts. And Simon's empty throw net lying limply on the deck was clear evidence that fishing conditions had not improved since then. That morning, Jesus had insisted on preaching from their boat until even the listeners on the shore were weary, and now he saw fit to issue instructions to an experienced fisherman! Who did this man think he was? But reminding himself of the need to show respect to a teacher, Simon curbed his resentment and responded politely in clipped tones.

"Master, we worked hard all night and did not catch anything. But because you say so, we will again put out our nets."

Rising with a grunt, Simon gestured sullenly to Andrew to hoist the sail. Then he pulled up the anchoring rock and took the tiller in hand, hearing the familiar creak of timbers and feeling fresh spray against his arms as he guided the boat away from the shore. When they were further out, he and Andrew again skillfully threw their smaller daytime nets. Simon could barely suppress a gloating grin in the anticipation of dismal failure. What did this teacher from Nazareth know about fishing? What an opinionated fool he would soon look!

Then a cloud passed in front of the white ball of sun, and bright shafts of gold burst across the lake. The surface around the small vessel started to tremble, then bubble, then boil, and the boat was suddenly lurching in the turbulent waters, dragged about by the seething nets. The two brothers raised jubilant cries as they strained to haul in the teeming masses of flashing, silvery bodies, and men on the pebbled beach raised their heads from mending and washing nets. They sent up their own loud cheers when they realized what was happening and raced excitedly to the water's edge to push out their craft. An elated Andrew signaled urgently, yelling for James and John to bring out their own boat with its hired hands, and he clapped his brother on the back, sweat rolling down his grinning face.

Amid the joyous uproar, Simon dropped his hands and turned slowly to where Jesus was standing patiently in the prow. Simon's eyes met an intense gaze that seemed to swallow time and thought. A wordless understanding flooded him, filling him with the illumination of truth. His heart pounded painfully within a deep hollowness that was both burning and sweet. He took a few shaky steps, then his knees buckled and he collapsed at Jesus's feet, sobbing as he had never done before.

An appalling sense of guilt threatened to crush the breath out of him.[18] With brutal clarity, he saw his resentment and cynicism and knew them for what they were—reluctance to surrender control and resistance to everything that was being freely offered.

"Lord, leave me," he groaned. "Go away from me, for I am a sinful man," he wept. "A sinful man!"

Strong arms embraced the burly fisherman as powerful shudders wracked his body and a tumultuous, bewildering sensation arose within him—that he was somehow broken and yet somehow healed. Then a voice of infinite compassion and tenderness coursed through his consciousness.

"Kefa. Peter. You will be my rock. Follow me, and you will be for me a fisher of men."

A fisher of men. Simon did not know what that was. But one thing he did know with deep conviction—his life was forever changed.

7

The Lame Shall Leap like Deer

THE WHITE KID LOOKED up and bleated feebly as Rachel descended the narrow stone steps that led steeply from the rooftop down to the small courtyard below. Even beneath the awning it was too hot up there in the midsummer sun, and now that Abba's clean clothes were laid out to dry, she could seek a cooler spot.

From habit she opened lids to monitor levels in the large stone jars that held wine, oil, and water. Then she poured drinking water for the kid and its mother and checked the lone oak tree that grew in one corner. It was almost time to pick the female kermes insects from the branches and use the coloring in their body and eggs to make *shani*, the valuable scarlet dye that provided a welcome seasonal income. Crossing the small yard, she settled on the cool earth in a shady corner by the clay stove, lifted a cake of dried dung and straw from the fuel pile, checked for scorpions, and placed it in preparation for a small fire to parch chickpeas.

Rachel had an additional reason for moving down from the roof: her Abba was exploring scripture with his students, the drone of animated voices rising and falling inside the house like a shifting swarm of bees. Closing her eyes in concentration, she tried to make out snatches of the conversation, torn between her desire to learn and her bitterness that as a woman she was not welcome to participate, no matter how much scripture she knew. Women could not attend a house of study, and Rachel was bitterly familiar with the popular statement that a man ought to thank God for three things: that he was a Jew, that he was not ignorant of the Law, and that he was not a woman. But no one could prevent her from picking up scraps of debate as crumbs from under the table of those fortunate enough to be born male. Then her expression softened as her Abba's raised voice floated through the open window.

"Carry Isaiah's words with you, my sons, which provide God's sure promise. It is written:

> Behold, your God will come with vengeance,
> With the recompense of God;
> He will come and save you.
> Then the eyes of the blind shall be opened,
> And the ears of the deaf shall be unstopped.
> Then the lame shall leap like deer,
> And the tongue of the dumb sing.

This is indeed a great and wondrous hope—God Himself shall come to save and heal us. Meditate with faith upon this promise and give thanks. Now, *shalom* until our next time together."

The traditional greeting signaled the end of the lesson, and Rachel scrambled hastily to her feet in frustrated disappointment. She was too late to hear the teaching, and she wanted to avoid these young men who had such high opinions of themselves. But she was only halfway to the roof steps when the door opened and Benjamin exited the modest home, laughing in natural exuberance as he grasped Daniel fondly by the shoulder.

Rachel had watched the two scholars grow up together in a traditional study pair, and they aroused in her a complex response in which affection and admiration were soured by resentment that they could pursue formal studies that would never be open to her. Her resulting envy was a simmering emotion that required little provocation to burst its restraints. The two scholars caught sight of her and stopped abruptly.

"*Shlama*, Rachel," came their dual greeting.

She hesitated, frowning. Now she was trapped. It would be disrespectful to ignore Abba's guests. Pulling her headscarf quickly over her forehead, she dropped her head modestly and greeted them briefly.

"*Shlama*."

But as she turned back toward the stairs, Daniel stepped forward quickly, cutting off her retreat as the sunlight inflamed the reddish tint in his short beard.

"Rachel, I was wondering," he said awkwardly, "uhm, how have you been?"

The lame question hung in the air as the vertical line between Rachel's eyebrows deepened.

"In what way?" she challenged, still looking down. She was well aware of how abrupt she sounded, but she had no wish to be patronized.

"Uhm," Daniel flushed slightly and stammered. "Generally, I mean? I mean, you, aaah, you look well."

Benjamin's explosion of laughter startled the kid into more pathetic bleating. He moved closer and laid a hand familiarly on Rachel's arm, tilting his head back and narrowing his eyes as he peered down teasingly into her face.

"You must forgive my friend, Rachel. Sometimes his very wits forsake him. Perhaps this is the effect of your Abba's weighty teachings, yes? Perhaps something else? But surely, no harm is meant."

Rachel's dark eyebrows contracted into an even deeper frown and she turned her head with slow deliberation to stare fixedly at the hand still clasping her arm. Benjamin chuckled, but the chilly atmosphere slowly trickled into his consciousness and he hastily removed his hand, pretending to wipe something from his dark woolen cloak.

"So, you will forgive our Daniel, yes?" he continued lightheartedly. "He is a clumsy fellow, this is true, but I can testify that he has a good heart. It's just that in the presence of such a beauty . . ."

Rachel sensed the menacing darkness rising. Was Benjamin actually *winking* at his intrusive friend? Her tongue felt furred with a metallic tang and her voice sounded muffled as if coming from a distance.

"It is not for us to forgive, sir," she almost spat in restrained vehemence. "Only God can forgive. Do you not recall the Midrash on Psalms? It is written: 'There is no one but You who can pardon sin.'[19] Not even the Messiah will personally forgive transgressions! Your request for my forgiveness is therefore irreverent . . . and . . . and irrelevant and . . ."

Words failed Rachel as she quivered with repressed anger that threatened to explode into physical reaction. Turning abruptly, she walked stiffly around the frozen, wide-eyed Daniel, forcing herself not to rush up the stone steps in her desperation to withdraw from the source of her fury. Men! Always prodding and poking and trying to get a rise out of you. Treating you like a harmless, ignorant plaything. As if they had the right to impose their nonsense on you in your own home! Was she nowhere safe from their stupid clowning?

An unwelcome image flashed before her, and she almost stumbled over the last step onto the rooftop. A bristled face loomed up, bleary-eyed and leering—*such a pretty girl, just like your beautiful mother, come on now, smile that toothy smile for Uncle Ahab* . . . Rachel shuddered and made pushing motions with her hands, gasping and praying mentally as she tried to fend off imagined clumsy pawing. Despicable, hateful men! She closed her eyes and collapsed against the rough wall, softly but vehemently panting out the reassuring words of Isaiah. *"Behold . . . your God will come . . . with vengeance . . . with the recompense of God . . . He will come . . . and save you."*

Rachel cared nothing about the prophet's promises for the blind, the deaf, and the leaping lame. But she regularly prayed for liberation from servitude to men and for God's vengeance on all who oppressed and belittled her.

"Master, our teacher sends us to ask, 'Are you the one who is to come, or should we expect another?'"

Jesus had by now called his chosen twelve to leave their homes and work alongside him as he moved throughout Galilee and the surrounding regions, teaching in synagogues and curing all manner of sickness. And a multitude had come out to find him, traveling from Jerusalem and other Judean cities, from the ten largely gentile cities of Decapolis, and even from the seaport cities of Tyre and Sidon. Crowds clamored to touch the traditional *tziztit* tassels of his garment because healing emanated from him, and trickles of people from diverse sources were gradually forming a powerful stream of faith.

A mixture of these seekers now crowded together in a house in Capernaum. A few hands absent-mindedly brushed away settling flecks of dust as people peered around each other to watch the interaction between Jesus and two disciples sent by the imprisoned John the Baptist. The question hung in the dusty air: "Are you the one who is to come?"

People exchanged meaningful glances and mumbled among themselves. How would Jesus answer the Baptist's question? Would he now openly declare that he was indeed the expected Messiah? But none of his teachings included the messianic promise to free the Jewish nation from foreign rule, and perhaps the Baptist was wondering how he could have ended up in the Machaerus dungeons if Jesus was indeed the expected liberator. Even Jesus's brothers accused him of being out of his mind, so perhaps he was merely a deluded fool after all. And yet what about his many healings? How could these be the work of a crazy man? The confused mutters slowly subsided as Jesus tilted his head slightly and regarded his questioners intently.

"Does your master not know?" he asked softly. Then his voice carried through the hushed room as he paraphrased the ancient prophecy of Isaiah. "Go back and report to John what you have seen and heard: the blind receive their sight, the lame walk, the lepers are cleansed, the deaf hear, the dead are raised, and the good news is proclaimed to the poor! And blessed is anyone who does not stumble on account of me."

The Baptist's two disciples looked nonplussed but nodded respectfully. As they left the house, Jesus turned to address the gathering. "Those of you who went out to see John baptizing in the Jordan, I ask you this: what did you expect to find in the wilderness? A weak reed that is easily swayed by the wind? A man in soft clothing? A prophet? I tell you, the Baptist is more than a prophet. This is he of whom it is written: *'I will send my messenger ahead of you, who will prepare your way before you.'*"[20]

Jesus's voice grew stronger.

"But I say that this generation is like children in the marketplace who cry out to each other, 'We played the pipe for you, and you did not dance. We sang a dirge, and you did not cry.' For John the Baptist did not eat bread or drink wine, and you say, 'He has a demon.' Then the Son of Man comes eating and drinking, and you say, 'Here is a glutton and a drunkard, a friend of tax collectors and sinners.'[21] On what do you base your judgments?"

People shuffled uncomfortably under the teacher's criticism. Then some looked up as more dust drifted down from the roof. Now voices sounded above them. What was happening up there? Rough wooden beams that reached across the length of the room suddenly vibrated, sending down showers of dirt, and there was a collective gasp as fingers poked through the woven branches overlaid with straw and clay. Then a whole section of the roof was torn aside to reveal two faces frowning down.

"Is he still there?" called a weak, disembodied voice from somewhere on the roof.

"I don't know yet. Is the healer called Jesus down there?"

Hands pointed to the center of the room.

"Right," came the decisive response. "We're coming down."

There were mild shrieks as more roofing was pulled away and dusty sunlight spilled into the crowded room.

"Make way! Make way!"

People pressed backward, ignoring muffled protests as toes were trodden on and bony elbows dug into ribs. A small pallet briefly blocked the light and then began a short jerky descent, steadied by helping hands until it settled among the surprised and curious crowd. A feeble arm reached up from the pallet toward the silent figure of Jesus.

"Lord. Lord. I had no other way to come to you. I know you can heal me. Please, Lord, have mercy on me."

Everyone waited in tense anticipation. What would the healer do? The man on the stretcher was familiar to many, and he had been paralyzed since his youth. Could anyone ever help him? Jesus bent over and gently touched the man's raised hand, gazing with compassion into rheumy, hopeful eyes sunk in a tear-stained face. Then he nodded briefly and said, "Friend, your sins are forgiven."

Voices crackled through the crowded room like fire in dry brushwood.

"What did he say?"

"Why does this fellow talk like that?"

"He's blaspheming!"

"Yes! Who can forgive sins but God alone?"

"Who does he think he is?"

Visiting teachers of the law bristled with animosity and resentment. The disturbing rumors they had heard in Jerusalem were all too true: this Galilean teacher thought he could claim God's divine right of forgiveness!

Jesus straightened up to face the growing commotion. Among the crowd, he recognized men who had criticized him harshly for healing on the Sabbath, and he knew all too well that they would prefer him to fail rather than see a crippled man healed. Jesus surveyed his challengers with anger, grieved by the hardness of their hearts as he responded decisively.

"Why do you raise such objections? Which do you think is easier: to say to this crippled man, 'Your sins are forgiven,' or to say, 'Stand up and walk'? Therefore, I do this thing now so you may know that the Son of Man has authority on earth to forgive sins." Raising his hands over the pallet, Jesus said firmly, "I tell you, arise, take up your mat, and go to your house."

People shrunk back as the prone man groaned and pushed himself into a sitting position. There were shouts of surprise and alarm as he grabbed hold of a neighbor and awkwardly heaved himself up to stand before them all. Conflicting expressions of shock, delight, and confusion flickered across the haggard face as his hands traveled wonderingly over his newly strengthened body. Slowly, tentatively, he raised his right leg, set it back down, raised his left leg, and set it down. Then with a joyous "*Hallelujah!*" he flung out his arms in delight and knelt weeping at Jesus's feet.

His friends above whooped with glee, and elation rippled through the house, erupting into laughter, clapping, and cries of delight that mingled with murmurs of astonishment. Many glorified God, saying in amazement, "We never saw anything like this!"

But as the grateful man bundled his stretcher under his arm and pranced away, menacing mutterings rumbled among the general celebration, sounding very much like the threat of an approaching storm.

8

Everyone Is Looking for You

EACH LOUD SOB WAS quickly muffled, absorbed by plush wall tapestries and deep fur rugs. Benjamin stared coldly at the shards of a once precious vase scattered across the tiled floor. He drew in a long slow breath, a muscle in his jaw flexing in time with his opening and closing fists. How long was he to tolerate this behavior?

Running a hand through his tousled hair, he stalked out onto the balcony to gaze down blankly at the sumptuous gardens and delicately arched bowers, deaf to sounds trickling up from the street. A cool western breeze drove light fleecy clouds across the sky, and Benjamin raised his head to drink in the glorious sight of the Temple—a glittering mass of silver, gold, and snowy marble that dominated the landscape as a symbol of holy purity.[22] Benjamin sighed deeply and compressed his lips in bitterness. Daniel was dead right to avoid marriage. Women ensnared you with their wiles and promises of unimaginable delights, then they tried to mold you and control you. Always the complaints and demands. Never enough of this, always too much of that.

And his wife Abigail did not appreciate the value of his studies. The only people more despicable than the Roman occupiers were the ignorant *am ha-aretz*—the people of the land. Did she not realize that for a man such as himself, mastery of Scripture and the Law was the highest possible calling? Nothing else could qualify him to be a worthy son of God. Even his family's wealth from their wine estates was meaningless: its only value lay in freeing him from the demeaning task of earning a living, allowing him to focus on his learning. His recent work with Rabbi

Hilkiah on prophecies of the long-awaited Messiah was far more precious than gold or possessions.

But instead of receiving due admiration and respect for his hard-earned knowledge, Benjamin had to endure Abigail's constant whining about her needs. He glowered as he thought of her moaning bitterly that he preferred to be with stodgy scholars rather than her. And instead of being grateful for servants who did the household work, she complained about being bored and nagged endlessly for more entertainment. All her friends went to the seacoast in the hot season, all her friends attended the games at the amphitheater, and all her friends wore kohl around their eyes. Her happiness was his responsibility. He had professed to love her. Why was he making her life so miserable? He was a hard, uncaring beast . . . !

Benjamin had heard the tragic litany so many times that Abigail's accusations now flowed over him without effect, and even the dramatic destruction of expensive items left him unmoved. Early in their marriage, his passion for her creamy olive skin, heady scent, and soft, secret flesh had overpowered him, bending him to her will and rendering him anxious to coax back a sweet smile and a pliant body. Her pitiful weeping had then twisted his belly with anxiety and remorse. But in the place of these emotions, there now lay only a cold stone of unyielding resentment. After all, what was the worth of a man who could be bowed by the fickle moods of a woman?

Yet even now, as Benjamin turned back inside and glimpsed the silk tunic slipping down Abigail's smooth shuddering shoulder, his traitorous loins stirred. Disgusted by the weakness of his body, he stiffened his back and marched determinedly from the room.

In a precious moment of solitude, Jesus stood on a cliff edge overlooking Capernaum, his soul deeply overshadowed by sorrow. His cousin John the Baptist was dead.[23] Beheaded by the unstable and paranoid Herod Antipas. With arms raised, Jesus prayed to his Father, intensely aware of both the tranquility of the moment and the formidable threat that lay ahead. His lips moved slightly as he fervently poured out his heart, drawing strength for the coming trials. Then the sound of voices disturbed his concentration. His fishermen disciples John and Simon, now called Peter, were laughing as they approached the silent figure.

"Lord!" John called out in loud rebuke. "We have been seeking you. Everyone is looking for you, but we had no idea where you were!"

Peter bustled up importantly. "We need to go Lord," he said shortly. "There is much that we must . . ."

But his words faded as Jesus turned slowly and placed both hands firmly on his shoulders. "Yes, Peter. There is indeed still very much that must be done."

The two watched in silence as their teacher raised his eyes to the snowcapped mountains in the far north that formed bright white splashes between the hazy sky and the grey-brown curves of earth. His gaze briefly followed the soaring glide of three vultures then dropped to scan the Sea of Galilee that stretched out below them, a swathe of diamonds shimmering on its surface.

Whitewashed buildings were scattered randomly around the shoreline that was vibrant with fishermen at work among storks and pelicans while crying gulls skimmed the wind-sculpted waves. Further out, the dark blue waters teemed with merchant ships, passenger ferries, Roman war vessels, and the billowing sails of bobbing fishing boats. Around the lake stretched fields, orchards, and vineyards that extended into the surrounding valley, dotted with watchtowers, storage granaries, and figures hoeing, plucking, and reaping under the bright sun of summer's end. And caravans of camels and donkeys, loaded with trade goods from as far as India and China, plodded stoically along the *Derech HaYam*.

Sounds of the many activities floated up to the men on the cliff—shouts from the small harbors and bays, shrieks of seabirds as they dived and squabbled, patient lowing of cattle, and monotonous chanting of camel drivers. Jesus closed his eyes and repeated softly, "Yes, there is much to do. I must yet preach the news in many other towns."

Peter and John waited patiently, unsure how to interpret Jesus's subdued tone. Then more chattering disciples appeared over the rise. It was a while before the ragged group gathered a new direction to follow their teacher who was already descending the rocky hill toward the crowd that impatiently awaited his teaching and healing. But another two of his disciples held back, reluctant to be drawn into the throng.

Judas Iscariot leaned against a tree with arms folded, a dissatisfied scowl darkening his sharp features. As a Judean from the town of Kerioth,[24] he was frustrated that their teacher surrounded himself with so many provincial Galileans.

"I cannot comprehend," he grumbled bitterly, "why the master wastes precious time on these peasants. So many important things must urgently be put in place if he is to lead our nation to freedom."

His companion, Simon Zealotes—the zealous one—nodded in firm agreement.[25] "Correct," he said, scratching his dark beard. "How can these ignorant country people be of any use in a movement to liberate Israel? Take Simon called Peter and his brother Andrew, for example, and those two sons of Zebedee: nothing but fish, boats, weather, nets, salt—I have to walk away in exasperation! They simply do not have the necessary focus or an adequate understanding of political realities. It's no use sitting around nodding happily while Jesus speaks about birds and lilies—this will contribute nothing to unseating these abhorrent Romans!"

"You're so right, Simon! And why has Jesus allowed Matthew to join us? He's one of those disloyal men who help to impose the Roman burden on us by collecting taxes: bridge tolls, road tolls, gate tolls, harbor taxes, salt tax, grain tax, customs duties . . . the list is endless!"

Simon growled in shared animosity. "Men like him are merely licensed robbers who charge extortionate taxes and kept the profit!" he agreed. "And they even use torture and imprisonment to force our people to pay!" He ground his teeth in fury. "They're traitors who have no shame that they enrich themselves on the backs of their own countrymen."

"Yes!" Judas agreed passionately. "It might be useful that Matthew can write, but this hardly outweighs the fact that he collaborates with the enemy. We should rather be recruiting respected men who are known to be dedicated to the restoration of Israel's freedom."

"Jesus is clearly biding his time," Simon commented. "And perhaps at this stage he is wise to pretend that his kingdom is not of this world. But that must soon change."

Judas nodded, pleased to have found a firm ally in Simon Zealotes, who clearly understood what was at stake. "Indeed!" he said fervently. "With enough armed support we can declare Jesus to be king of the Jews and boot out that sycophantic sell-out, Herod Antipas. A great uprising could finally see the *goyim* chased out of Jerusalem and hopefully out of the entire holy land of Judea!"

Judas's heart raced as he nursed his vision of a liberated Israel, once more an independent nation free from brutal heathen control. He stealthily hefted the bag of communal money that had been entrusted to his care, assessing its value. This would be far more useful for purchasing allies and arms than providing alms for the idle poor! Excitement tightened his throat as he made a mental tally of the people committed to his idea of revolt.

"Many have already pledged to rise in support of Jesus," he noted tensely, "and all we have to do is fan the flames of patriotic nationalism."

Simon grinned fiercely. "As the heroic Maccabees once broke the control of King Antiochus, so will our uprising shatter the iron grip of Pontius Pilate!"

But their musings were interrupted as a voice hailed them from below. Judas's forehead creased in annoyance and he raised an arm in brief response.

"Yes, yes, we're coming," he muttered. "But so, too, is the time for meaningful action."

9

I Am the Good Shepherd

"*SHALOM, WORTHY TRIBUNE.* I meant no disrespect, but an officer ushered me into your room. I was unaware that you were not as yet present."

Lucius's Jewish visitor bowed courteously, his broad beard flattening against a grey cloak as the Roman's face relaxed into the vestige of a smile.

"No need to apologize, Joseph," he said. "I gave instructions that you were to be led in as soon as you arrived. I regret to have kept you waiting, but there is always much to attend to, and the time . . ." Lucius opened a hand, leaving his sentence unfinished.

"Ah, yes," came the mild response. "Time rudely ignores us mortals and marches heedlessly over our many distractions as if they are of little importance. The sun rises and the sun sets, whether we weep or rejoice."

Lucius could not resist a mildly mocking response to the calm sing-song voice. "But not of course," he said with exaggerated solemnity, "without the permission of the One God."

Slight crinkles appeared at the outer corners of Joseph's eyes as he pulled absently on his right earlobe and responded gravely, "But of course—not."

Lucius laughed briefly and the two men took their seats. For some reason, this particular Jew had gradually managed to erode the tribune's usual reaction of frustration and suspicion. To Lucius's great surprise, Joseph had proved to be a reasonable man and even tolerably good company in addition to being a valuable source of information. Lucius lived by the maxim of his experienced father: "*Your enemy's ignorance is an advantage. Your own poses a serious threat.*" On reaching his new post in Jerusalem, Lucius had sought someone to instruct him on the subtleties of local culture, beliefs, and politics. The temple priests were largely pro-Roman, and their leader Caiaphas had recommended this Joseph from Arimathea, a member of the Sanhedrin, to instruct Lucius in their ways. And like most Jews the tribune met, the man spoke a form of Greek, the common language of the Empire. Lucius clicked his fingers for his dark-skinned Nubian servant to pour two goblets of wine, aware that only one would be touched. Then he turned to his guest with a sense of anticipation.

"Today, Joseph, I wish you to explain why you Jews worship only one god." The tribune leaned back, took a deep draught of the sweet liquor, and waved his free hand to emphasize his points. "We have gods of war and goddesses of love, deities for the home and deities for public life. In this way, we are well supported. But you people have only one formless god who laid down strict laws from a mountain in times past. Why do you choose this invisible god? How can he be of use to you? Can he lead you into battle? Can he bless your crops? Can he provide you with children?"

Lucius narrowed his eyes and thrust out his chin in a habitual gesture of interrogation. Unhurried, Joseph raised his eyes to the ornately decorated roof as shouts and drilling instructions wafted up from the fortress parade ground below.

"Yes," he stated quietly.

"Yes? What do you mean, 'Yes'?"

"Yes." Joseph looked back at his host. "God can and indeed does lead His people in battle, provide us with descendants, send down rain on the just and unjust alike, and control the very sun and stars."

"Well, of course, your god must be all-powerful, as is Jupiter. But surely other gods can also provide benefits? Why do you restrict yourself to this one deity?"

"Ah, there you touch on something central to our belief, Tribune." Joseph placed a hand on his chest. "Our relationship with God requires sustained fidelity on our side. We are assured of God's faithful loving-kindness to His people, but this depends on our own commitment and loyalty, as in a sacred marriage covenant. You see, Tribune, all Israel—the collective nation that includes each one of us—is meant to be a spotless bride for our Bridegroom. Our relationship with God should be a joyous bond of mutual love and fidelity. Yes, a marriage." Joseph nodded slowly and pressed his hands firmly together, palms and fingers meeting in a vertical line.

"You mean—you think of yourself as a *bride*?" Lucius grimaced in distaste and shifted forward in his chair. "Is that not demeaning for a man? Do you not rather wish to be a strong husband yourself?"

Joseph shrugged expressively and opened his hands. "Each of us takes on many roles, Tribune. For example, in this room, you are a student who wishes to learn from me, but outside you take charge, not advice. Not so? Here in your fortress, I am a Jewish subject under Roman occupation, but in the Holy Temple, I am a son of David who is beyond your legislation. To my wife, I am the husband who leads, but in the eyes of God, I am his beloved child and, yes—his wife, as part of collective Israel. We are taught: '*Your Maker is your husband*,' and '*as the bridegroom rejoices over the bride, so shall your God rejoice over you.*'"

Lucius sat back and shook his head, laughing in scornful amusement. "Well, you won't find one Roman worth his salt who would choose to see himself as a 'wife' to any god! It is a very odd notion, Joseph. Very odd, indeed. But perhaps I should not be surprised. After all, I have also learned that you are happy to be called sheep! Is this true, Joseph? Sheep?"

Joseph's hands came together again, this time with fingertips touching and thumbs supporting a chin hidden under a full beard as he nodded thoughtfully. "Of course, you would prefer to think of yourself as more than a sheep—a lion perhaps? A feared and powerful creature. But why do we admire a lion more than a sheep? A lion can tear, yes, destroy, yes. But can it recognize and follow a superior intelligence? Can it reach beyond its limited nature by relying upon something greater?"

Joseph's hands opened once more, palms up as if waiting to receive something. "As a man of experience, Tribune, you know very well that human nature is imperfect. Despite our intelligence, we have all erred at some time in the past and will err again in the future. As Isaiah so correctly wrote, '*All we, like sheep, have gone astray; we have turned, every one, to his own way.*' Each of us has been drawn off course by greed, by fear, by false hopes, or poor judgment. Who has not reflected on their decisions and wished they had been shown a clearer path through the confusion? If we admit this frailty, do we risk being humbled? Perhaps. But what do we risk if we refuse to admit it? Where does true wisdom lie, Tribune: in stubborn overconfidence and misguided self-reliance?"

Lucius frowned impatiently. "No, Joseph, of course thoughtless arrogance is not wisdom. But neither is blindly following like a sheep!"

"Ah, but that must surely depend on *what* you are following. If I have a lamp and you do not, why would you refuse my light and stumble away in the dark? God's word is a lamp to our feet, so in our faith we are not sheep following another stupid sheep—we are creatures who are safest in the arms of a dedicated Shepherd who alone knows the right path. God describes both Himself and His promised Messiah as loving shepherds who will finally lead us to a place of rest." Joseph's eyes took on a far-off look. "Hear God's words, Tribune:

> *I will feed My flock, and I will make them lie down.*
> *I will seek what was lost.*
> *I will come to give rest to Israel.*
> *I will establish one shepherd over them,*
> *and he shall feed them.*

Yes, Tribune, we are God's precious sheep. And we take immense comfort in the knowledge that we are what we are in His eyes: no more, but—this is important—also no less."

Lucius raised a skeptical eyebrow and fell silent. Yet despite himself, he felt a strange power emanate from the ancient verses. Absently swirling his wine, he stared blankly at the intricate mosaic floor and murmured thoughtfully, "Bridegroom. Shepherd. Bringer of rest."[26]

"Come to me, all who are weary and burdened! Take my yoke upon you and learn from me, for I am gentle and humble in heart, and you will find rest for your souls.[27] I am the good shepherd, for the Son of Man has come to seek and save the lost."

Jesus's words resonated off the rocky surfaces of the Capernaum countryside, ringing in the ears of those who sat patiently on the ground to hear the renowned teacher. But a group of Pharisees stood to one side, clothed in elaborate headdresses and long prayer shawls, muttering and shaking their heads in sour disapproval. This was blasphemous talk! All Israel knew that God alone would be the source of rest and salvation, not some self-proclaimed preacher from the back of beyond! This fellow was not associated with any recognized school, and he showed no respect for their distinguished traditions and leadership.

The Pharisees conferred intensely with another group of disgruntled listeners: the Herodians. The two factions were political opponents, with one group aiming to establish Herod Antipas as King of Judea and the other hoping for the restoration of the kingdom of David under the promised Messiah. But they now shared a common desire to silence the pestilential but popular Galilean who urged people to follow his radical teachings. They glared intently while Jesus continued to teach, determined to catch him out and prove him inadequate in front of his admirers.

"And I have other sheep that are not of this sheep pen," Jesus called out. "I must bring them also. They too will listen to my voice, and there shall be one flock and one shepherd—"

"You say you are a good shepherd!" a Herodian interrupted loudly. "But why is it that John the Baptist's disciples fasted and the disciples of the Pharisees fast, but yours do not?"

Heads turned to trace the source of this challenge. Was it true that Jesus's disciples did not fast? Why was this so? The crowd looked back to the raised slope as the teacher's answer sounded through the clear air.

"How can the guests of the bridegroom fast while he is still with them? They cannot, so long as they have him. But the days will come when the bridegroom will be taken from them, and then they will fast."

The challenger glowered furiously and huddled in debate with his supporters as the crowd muttered in surprise. How could Jesus claim to be a bridegroom when that was God's role to His chosen people? And what did he mean that he would be taken away? Did this have something to do with the recent execution of John the Baptist? A current of anxiety circulated as people chattered uneasily.

"But I tell you," warned Jesus, "that the kingdom of heaven is like ten virgins who went out to meet the bridegroom. Five of them were foolish and unprepared, and they did not bring oil for their lamps. While they were away buying oil, the bridegroom arrived and the door was shut to them. Keep watch, therefore, and be always ready, for you do not know the day or hour in which the Son of Man is coming."

This prompted more puzzled murmuring. It seemed the bridegroom in the parable was also a "son of man" who would arrive unexpectedly. But what was that supposed to mean? Who was this bridegroom? Then a Pharisee raised another criticism.

"We also demand that you explain why you do not uphold the teachings of our elders. Are you too good for the traditions of our forebears? For your disciples do not wash cups and hands before they take food but instead eat with defiled hands!"

His colleagues raised a loud chorus of agreement, nodding their heads in solemn condemnation. Jesus sighed and looked down at his folded hands. Heads craned forward to hear the soft words that he seemed to speak only to himself.

"How correct are God's words in Isaiah: '*These people honor me with their lips, but their hearts are far from me. They worship me in vain, following merely human rules.*'"

Then he raised his head and responded firmly to the challenge.

"I say that you have set aside the commandments of God and instead hold tightly to your own traditions, which you teach as if they are doctrine! Why do you concentrate on the outside of the cup? How does it help to clean the *outside* but leave it filled with greed and self-indulgence? Rather clean the *inside* and then the outside will also be clean."

Jesus opened his arms and appealed passionately to the seated throng.

"Listen to me, everyone, and understand this. Nothing that enters you from outside can defile you. No! For it merely goes into your stomach and gets expelled. It is what comes out of your heart that defiles you—evil thoughts, sexual immorality, murder, greed, blasphemy, and foolish pride. After all, a tree is known by its fruit. Do people gather figs from thorns or grapes from a bramble bush? No! In the same way, a good man brings out that which is good from the treasure of his heart, and the evil man brings out that which is evil. For your mouth speaks out of the abundance of your heart."

The restless mumbling grew louder.

"And woe to you hypocritical Pharisees and teachers of the law!" Jesus continued loudly. "For you weigh the smallest amount of herbs and spices for tithing, yet you neglect the heart of God's law, which is justice and mercy. You are blind guides who strain out a gnat but swallow a camel!"

His voice lifted above the growing clamor.

"Yes, you may protest! But I say you are like newly whitewashed tombs that appear beautiful but hide the unclean bones of the dead." He pointed to his furious antagonists. "I tell all of you here, do not be as these Pharisees! For they load heavy burdens of their own laws onto people and will not lift a finger to help them. And everything they do is designed to make a good impression. Yes, they make their phylacteries wide and their tassels long, they love places of honor at feasts and the best seats in the synagogues and to be greeted with great respect in the marketplace. But inwardly, they are full of hypocrisy and wickedness!"

"*No!*" A shout of indignation exploded from Jesus's Pharisaic critic. "It is *you* who are wicked and *you* who makes false claims. It must be through Beelzebul, the prince of demons, that you drive out demons!"

"But how can that be?" Jesus shook his head resolutely. "Any kingdom divided against itself will be ruined, and a house divided against itself must fall. So if Satan is divided against himself, how can his kingdom stand? This makes no sense. But if I drive out demons by the finger of God, then you must know that the kingdom of God has come upon you!"

The challenger bellowed in rage and wrenched at his costly cloak as if to tear it in protest. "How dare you claim to work through the finger of God! This is how God Himself acts! With His finger, God wrote His commandments on stone tablets and unleashed plagues upon Egypt. You have no right to use this divine symbol. You are a false teacher who leads others astray!" The man shook his fist violently and appealed in fury to those around him. "How can this arrogant nobody use holy images to describe his works? Do not listen to him! I warn you to reject his blasphemous words! This outrage will not be tolerated!"

Fuming and muttering fiercely, the spokesman and his group stalked off, leaving many in the crowd feeling bewildered and doubtful. Surely it *was* blasphemous to claim to act through the finger of God! And why did Jesus reject the respected traditions of the Pharisees? Many of his teachings were certainly strange, and perhaps they were indeed dangerous to hear. Ripples of conflicting opinions spread rapidly.

"This man is just a trouble-maker! See how he creates disorder wherever he goes."

"Yes, ignore him! He's just a crackpot preacher who doesn't know what he's talking about."

"But I say he is a good man."

"No, he deceives the people!"

"And why does he promise that people will eat and drink in *his* kingdom? Does he plan to overthrow the Romans?"

There was much uneasy chatter, but no one wanted to be heard saying anything openly about the Nazarene. Some people had already drifted away, reluctant to be drawn into the growing enmity between this controversial figure and the established Jewish leadership. Looking around at those who remained, Jesus resumed his teaching.

"Do not think I have come to destroy the law or the prophets. I did not come to destroy, but to fulfill. For not one *yod* or tittle shall pass from the law until all things are accomplished.[28] But I also tell you that unless your righteousness exceeds that of the scribes and Pharisees, there is no way you will enter into the kingdom of heaven."

A voice called out, "Good teacher, what then must we do, that we may work the works of God?"

Jesus placed both hands on his chest and answered earnestly. "This is the work of God: that you believe in him whom he has sent. I have come down from heaven, not to do my own will, but the will of him who sent me. And this is the will of my Father who sent me: that everyone who believes in the Son shall have eternal life."

There was a roar of mocking laughter.

"Ha! Isn't this Jesus, whose father and mother we know?"

"Why then does he tell us, 'I have come down from heaven'?"

"And who does he think he is to promise us eternal life?"

"He who has ears to hear, hear this," Jesus responded loudly above the commotion. "I am the bread of life. Your fathers ate manna in the wilderness and they died,[29] but I am the living bread that came down out of heaven! If anyone eats of this bread, he will live forever. Yes, the bread that I will give for the world is my flesh. Whoever eats my flesh and drinks my blood will live in me, and I in him!"

The muttering was now tinged with shock and revulsion.

"How can this man give us his flesh to eat?"

"This is a hard saying! Who can listen to it?"

"We are not even allowed to eat animal blood!"

"What nonsense is this?"

"Does this teaching cause you to stumble?" Jesus persevered. "Then what if you would see the Son of Man ascend to where he was before? It is the spirit who gives life. The flesh profits nothing. The words that I speak to you are spirit and life!"

But the trickle of desertion became a fast-flowing stream as many threw up their hands in disgust at the bizarre teaching and stomped off. Jesus turned to his closest followers seated around him.

"To you whom I have chosen," he said solemnly, "it is given to know the mysteries of God's kingdom, but to those who are outside, all things are done in parables. This is in keeping with God's words to the prophet Isaiah that '*seeing they may see, and not perceive; and hearing they may hear, and not understand, lest perhaps they should turn again, and their sins should be forgiven them.*' Take heed therefore how you receive my words, because whoever does hear, to him more will be given; but whoever does not hear, from him will be taken even that which he thinks he has."

Gesturing to the dissipating crowd, Jesus asked his disciples simply, "And what about you? Do you also wish to leave?"

But Peter replied confidently, "Lord, to whom would we go? You have the words of eternal life. And we have come to know that you are the Messiah, the Son of the living God."

10

The Stone the Builders Rejected
Has Become the Cornerstone

THREE NOSES SNIFFED APPROVINGLY as a mouth-watering aroma filled the room.

Rabbi Hilkiah inhaled deeply and let out a deep sigh of appreciation. "Ah, Daniel," he said warmly, "you do not know what you are missing. You should imitate your namesake and brave the lion's den! Dive into the unknown and take a wife when you visit your friends in Capernaum next week.. Tell him, Benjamin, how wonderful is married life. Choose wisely and you will not regret it. But do not be tempted by superficial beauty, my son." The rabbi shook a bent finger in warning. "Remember: 'As a ring of gold in a swine's snout, so is a lovely woman who lacks discretion.'"

Benjamin gave an abrupt snort and Daniel smiled affectionately, idly smoothing his beard that glinted red in the light streaming through the small window. Their rabbi could always find a verse of scripture to support his advice. But Daniel was unconvinced about the benefits of marriage. He had seen too many women change from doe-eyed submission to shrill dominance, and Benjamin's wife was a clear warning.

"But do not forget," he countered with a wry smile, "it is also written: 'Better to dwell in a corner of a housetop, than in a house with a contentious woman.'"

"Well, of course, of course," Hilkiah waggled his head. "But a gentle woman is a great blessing in any man's home. Not so, Rachel?"

Rachel looked startled and confused as she appeared in the low doorway with a board of flatbreads and a steaming bowl of stew. Her cheeks reddened with embarrassment and annoyance at being thrust into an unknown situation. She respected and loved her Abba, but he was often insensitive to her position as a woman among these condescending men.

Daniel stood up swiftly and stepped toward her with an outstretched arm. "Please let me take that, Rachel. Do not mind your Abba, he was only teasing me about something. These delicious smells have had our stomachs rumbling in anticipation, so we thank the Lord Almighty for the blessing of your hands."

Daniel's tone was warm and earnest, but Rachel turned her back on him and dumped the meal hastily onto the low table. Oblivious to her discomfort, Hilkiah tried to draw her in.

"Today, we have been discussing God's vineyard, Rachel, which you and I spoke about just yesterday, hmm? This represents God's people: '*For the vineyard of the Lord of Hosts is the house of Israel and the men of Judah are His pleasant plant.*'"

As always, the air seemed to take on a different vibration when the rabbi quoted scripture, and Rachel turned to listen. Then she glared as Daniel interrupted clumsily.

"And also the cornerstone, Rachel. We are exploring the messianic imagery of the cornerstone. You might have heard of this."

It did not sound to Rachel as if Daniel was at all sure she had heard this scripture. He probably regarded her as an ignorant woman who only knew how to cook and weave and grind and sew. Compressing her lips, she adopted a wide-eyed expression of innocent attentiveness.

"Really? How interesting."

"Oh yes, very," Daniel responded eagerly. "I can show you the verses some time if you like, where Isaiah predicted that God will lay an essential foundation stone on which some will stumble."

Smiling sweetly, Rachel backed slowly toward the door. Then she looked up at the roof in imitation of her Abba, closed her eyes, and with a deepened furrow between her eyebrows, confidently intoned the words of Isaiah:

> So this is what the Lord God says:
> "See, I lay a stone in Zion, a tested stone,
> a precious cornerstone, a sure foundation;
> the one who believes will never be shaken.
> He will be as a sanctuary,
> but a stone of stumbling and a rock of offense
> to both the houses of Israel."[30]

Looking down, Rachel was gratified to see the surprised expressions of both students. "And an important foundation stone is also mentioned in a psalm about the Messiah," she stated confidently. "It is written: '*The stone the builders rejected has become the cornerstone!*' It seems significant to me that the word for stone—*eben*—is composed of two words: *ab* for father and *ben* for son. What father and son do you suppose can form this precious cornerstone of salvation? Hmm? I was just wondering . . ."

Rachel arched her eyebrows in query and opened a hand to invite an answer. Then without waiting for a response, she turned sharply and left the room with a thin-lipped expression of satisfaction.

"A man planted a vineyard, put a hedge around it, dug a pit for the winepress, and built a watchtower."

People sat and reclined on the moist ground as they listened keenly to the teacher, and heads nodded in understanding of these symbols. The vineyard owner was, of course, the One God of all creation. And each Jew knew they were the precious fruit of God's vineyard, from Abraham, through Moses and David, down to the present generations. Children splashed in muddy puddles of autumn rain, their delighted squeals piercing the cool air as Jesus continued the parable.

"Then the man rented out the vineyard to tenant farmers to care for the vines. At harvest time, he sent a servant to collect his share of the fruit. But the farmers seized the man, beat him, and sent him away empty-handed. When the owner sent yet another servant, they threw stones at him, struck him on the head, and sent him away badly treated. Many other servants were also beaten, and some were even killed."

Listeners continued to nod. God's prophets were His servants and, shameful though it was to admit, many of these messengers had been killed by the leaders of Israel and Judah throughout their history. But Jesus's next words had the crowd glancing at each other uncertainly.

"But the vineyard owner had one man left to send—his beloved son. He sent him last of all, saying, 'They will respect my son.'"

A son? What son? God has no son! Now the parable seemed hopelessly confusing. Was the vineyard owner perhaps not God after all? Eyebrows contracted quizzically and heads inclined as people concentrated on Jesus's next words.

"The wicked tenant farmers said to one another, 'This son is the heir of the wealth of the vineyard. Come, let us kill him, and the inheritance will be ours!' So they took him, killed him, and cast him out of the vineyard."

A black cloud of crows swooped low overhead, casting swift dark shadows and cawing harshly as the teacher posed a question to the scattered listeners.

"What, then, do you think will happen? What will the Lord of the vineyard do to these disloyal farmers?"

Faces were blank and nonplussed. Jesus lifted an arm and swept it slowly across the silent group. All eyes followed his finger until it stopped, pointing directly at a small knot of priests and religious teachers in long cloaks and richly ornamented mantles.

"I will tell you what the Lord will do," he said firmly. "He will come and destroy those greedy farmers, and he will give His precious vineyard to others! Have you not read this passage: '*The stone the builders rejected has become the cornerstone; the Lord has done this, and it is marvelous in our eyes*'?"

The crowd gasped—this was a well-known messianic verse! There was a hum of speculation. What was this teacher trying to say? Who was the murdered son supposed to be? Was he also God's promised Messiah who would first be rejected but then form the cornerstone of faith? And who were the disloyal tenant farmers that the Lord would destroy?

But the antagonistic priests and teachers understood only too well that Jesus was directing the parable against them. They made muted but furious gestures and moved off, muttering in great offense. As Jesus watched their retreating backs, his voice carried on the crisp breeze.

"Listen to what I tell you. The kingdom of heaven is like a man who sowed good seed in his field. But while everyone was sleeping, his enemy came and sowed weeds among the wheat. Both are now growing together until the harvest. But beware! At that time, I will tell the reapers: first gather up the weeds and bind them in bundles to be burned, then gather the wheat and bring it into my barn!"

Jesus's voice softened as he addressed his closest followers. "And you must hear this: I am the true vine, and my Father is the farmer. As a branch cannot bear fruit by itself unless it remains in the vine, so neither can you, unless you remain in me."

Then he and his disciples moved off while the crowd continued to debate the possible meaning of his strange parables. Leaning against a stone wall, Daniel stroked his beard that flared red in the sunlight as he thoughtfully watched the retreating back of the teacher from Nazareth.

11

Is Anything Impossible for God?

THE SOUND OF THE shofar vibrated across the city—one of many calls that would ring out during *Yom Teruah*, the solemn Day of Trumpets. As soon as three witnesses had sighted the fine sliver of new moon, the huge pyre on the Mount of Olives was set alight to provide a blazing signal for eager watchers who had replicated the flame from peak to peak in ever-widening circles until Jews throughout Palestine and beyond knew that a new month had officially begun. The first of Tishri had arrived!

A warm desert wind tugged at the edges of Rachel's shawl as she leaned avidly forward against the stone balustrade of the upper balcony, thrilling at the exhilarating shofar call. A few steps to her left, Benjamin raised his head and shouted boldly.

"Sing for joy to God our strength! Shout aloud to the God of Jacob!"

Despite her usual reserve, Rachel couldn't help smiling at his boyish enthusiasm, and she instinctively extended his quotation from the psalm, her voice quaking with excitement.

"Sound the ram's horn at the New Moon, and when the moon is full, on the day of our festival!"

Laughing in delight, Rachel drank in the glorious world that stretched out before them, painted with the fiery palette of autumn: vivid reds of sprawling grapevines, brilliant yellows of pomegranate trees, and blazing orange and crimson of cyprus and terebinth. But the most magnificent sight of all was the Temple. Rachel's cloak slipped back to reveal shapely arms as she raised them reverently toward the imposing structure on the Temple Mount, surrounded by its vast courts and colonnades. It was the most sacred place in the world: the meeting place of heaven and earth, and symbol of the glorious Presence of the Holy One Himself. Rachel exhaled slowly in audible wonder.

"Look," said Benjamin softly, drawing nearer. "You can just make out the *kohen* and his shofar there at the Royal Stoa."[31]

Extending his arm, he pointed to the western corner of the red-roofed colonnade that ran along the entire southern length of the Temple Mount, towering above street level atop vast retaining walls. Half closing his eyes, Benjamin whispered from scripture, *"May your eyes be open toward this Temple night and day, this place of which you said, 'My Name shall be there!'"*

And once again, Rachel provided the next verse: *"So that you will hear the prayer your servant prays toward this place."*

She slowly lowered her arms and turned her head, catching her breath as she met Benjamin's ardent look of admiration. Almost giddy from a rush of fiery pride, she quickly looked down and pulled the shawl further over her flushed face as the exhilarating realization struck her: Benjamin *saw* her! He *recognized* her as a kindred spirit! She peered up cautiously to meet his intense gaze, and her heart raced. Perhaps he was even *attracted* to her. But she abruptly pulled away at the brisk clack-clack of wooden sandals on the flagstones and the sound of a woman's voice.

"Revered Rabbi Hilkiah, how very kind of you to grace our humble home. And Rachel, you are both most welcome. I wonder, has my husband thought to offer you refreshments, perhaps? Has he pointed out the palace of the high priest? There is a marvelous view of it from out there. And you can also see King Herod's Palace. Do you know, just before the recent *Pesach*, I saw Prefect Pilate arrive with his entire entourage from Caesarea to reside there—quite a splendid sight. But do come in out of the sun, you two."

As Rachel and Benjamin stepped back into the cool room, Benjamin opened one hand toward the elegant new arrival. "Rabbi Hilkiah, Rachel," he said with an edge to his voice, "this is my wife Abigail, who it seems waits for no introductions."

"Don't be foolish, Ben," Abigail responded sharply. "Who does not know of the famous Rabbi? And Rachel—well, there has been no *end* of talk here about your accomplishments. And here is the proof of it—you are so quick to complete my husband's words. How *do* you find the time for all this scholarly work as well as the care of your home? I'm sure I could not manage it. But then, there is always so much important work to do in a household such as this. Of course, I am fortunate that the market is so close, and the slaves can get anything we need from there, you know, even purple cloth, pearls, frankincense, ivory—But do forgive me, Rachel, you must be quite exhausted. It is such a long walk up here from down in the valley. Do feel free to rest your tired feet."

Rachel's eyes narrowed at the pointed reference to her residence in the lower and poorer southeast section of the city, with its noisy maze of alleyways crammed with houses of rough stone, mud, and crumbling bricks aged yellow-brown by the sun. She felt intimidated in general by the wealthy Upper City with its orderly grid of broad avenues, opulent palaces, and impressive white mansions with decorative marble columns, bubbling fountains, and formal gardens. And in particular, she was overwhelmed by Benjamin's luxurious home. This was her first invitation into the house, and she had found herself gawking at the intricate mosaics, lofty carved ceilings, silver goblets on ornate wrought-iron tables, and arched windows with deep cushioned seats backed by intricate stone latticework. Sensing her unease, Benjamin had been reassuringly warm and gentle. But his wife's barbed comment made Rachel once again uncomfortably aware of a fraying edge on her shawl and the sheen on her Abba's well-worn cloak.

There was an awkward silence. Then Benjamin spoke out abruptly, inclining his head politely toward Rabbi Hilkiah who leaned back in a large padded chair with hands folded solemnly across his midriff. "It is my privilege to celebrate this important day with my rabbi, Abigail. I thank him and Rachel for being so gracious as to join me here."

"Indeed, my young scholar," Hilkiah intoned gravely, sighing deeply and nodding his head. "This is a most significant day. The shofar that now sounds from the Temple once called all Israel to Mount Sinai where God manifested His Holy Presence in smoke and fire to establish His covenant with us. This call must again stir our spirits and prepare our hearts for *Yamim Norai'm*: the Ten Days of Awe that start today and provide us with a much-needed period of prayer and repentance. Yes, *teshuvah*—turning back to God—is of great importance. We must spend time in humble self-reflection to prepare for the arrival of *Yom Kippur*, the great Day of Atonement when God will do the impossible: cover our iniquity of the past year."

Such a solemn speech from her Abba would usually bring scripture tumbling out of Rachel, and she suspected that Benjamin burned to respond. But somehow, the presence of the stylish woman in white silk stifled any enthusiastic response about the significance of the first day of

Tishri. Instead, the room lapsed into another cold silence until Benjamin cleared his throat and spoke again.

"Rabbi Hilkiah has been kind enough to bring a scroll that he believes will interest me."

"Yes, yes, I believe it will, Benjamin, following our explorations into the promised Messiah. And I do try to leave my comfortable nest now and then, with Rachel's competent guidance through the streets. Come, child, take this."

Hilkiah dug under his cloak and produced a small roll of papyrus. As Rachel moved forward, Abigail sighed gently, rearranging her headscarf with a dainty hand and managing to loosen glossy black curls adorned with pearls, which fell prettily over a forehead defined by delicately arched eyebrows. Her light voice floated across the room.

"You are indeed fortunate, worthy rabbi, that Rachel has so much free time to assist you. And Rachel, I am sure you are grateful to be needed somewhere. But please excuse me—I must check on the kitchen servants. They will soon bring in something tasty for you all."

Abigail swayed across the room with a sultry grace, arching her back as though her body held a precious secret. Placing a slim hand on Benjamin's arm, she smiled up sweetly as she murmured, "Unless you would prefer me to stay awhile, my husband?" But Benjamin merely mumbled something incoherent and stared out at the distant Temple. Abigail hesitated, then removed her hand sharply and turned with a brittle smile.

"Excellent, then. Excellent," she said brightly. "Refreshments in a moment for our most honored guests."

Rachel kept her eyes on the scroll in her hand while footsteps clacked across the floor. Then a smooth hand was laid upon hers and a voice whispered close to her ear.

"I do apologize if I seem distracted, Rachel, but I have so many responsibilities as a wife. Fortunately, a husband like Ben makes it all worthwhile. I must say that I have no cause for complaint regarding his . . . attentions." Abigail turned her head to regard the figure still staring out of the window. Then she drew her eyes back to Rachel, her mouth puckering in an affected expression of pity. "Oh, I *am* sorry, I forgot that you are quite alone now. Almost two years, I think? At least you have your many little scrolls and your old scriptures. I am sure they must provide perfectly . . . satisfactory . . . comfort."

Cool fingers patted Rachel's hand three times in accompaniment to the last words. Her vision became grey and blurry and she blinked, biting hard on her tongue as the rapping of wooden sandals on stone faded away.

A blood-curdling shriek tore through the agitated group, and alarmed bystanders retreated hastily from the rigid body on the ground. The boy's back arched in agony and his mouth opened in a wide, spittled grimace as his teeth ground violently and tears made dusty streaks down his gaunt face.

"I can't stop it," sobbed his father in distress. "Some spirit seizes him and throws him into these fits. Help! In the name of God, please help him!"

Andrew and Peter grappled with the small wiry body while John and James again loudly commanded the spirit to come out of the boy, groaning in distress and panic, confounded by their dismal failure.

Jesus had only recently dispatched his chosen *apostolos*—ones sent forth—to preach the good news. The twelve had worked in pairs: Andrew with his brother now called Peter; James and John, the sons of Zebedee; Philip and Bartholomew; Thomas with the tax collector Matthew; Thaddaeus and James, the son of Alphaeus; Simon, called the Zealot, with Judas Iscariot. Jesus had empowered them to drive out impure spirits and heal every disease, and their success had been tremendous, exceeding all expectations. When they returned, buoyant with optimism and confidence, Peter had laughed as he boasted, "Lord, even the demons submit to us in your name!"

But now they were at their wits' end, shouting ever louder as they struggled to contain the wild limbs of the thrashing child. The father's wails mingled with other horrified cries, and critical scribes added to the clamor by shouting disparaging comments about the futility of these attempts by Jesus's foolish disciples.

Then a shadow fell over the scene, and the throng parted. All faces turned toward Jesus, many expressing hope but some twisted with antipathy. "You unbelieving generation!" he murmured. "How long must I remain with you?" Turning to the boy's father, he asked, "How long has he been like this?"

"From childhood," moaned the despairing man. "This spirit has often thrown my boy into fire or water to kill him. But if you can do anything, I beg you to take pity on me and help us."

"Why do you ask, 'if'?" Jesus inquired softly. "Everything is possible for one who believes."

Immediately, the father clutched Jesus's arm and exclaimed frantically, "Yes! Yes, I believe! I do! Help me overcome any unbelief!"

Then Jesus's authoritative voice rang out, rebuking the spirit, and the exhausted boy crumpled into stillness. Stooping down among the panting apostles, Jesus gathered up the limp form and passed him to his weeping father.

"Take him home," he said gently. "Your son is healed."

Then he turned to his distraught, disheveled followers and with a simple gesture indicated for them to accompany him as he moved away from the excited crowd. The downcast group trailed behind their teacher until they reached Peter's home where they often gathered, and Jesus waited patiently as they arranged themselves around him on low stools and cushions.

"Do you have so little faith?" he asked them somberly. "Truly I tell you, if you have faith as small as a mustard seed, you can say to a mountain, 'Move from here to there,' and it will move. Is anything impossible for God?"

Burning under the rebuke, John exclaimed, "Teacher, we saw someone driving out demons in your name and we told him to stop because he is not one of us!"

Jesus shook his head slightly and raised his hand. "No. Do not forbid this, for there is no one who shall do a mighty work in my name who shall readily speak evil of me. But I warn you: do not rejoice and become proud because some spirits have submitted to you; rather rejoice that your names are written in heaven.[32] For I know your hearts. I know that you contend for positions in my kingdom, saying among yourselves, 'Who is to be the greatest?'"

The men furtively shared guilty looks of surprise. How did the master know such things? For they had indeed argued recently over this question, competing for imagined authority in the future kingdom. Ignoring their disconcerted expressions, Jesus leaned forward and spoke urgently.

"Listen carefully now to what I say. You know that the rulers of the Gentiles lord it over them, and their high officials exercise authority over others. This must not be so with you. Instead, whoever would become first among you must be as a child and a servant. Remember my words when I am no longer here to guide you. I have told you that I must go to

Jerusalem to suffer many things and be rejected by the elders, the chief priests, and the teachers of the law.'"

"And yet here you are, teaching in perfect safety!"

Heads whipped round at the sharp voice behind them. In the doorway stood James, one of Jesus's skeptical brothers, his arms folded and a sardonic smirk playing across his face. Peter glowered angrily. He bitterly resented these ignorant siblings who had no idea who Jesus was. They had even publicly accused him of having lost his mind, and their scornful disbelief was infuriating. Why had this brother followed them now? Peter stood up and watched suspiciously as James strolled slowly into the room, addressing Jesus with mock gravity.

"If your work is so important, brother, I suggest you return to Judea so that people there may also see the mighty acts you perform. Surely no one who wants to become a public figure would act in secret, hmm?" James swept a questioning gaze across the seated disciples before turning back to Jesus. "The Day of Trumpets is now past, and the Feast of Tabernacles is not far away—a time of great pilgrimage to Jerusalem. A man who does so many remarkable works should surely show himself there to the world. What a perfect opportunity it will be for you to spread your fascinating message, brother, that in your very person God's kingdom is breaking in upon us!"

Peter gave a low growl and made a movement to confront James. But Jesus grasped his arm in restraint and shook his head sadly as he responded.

"My time is not yet come. For you, any time will do because the world cannot hate you. But it hates me because I testify that its works are evil."

James's thin smile was patronizing and insincere. But Jesus knew that the time was indeed approaching when he would have to set his face toward Jerusalem. The completion of his Father's work drew ever nearer.

12

Let Anyone Who Is Thirsty Come to Me and Drink

Bam! Startled students glanced warily at each other as their revered teacher emphasized his words with repeated blows on the low table.

"*This . . . man* is . . . *not* the . . . *promised . . . Messiah!*"

Rabbi Hilkiah reached for his staff and struggled up awkwardly from the stone bench to look down with stern disapproval at his wide-eyed study group. They had never before seen their rabbi so exasperated. Holding up his right fist to enumerate his arguments, Hilkiah shook his head fiercely with the extension of each finger.

"*Will* the Messiah come from Nazareth? No! *Will* he be a humble tradesman who wanders the shores of Galilee gathering illiterate fishermen as followers? No! *Will* he go about healing Gentiles? No! *Will* he associate with sinners, tax collectors, and immoral women? No! *Will* he be concerned with exorcising foul spirits? Again, no!"

Adopting a calmer but still insistent tone, Hilkiah raised his left hand to count his further arguments.

"And does this Nazarene do *anything* the Messiah is expected to do? Hmm? Does he promise to liberate Israel from Gentile rule? No!"

Daniel gently interjected, "But Rabbi, Jesus says that his kingdom is not of this—"

"*Does* he promise to perfect the Temple? No! *Does* he speak of bringing our dispersed brothers back to Palestine? No! Do not think I am ignorant of what this man teaches. He has been much discussed by your respected elders and we know that we judge righteously. So why," the rabbi pleaded in almost plaintive desperation, "*why* do you allow yourselves to be led astray by this obvious and dangerous imposter? Have you not heard his outrageous claims? He openly declares that anyone who loves their son or daughter more than him is not worthy to follow him! Who does he think he is? Our prophets have always prefaced their message with, 'Thus says the Lord,' but does the Galilean follow this respected tradition? Oh, no! He baldly states: 'Truly, *I* tell you!' But who is this man to tell us anything at all? He follows no acknowledged school. And is he not aware that 'Amen, Amen' is used to confirm another's words, not one's own?"[33]

The five young men nodded in respectful agreement, but Hilkiah's voice continued to rise in growing outrage.

"Furthermore, this charlatan blatantly breaks our Shabbat laws and insults our traditions. And how . . . how *dare* he call God his Father, making himself equal with the Holy One?[34] Do these . . . do these *sound* to you like the words of a sensible man? Or a respectable teacher? Who would speak like this but a . . . a raving lunatic?" Hilkiah spluttered in passionate, bubbling fury. "What is the *use* of studying scripture if you can be so easily misled? The *am ha-aretz* I can understand—what do the peasants of the land know about such matters—but *you*!"

The students looked down sheepishly as their teacher shuffled back to the bench, shaking his head in sorrowful anger and muttering bitterly. "Do you know that this man even rejects Moses's permission for divorce? And he has the audacity to think he can improve on commandments received directly from God!" Hilkiah grunted as he lowered himself carefully onto the seat. "Apparently, it is not good enough that we do not murder—no, we must not even entertain a single angry thought! And if you just once cast an admiring look upon a woman, you have already committed adultery! Is this reasonable? Must we stone every man in Judea? Hmm?"

Hilkiah stamped his staff on the ground for emphasis. But the rhetorical question received no answer.

"This madman berates learned teachers and urges ordinary people to be even more worthy than ourselves! I tell you now that no good will come of his folly. His growing popularity will only lead to yet another tragedy that our nation has seen all too often. Have you already forgotten the brutal destruction of those who followed false leaders? Think about that other deluded Galilean called Judas, or Athronges who put a crown on his head and declared himself king. Where are those men now? And where are their confident, adoring followers, hmm? Dead! Killed by the

Romans! I warn you again that this Jesus brings nothing but dissent and danger." Hilkiah held out his hands in appeal, striving to adopt a gentler tone. "Come now. Let us have no more of this nonsense. We will continue our study—"

"But, Rabbi, if you would only hear Jesus talk! No one speaks like him, with such—"

Bam! The rabbi drew in a deep breath and glared down at the clay floor, his outstretched hands slowly closing into clenched fists as he forced out his words. "*No*, Daniel! I will tolerate *no more talk* about this blasphemer. Anyone who even *speaks* the Nazarene's name is no longer welcome in this house! Not. Welcome."

For several minutes, Hilkiah's labored breathing was the only sound in the hushed room. Then he opened one hand and looked up. "Now— with your permission," he said, controlling a quaver as he spoke, "we will continue to explore the significant rituals of the Feast of Tabernacles, the last of our seven appointed times." The rabbi leaned back against the wall, and the tension gradually eased from his voice as he relaxed into the familiar comfort of imparting his extensive knowledge to others.

"As we were discussing, the Temple lamps burn continually to symbolize the Great Light that Isaiah prophesied will bring illumination to those who dwell in spiritual darkness. And remember God's promise that one day He will fill His people with His Holy Spirit: '*I will pour water on the thirsty land, and streams on the dry ground; I will pour out my Spirit on your offspring, and my blessing on your descendants.*' This water is the only true source of life, and it will be freely poured out in the days of the Messiah when '*with joy you will draw water from the wells of salvation.*' So, my young scholars, what does it symbolize when water and wine are both poured out on the altar during the water libation of Tabernacles? Hmm?"

Oblivious to the lack of response, the rabbi pressed on confidently.

"Water and wine together symbolize the life and the joy that are associated with the Holy Spirit. On no other festival has God specifically commanded us to be joyful. This is why we regard the spring *Pesach* festival as the time of liberation and new planting, and the autumn Tabernacles as the time of joyful final harvest. Do you see? Is this not a wonderful celebration?"

Hilkiah nodded encouragingly at his students.

"Tomorrow is the seventh day of the feast: *Hoshanah Rabbah*, the Great Salvation. Following closely after *Yom Kippur*, this will be our last opportunity in the year to repent and be restored to God, and we will all call upon Him to redeem us. What a tremendous day of celebration it will be! Well might Tabernacles be called the greatest and holiest feast of the year!"

But the rabbi's fervent words fell like stones into a deep well of silence. All enthusiasm seemed to have seeped out of the subdued young men who sat dumbly at his feet.

The autumn harvest was now fully underway, and the fragrance of apples and pomegranates permeated the sweet air. Skillful fingers rapidly plucked swollen grapes from the vines, and laughing children scrambled to collect dates and figs that would be transformed into sweet cakes and delicious syrup. Men shook and beat loaded olive branches, and women carried heaped baskets across the soft earth to where donkeys plodded in patient circles, rotating flat stones that pressed the fruit to an oily pulp.

Many thousands of pilgrims had poured into Jerusalem for the week of Tabernacles, also called *Sukkot*. The inhabitants of the city were mindful of the saying, "Be not forgetful to entertain strangers," and their hospitality was legendary. A few homes still hung a curtain across their doors to indicate that there was room for late festival guests.

As instructed in the Torah, people had been living outside in *sukkot* booths to commemorate the time when Israel wandered the desert in complete dependence upon the Great Shepherd. These temporary shelters, constructed from branches and gaily festooned with flowers and vines, had sprung up on every street, square, courtyard, and rooftop until the entire city was transformed into a vast leafy carpet that spread out across the hillsides within the limits of a Sabbath-day's journey, to include nearby towns such as Bethphage and Bethany on the Mount of Olives. A festive excitement pervaded the air: youngsters played exuberantly in the streets, old friends and returning relatives greeted each other joyously, rabbis preached to large groups, and shofar calls reverberated across the city.

On this seventh day of Great Salvation, Rachel hugged her shoulders and shifted excitedly from one foot to another, uplifted by the contagious enthusiasm of the pilgrims. Singing and dancing had gone on all night on the Temple Mount beneath enormous candelabra that illuminated the entire city. Now, buoyant with anticipation, a great crowd had gathered at the southeastern Pool of Siloam, which was fed underground from the

Gihon spring in the Kidron valley. A tremendous shout filled the air as a priest raised high a gleaming golden jug, filled with purifying, living water.

Then the priests turned and started to retrace their steps, pacing with ceremonious dignity back up the Tyropoeon valley toward the House of God, impressively arrayed in turbans, linen breeches, and long tunics adorned with wide sleeves and broad sashes. The wedding-like procession was accompanied by Levitical singers who also provided the jubilant sounds of tambourines, flutes, and lyres. Rachel allowed herself to be swept along as the throng made its way up the wide paved road lined with thousands of clapping, dancing people in festive clothing. The celebrants paraded noisily past houses and the Lower Market, gathering more children and excited pilgrims along the way, until their arrival at the Temple Mount was heralded by the ritual call of three shofar blasts.

The babbling crowd flowed along the base of the southern retaining wall, and some people ascended the wide steps toward large entrance gates that led up through underground ramps into the Temple precincts. But Rachel remained at street level for a while, enjoying the profusion of luxurious costumes from Arabia, Medea, Persia, Spain, and even India. Richly colored robes were ornamented with embroidered shawls, jewel-studded girdles of finely-wrought metal, tinkling anklets, and elaborate headdresses that held rows of gold and silver coins. Among the ostentatious display of wealth, ragged beggars shook their clay cups and cried out for mercy, pilgrims descended stone steps into sunken *mikvot* baths for ritual purification, and shoppers haggled loudly for souvenirs. Some goods were displayed in temporary booths, while others were laid out beneath arched stone structures that supported a large staircase at the corner of the western retaining wall.

Rachel was jostled against the cold stone wall as she carefully paced up these steps that ascended steeply, first leading the pilgrims away from the Mount then changing direction twice to sweep back across the great vaulted arches and over the street below. The voluble throng spilled out into the extensive Temple plaza, and Rachel observed her surroundings eagerly, from the green Mount of Olives in the east to the looming Antonia fortress on the northwest corner of the Mount, and her heart soared at the closeness of the Temple that shimmered brilliantly as if it was itself a source of light.

Then she turned to admire the towering columns of the Royal Stoa that opened into the plaza. The long colonnade was the hub of commercial transactions on the Mount, and high windows in its raised central aisle poured light down into its bustling corridors. Various tongues from guttural Germanic to liquid Parthian competed to be heard; soothsayers provided arcane information in their booths; sacrificial animals cooed and bleated; coins clinked at the tables of merchants and money-changers as sacrifices were purchased and currencies were exchanged for the acceptable Tyrian shekel and half-shekel. Strolling past the hubbub, Rachel smiled wryly as she thought of how her Abba railed against the irreverent nature of this rowdy center.

Then she briefly closed her eyes, savoring the rich fragrances of incense and aromatic wood smoke. But as she entered the Court of Women, she was assailed by a haunting sadness. Boisterous gaiety surrounded her as families and acquaintances clasped arms and chattered gaily, but she had no part in it. If only she had a sister or friend to share this important day with. But she was totally alone.

To distract herself from welling self-pity, Rachel idly noted the four unroofed chambers in the corners of the women's court. In the southeast chamber, Nazirites cut and burnt their hair at the end of their *nazir* period; the northeast room held wood for the altar fires; the northwest chamber contained the *mikvah* bath where purified lepers washed before presenting themselves to the priests; the southwest chamber stored wine and oil for altar offerings. And along a wall of this courtyard stood the public treasure chests with narrow necks and broad bases into which pilgrims were dropping their offerings according to each inscribed purpose: new shekels of that year, old shekels, pigeons and doves, burnt sacrifice, wood, frankincense, voluntary sacrifice, and gold for propitiation.

Rachel yearned to be even nearer the Temple, but women were not permitted beyond this court. She could only stare admiringly at the grand sweep of semicircular steps leading up to the gleaming bronze doors of the immense Nicanor Gate, which opened into the Court of Israel and the Court of Priests with its great altar of sacrifice from where dark smoke was now billowing into the sky.

Pushing through the press, Rachel climbed the steps to one of the temporary balconies that had been erected along the walls of the women's court for the *Sukkot* celebrations. The buzz of anticipation increased as the time for the important water-pouring ceremony approached, and Rachel's eyes flickered across the crowd in the hope of spotting at least one friendly face. Her father would be in the Court of Israel, but some of his students might be in the common section. She thought she had glimpsed Daniel on the outside stairs, but she could not be sure.

Then a great roar announced the approaching climax of the week-long festival. Together with thousands of pilgrims, Rachel praised God with heart and mouth and hands. Shouting "*Hoshiana*—save now!" they enthusiastically shook their *lulabs* woven from myrtle, willow, and palm branches. Accompanied by the loud cheering, barefoot priests reverently circled the altar for the prescribed seven times, then slowly ascended the ramp onto the enormous platform, and with perfect timing, two of them ceremoniously poured wine and living water into the spouts of two bowls.

A triumphant blare of trumpets announced the performance of the libation ritual, and the Levites on the curved steps of the Nicanor Gate burst into song. The air vibrated with the glorious sounds of harps, lyres, cymbals, and flutes as their resonant voices chanted from a Psalm of Ascent:

> *Israel, put your hope in the Lord,*
> *For with the Lord is unfailing love*
> *And with him is full redemption.*
> *He himself will redeem Israel*
> *From all their sins!*

Then the gathered pilgrims joyfully chanted antiphonal responses to the great praise psalm of the choir:

> *Give thanks to the Lord, for he is good:*
> His love endures forever!
> *Let Israel say:*
> His love endures forever!
> *Let the house of Aaron say:*
> His love endures forever!
> *Let those who fear the Lord say:*
> His love endures forever!

Elated by the deeply stirring verses, the crowd sent up a final shout of jubilation, and tears of humble gratitude ran down Rachel's face. Everyone gradually quietened down in anticipation of the sacrifice, with souls yearning collectively for God's promised redemption.

Then Rachel noticed something curious. A ripple seemed to be spreading out in the crowd below. Raised arms were slowly being lowered and heads were turning inward toward a voice that raised itself above the background hum. Rachel peered down to identify the focus of attention: a man in a dark homespun cloak was speaking loudly in the middle of the women's court, gesturing with expressive hands. His head was raised, and his voice floated up as he turned to address the throng, repeating his message with uplifted arms.

"Again I say to you, let anyone who is thirsty come to me and drink. Whoever believes in me, as scripture has said, rivers of living water will flow from within them!"

Rachel shivered. The voice was strangely moving, vibrant with compassion and tenderness. There was a stir of confusion and some mutterings of disapproval. It was unheard of for any teacher to interrupt these holy celebrations. And what was this strange fellow claiming? The murmurs grew in strength.

"What does he mean, 'Come to *me* and drink'? Drink what?"

"Living water represents God's Holy Spirit, so how can this man provide it?"

"Yes, God is the only source of that water!"

"I know this man!" exclaimed a woman behind Rachel. "This is the teacher from Galilee who has been challenging our traditions."

"Yes, it is Jesus the Nazarene," came a confirmation. "I have heard him teach."

"Then isn't he the one our leaders are trying to kill? Yet here he is, speaking boldly in public, and no one is saying a word to him."

"Could they perhaps think he is the Messiah after all?"

"But we know where this man comes from," someone else countered. "And when the Messiah comes, no one will know where he is from."

"Well, when the Messiah does come, will he perform more signs than this man?"

"And how does he teach so well, having never been taught?"

"Yes! I say that a great prophet has arisen among us!"

"Or perhaps God has visited his people!"

"No! The man is clearly insane and possessed by a demon! Why do you listen to him?"

"But how can a crazy man open the eyes of the blind?"

There was a deep rift among the people. Some were impressed by the teacher's commanding presence and his reputation for healing, while others were infuriated by his bizarre claims and uttered threats against him. But no one laid a hand on Jesus as he made his way slowly through the crowd toward the gates, followed by many curious and excited pilgrims.

Rachel felt powerfully drawn to the departing figure who seemed so ordinary in his plain garments and yet so inspiring at the same time. What did he mean that he could give them living water to drink? What was he promising to provide? Was her Abba correct that the Galilean was merely a deluded troublemaker? But why did the teacher seem so confident and exude such authority? Questions tumbled around Rachel's head in confusion while her innermost being strained with longing to be near this enigmatic man and hear his words.

Then it struck her that this teacher not only offered to provide living water but also claimed to be the bread of life and even light itself! The psalmist's words rose in Rachel's mind: "*For with You is the fountain of life; in Your light we see light.*" Surely Jesus wasn't claiming to be like God! But was it merely a coincidence that the furnishings of the Temple included a laver of purifying water, a menorah of light that was never extinguished, and the Bread of God's Presence? Rachel longed to discuss this with her Abba, but she knew that could not happen. Who was this fascinating teacher from Nazareth? And what would be the consequence of how his teachings were received?

13

He Was Lost and Is Now Found

"Why did you not bring him in?"

The unanswered question hung heavily in the menacing silence. Sunlight streamed through the high windows, bouncing off the polished surfaces and tiled floor of the apse in the Royal Stoa. The four Temple guards glanced furtively at each other, intimidated by the semicircle of seated priests, elders, Pharisees, and teachers of the law. In particular, they avoided the scowl of the high priest, Caiaphas, who cut an imposing figure in his fine linen embroidered with gold, purple, and scarlet thread.

"I ask you four again," Caiaphas repeated stolidly, staring intensely at the guards. "Why did you not bring him in? You were sent to arrest Jesus of Nazareth, yet you return to me emptyhanded. Why did you not obey your orders to bring in the Nazarene? Answer me!"

One officer reluctantly mumbled something.

"Speak up! What did you say?"

"Respectfully, *Kohen HaGadol*, I have never heard . . . No one ever spoke the way this man does."

His three companions quickly nodded in agreement but stopped abruptly when the high priest snorted in disgust.

"You mean he has deceived you also? Do any of the rulers or the Pharisees believe in this man?" Caiaphas gestured broadly to the seated gathering. "No! He can only persuade an ignorant mob that knows nothing of the law—there is a curse on those peasants!" Caiaphas flicked his hand dismissively. "Take these men away. I will deal with them later."

Animated chatter sprang up among the council as the subdued officers were ushered out. Then Caiaphas spoke out loudly, gesturing angrily with a raised fist.

"This Galilean dares to heal *goyim* and heathen Romans in the holy name of the Lord God! He criticizes our teachings, challenges our sacred traditions, and tells stories about Samaritans who are nobler than our priests! He even claims to be greater than Solomon and Abraham! What gives this oaf the right to act in such an offensive manner?"

A scribe rose slowly from his chair, smoothing his curled beard as he nodded in solemn agreement. "Indeed, Caiaphas, you speak justly. For this workman from Galilee has no skill in the Law and no learning, yet he instructs his gullible followers to observe his *own* commandments. I have been reliably informed that the scoundrel compares our traditions to old wineskins that will be burst by his new teachings! This is unheard of. Where will this behavior lead? If any teacher can simply make up new injunctions, what will be left of our role? Of what value will be the hallowed wisdom that we accumulate and dispense to the people? Do we not possess the knowledge to deliver righteous judgment?"

"Quite right!" A loud voice rose above the assenting hum as the first speaker stiffly retook his seat. "No one can rightly question our proficiency or our purity—our decisions are based firmly on scripture and are aimed solely at pleasing God. Therefore, if we conclude that Jesus's claims are false, the people must accept our judgment. How can some uneducated worker from an insignificant town have the audacity to call us 'blind guides' and promise sinful tax collectors and harlots that they will enter into God's kingdom before us? We must ensure that this insulting challenger is decisively dealt with!"

A third member raised his hand. "I concur. The ignorant masses are easily deceived, but we who are closest to God's word are the recognized interpreters of Torah and the providers of truth. It is our heavy responsibility to make a hedge about the Law and protect it from such false teachers. I say that this imposter Jesus and his close disciples should be severely punished. By all rights, such abominations should die!"

Some of the council shifted uneasily in their seats and a few shook their heads. A grey-headed Pharisee spoke up mildly among the general murmuring.

"Your words are harsh indeed, Eleazar. It leads me to ask, does our law judge a man unless it first hears from him and knows what he does?"

Caiaphas snorted again. "Are you also from Galilee, Nicodemus, that you would defend this teacher?"

"I must support Nicodemus, my worthy friends," contributed Joseph from Arimathea, pulling distractedly at his earlobe. "After all, what is our true responsibility: to provide guidance to our people or to destroy them?"

Then the Pharisee Gamaliel stood and turned to face the council, his arms folded in voluminous sleeves.[35] As grandson of the highly esteemed Hillel the Elder, Gamaliel wielded substantial authority in the Sanhedrin, and heads inclined respectfully toward him.

"Men of Israel," he said gravely. "Our fellow councilor Joseph asks a crucial question. Consider carefully what you intend to do with this Jesus. We must recall that he is not the first teacher to be proclaimed as someone important. Remember Judas the Galilean who led a band of men in revolt? He was killed by the Romans, as were his followers. Therefore, in the present case, my advice would be that you leave Jesus and his followers alone—" Gamaliel held up a hand and raised his voice above the instant hiss of disapproval. "No, listen to my words. After all, if their action is merely of human origin, it will fail like previous messianic movements. But if their message is from God, you will not be able to stop them. In fact, you might find yourselves fighting against God."

"Perhaps so," Eleazar snapped, glowering grimly as Gamaliel returned to his seat. "But it is also true that many continue to flock to Jesus because they believe he performs miraculous signs. If we allow him to continue like this, more will come to support him, including even the *goyim*! Perhaps men will rise in his name, and as you so kindly remind us, Gamaliel, when superstitious and ignorant men attach themselves to a pseudo-messiah, the inevitable outcome is destruction!"

There was a loud buzz of agreement as Eleazar pursued his argument, gesticulating passionately with a rigid hand. "It might be that in this case Pilate will respond even more violently than ever before. And the Romans will not continue to support our position as leaders if we cannot be relied upon to keep the peace among our own people! Indeed, are we not taught that a prophet who leads a city astray must be killed?"

"With respect, Eleazar" Nicodemus interposed gently, "that injunction applies to the practice of sorcery or idol worship, whereas in the case of Jesus—"[36]

"Enough!" Caiaphas burst out, slamming a fist on the arm of his ornate chair. "Do you not see that Eleazar offers sage words of warning?

Jesus threatens both our position among the people and our accord with the Roman leadership. Surely it is better that one man should die for the people than for the whole nation to perish? From this moment we must consider the Galilean to be condemned to death! Who agrees?"

Caiaphas cast a fierce look around the room, focusing on each solemn face. Under the sustained challenge, hands were slowly raised until a majority was reached. "Good. We are decided," the high priest nodded in grim satisfaction. "Now, as our powers under Roman rule are severely curtailed,[37] we must devise a strategy for ending the influence of this Galilean before more of our people or even the *goyim* are led astray!"

"Listen, you proud children of Abraham—you sons and daughters of the Most High. Listen while I tell you more about what the kingdom of God is like. He who has ears to hear, let him hear!"

A flickering line of fire scribbled its way across a dark field as a farmer burnt the after-harvest stubble. High above, a vast flock of migrating storks slowly beat its way south, flashing white against the burgeoning blue-black clouds that promised early winter rain. But the seated crowd kept their eyes on the teacher in anticipation of an entertaining parable. Gusts of chilly, moist wind carried Jesus's voice across the sloping ground.

"A certain man had two sons. The younger said, 'Father, give me my share of your property.'"

Voices of condemnation immediately peppered the damp air. No decent young man would dream of demanding his inheritance while his father was alive! This was a highly offensive act. But the noisy reactions were quickly hushed as Jesus resumed.

"So the father divided his property. Then this son gathered all he had and traveled to a far country where he wasted his wealth in riotous living. When he had spent it all, there was a severe famine in that country, and he began to be in need. So he hired himself out to a citizen of that country, who sent him to feed the pigs."

This was even worse! There were loud groans of disgust that a Jewish son would disgrace himself and his family by working with swine. There was little hope for this reprobate!

"The son grew so hungry that he craved to fill his belly with carob pods that the pigs ate, but no one gave him any. Then the young man came to his senses and said to himself, 'Even my father's hired servants have bread to spare, yet here I am dying of hunger! I will go to my father and say: Father, I have sinned against heaven and against you. I am no longer worthy to be called your son; make me as one of your hired servants.' So the young man returned home."

"Surely the father won't let him into his house!" came a loud suggestion.

"Yes, it's too late for remorse now!" called another.

"The father must beat the son and disown him after such an insult."

"And break a pot in a *kezazah* ceremony to cut off the wastrel from the entire village!"

"Ssshhh! We cannot hear!"

Jesus proceeded with the tale, shading his eyes and pointing as if trying to make out an object in the far distance. "But while the son was still a long way off, his father, who had been watching for him every day, saw him and was moved with compassion. He lifted his cloak and ran out to meet him, falling on his neck and kissing him."

Shouts of surprise and groans of disapproval accompanied Jesus's teaching.

"The son said to him, 'Father, I have sinned against heaven and against you. I am no longer worthy to be called your son. Make me as one of your hired servants.' But the father said to his servants, 'Bring out the best robe and put it on my son. Put a ring on his finger and sandals on his feet. Bring the fattened calf and kill it so that we might feast!' And they began to celebrate."

People looked bemused and chatted among themselves. What was this parable supposed to teach? Did it describe God's love and compassion? It was indeed a wonderful tale of repentance and forgiveness, but if the father was God, who were the sons supposed to be?

"What about the other son?" came the question.

"Well," Jesus responded, "the elder son was in the field. When he came toward the house he heard music and dancing, so he called one of the servants who explained, 'Your brother has come home, and your father has killed the fattened calf because he has him back safe and healthy.' The brother was angry to hear this and would not go in."

"I'd also be furious!" called a boisterous voice. "That young brat burnt his boat when he turned his back on his family!"

There were laughs and shouts of agreement until Jesus raised his hand.

"The father went out to plead with the elder son," he continued. "But the son answered, 'I have served you these many years without disobeying you and you never gave me even a goat that I might celebrate with my friends! But when this son of yours comes home, who has wasted your property with prostitutes, you kill the fattened calf for him!'"

"That *is* unfair!"

"Yes, how can reckless behavior receive a greater reward than loyalty?"

"Exactly!"

"Well," said Jesus, "hear what the father said to this son."

Everyone fell silent to focus on the final message of the puzzling parable.

"'My son,' the father said to the older boy, 'you are always with me, and all I have is yours. But it is right that we now celebrate and be glad, for this brother of yours was dead and is now alive. He was lost and is now found.'"

Heads titled and foreheads wrinkled in thought as Jesus sat down and lifted a water skin to take a deep draught. There was a drone of muted discussion. "Was lost and is now found" was certainly a good line. But who was the lost son supposed to be, who rejected their father but finally came home in repentance? And who was the older son, who understandably resented the loving welcome given to his disloyal and foolish brother? The parable seemed to require more explanation or clues. Sometimes this teacher said too little rather than too much.

14

I Am Not of This World

Darkness set in as the door and shutters were firmly closed. Among muted whispers, a flint rasped in the gloom and light flared out from an oil lamp on the small wooden table. Daniel's gaze ranged over the tense expressions of the gathered men, noting some unfamiliar faces in the uneven lamplight as his brother Caleb spoke in a hushed voice.

"Welcome, comrades. It gladdens my heart to see how our numbers are swelling. Following our last meeting, I am pleased to report on the growing belief that Jesus is indeed the promised Messiah. It is said he can miraculously provide food, calm a tempest, heal all manner of ailments, and even raise the dead! Every day more men declare that they are prepared to rise in his name. Some of the teacher's followers in Galilee tried to take him and declare him king, but unfortunately he learned of their plan and withdrew into the mountains. Jesus continues to hold back, but if we do not strike soon against the Romans, our opportunity might be lost!"

"But Caleb," Daniel responded hesitantly. "Jesus does not declare a confrontation with Rome. He instructs the people to continue paying taxes, and he says his kingdom is not of this world—"

"This is of no importance, Daniel," Caleb interrupted tersely, shaking his head. "The Galilean might not speak politically, but he will be the perfect focal point for the uprising we have spoken of for so many years. No man has performed the miracles this one does! All Judea is talking about his remarkable powers, and we will never again be able to rally so many to our cause. Simon Zealotes, would you like to address us about Jesus's plans? We are keen to hear directly from one of his disciples."

All heads turned toward the tall, angular follower of Jesus. His dark eyes flickered across the group as he spoke. "Your support is highly valued, Caleb. However, during my time with Jesus, I have come to realize that he is reluctant to publicly pronounce his claim as Messiah. I suspect he lacks the grit to face the reaction this might provoke. And many of his followers prefer to talk about sharing cloaks and humbly serving one another rather than throwing off Roman tyranny."

Simon Zealotes briefly compressed his lips into a thin line of frustration before he continued.

"I and my fellow disciple Judas Iscariot have come to doubt that the teacher will make any move against our oppressors unless we provoke him into an open declaration or act of resistance. However, we believe that if we plan correctly, Jesus could be the answer to our patriotic prayers. For his own good, we must use his popularity to mobilize support and then force a confrontation with the Romans. We will rise up like Maccabees, the "hammer" of two hundred years ago. Like them, we will smash the *goyim* and liberate Israel!"

A roar of approval was quickly muted by Caleb's warning hand. "I can see why you are called the zealous one, Simon! You truly share the spirit of those of us who are jealous for the Law and determined to free our people from foreign oppression."

"Indeed, Caleb. But our liberation that is promised in scripture will not come about if we merely sit around piously waiting for the kingdom of God to arrive. We must act with commitment, expressing our zeal in the only way that counts—in armed conflict against the heathens who strip us of our land and our rights!"

"Well said!"

Simon punched his fist into an open hand. "This must be our rallying call," he whispered vehemently, "to reestablish the Maccabean kingdom that passed into the tainted hands of Herod the Idumean. Our nation has not experienced glory since that time, but there have been other heroes. We must fight like the patriot Ezekias who was beheaded by Herod, or his son Judas the Galilean who urged us to resist Roman taxation as a badge of servitude.[38] Just as they aspired to the throne, so must we now do all in our power to oust the collaborator Antipas and establish ourselves as an independent power under King Jesus!"

Among the restrained but enthusiastic response, Caleb's close friend Gideon spoke up. "All of us here are in accord with you, Simon. So what is the news from comrade Judas? Will he be joining us tonight?"

"No, Judas is being wisely cautious. He cannot risk associating with any suspected patriots in case this jeopardizes his negotiations with the Temple priests, who of course know nothing about our plans."

"Accepted. But when will be the time of our rising?"

Simon's voice took on an edge of excitement as he leaned forward. "Judas is developing a plan that will be sprung during one of our feasts, at a time when our armed supporters are dispersed among the thousands of pilgrims."

"What about the coming Feast of Dedication?" came a suggestion.

"Yes!" Gideon agreed vehemently. "Imagine the mood of the people as they commemorate the Maccabees' conquest of King Antiochus's heathen army and the rededication of the Temple that was defiled when a pig was slaughtered on the altar! The *Hanukkah* Feast of Dedication could provide a perfect opportunity to rouse nationalist fervor, with every home and shop displaying a light to symbolize loyalty to the Jewish cause."

Gideon's voice grew more passionate, accompanied by bitter murmurs around him. "We will remind our people how the murderous troops of Antiochus butchered our men, women, and children, forbade our Shabbats and festivals, and burnt our Torahs!"

"And tortured and killed those who continued to circumcise their sons or refused to bow to idols!" exclaimed another.

"And sold thousands of Jewish families into slavery!"

"Yes!" Caleb added hotly, slamming a hand on the table. "When the *Hanukkah* menorah is lit, with its eight lamps representing a new beginning, we could harness the bitterness of our people and promise a new life, cleansed from Roman pollution. The lamps are lit by the ninth *shemash* flame, and we will teach that Jesus is this *shemash* or servant that brings light! This light will be a new political dispensation—liberation from foreign subjugation!"

Spontaneous cheers were quickly hushed by Simon's glare as he interjected.

"No, Caleb! You must not do anything to precipitate action! Jesus does indeed plan to attend the *Hanukkah* celebrations, but comrade Judas must decide if this feast is to be the appointed time for you to mobilize your forces. It is vital that our strategy is not rushed. You all know your duty during this critical time of preparation: cautiously spread the word about the coming revolt to everyone you trust and encourage them to join us, collect whatever weapons you can, and await further instructions."

Each man nodded firmly and raised an arm. As fists met, the small room filled with fierce whispers of commitment and encouragement.

"God is our only Ruler and Lord!"

"We accept no other as Lord!"

"We will not submit to the Roman yoke of tyranny!"

"We are the ones with zeal!"

"We do not fear death!"

"Everyone who spills the blood of a pagan is like one who brings a sacrifice to the Temple!"

"Death to all Romans!"

A hand reached out and the lamplight flared and died, plunging the room into darkness. One by one, each man checked outside the doorway and slipped quietly past the posted guard until he, too, melted into the night. No one noticed the figure squatting outside with trembling hands held tightly over her mouth. Or the moonlight that glinted in the wide eyes of Rachel bat-Maoz.

The first winter rains had finally fallen. Gratefully sucking in the precious moisture, the thirsty earth had magically transformed it, casting it out in bright bursts of gaiety, sprinkling fields and hedges with pink and white cyclamen and red and purple splashes of anemones. Across the terraced hillsides around Jerusalem, industrious farmers took advantage of the freshly softened earth, guiding iron plows behind stoic oxen to break the stubble of the autumn harvest and unfold glistening slabs of rich red clay. Preparation was also being made for the winter feeding of livestock, and all manner of edible fodder was bundled into storerooms: hay, straw, shoots, stalks, gourds, and carob pods. And during the mild days that alternated between cloud and sun, the city bustled with excitement in preparation for *Hanukkah*, the Feast of Dedication.

On this calm morning, Jesus was teaching in the double portico known as Solomon's Porch, which ran along the eastern wall of the Temple Mount. He fell silent as a group of young mothers approached, their high-pitched voices imploring him to bless their children. Some disciples stepped forward and gestured irritably for the women to leave, but their teacher rebuked them firmly.

"No. Let the little children come to me, and do not hinder them, for the kingdom of God belongs to such as these."

Kneeling down, Jesus tenderly took each child in his arms and placed his hands on them in a loving benediction. Mothers wept with pleasure as they received their gurgling children to their breasts. Jesus smiled fondly.

"Truly, I tell you," he said, "unless you change and become like these little children, you will not enter the kingdom of heaven. Therefore, whoever takes the lowly position of a child is the greatest in the kingdom of heaven. And whoever welcomes one such child in my name welcomes me."

Jesus straightened up to address his followers, his voice carrying a note of reproach.

"Why do you call me, 'Lord, Lord,' and do not what I say? Not everyone who calls me Lord will enter into the kingdom of heaven, but only he who does the will of my Father who is in heaven. Be warned that a day is coming when many will tell me, 'Lord, did we not prophesy in your name, in your name cast out demons, and in your name do many mighty works?' Then I will tell them, 'I never knew you. Depart from me, you who work iniquity.'"

A Pharisee with a luxuriously oiled beard grunted scornfully and raised his voice in arrogant confidence.

"Who are you to be making such bold statements about yourself and the kingdom of heaven? You are the only witness to your strange claims, so your testimony is not valid!"

Onlookers listened intently as Jesus responded.

"Even if I do testify on my behalf, my testimony is valid. For I know where I have come from and where I am going, while you have no idea where I am from or where I am going because you judge by human standards. But in any case, my statements are indeed valid because I am *not* alone. Is it not written in your law that the testimony of two witnesses is accepted? Well, I testify for myself, and my other witness is the Father who sent me."

"Ha! Where is this father, then, as the other witness to your bizarre statements?" came the loud challenge.

"You do not know me or my Father," Jesus replied firmly. "But I tell you that soon I must go away, and you will look for me but will not find me. For where I go, you cannot come."

More people were wandering closer, attracted by the raised voices, and Jesus's ambiguous statement sparked speculation among the growing crowd.

"What does he mean he is going away?"

"Does he plan to kill himself?"

"Is that why he says, 'Where I go, you cannot come'?"

"You are from below," Jesus continued. "But I am from above. You are of this world, but I am not. And I have told you that unless you believe that I am, you will die in your sins.[39] If you held to my words, you would know the truth, and the truth would set you free. But instead you seek to kill me—a man who has told you the truth that I have heard from God!'

"Indeed!" came a mocking shout. "What world do you think you are from, then?"

"Yes, and who do you imagine is trying to kill you?" laughed another. "You are a mad man possessed by a demon!"

But Jesus shook his head calmly. "No, I speak truly: many of you know about the plots against me. But if God were your Father, you would love me, for I have come from God. Why is my language not clear to you? Because you are unable to comprehend what I say! When I tell you the truth, you do not believe me because you do not belong to God!"

Jesus's challenge provoked outraged cries from the listeners. How dare this teacher deny that they were children of God!

"So who do you claim to be, then?" a peevish voice burst out. "How long will you keep us in suspense? If you are the Messiah, tell us plainly!"

"I have told you," Jesus answered clearly, "but you do not believe! And the works that I do in my Father's name bear witness about me, but you deny them because you are not among my sheep and do not recognize my voice. If I do not do the works of my Father, then do not believe me. But if I do them, you must believe my works that you have seen with your own eyes,[40] so that you may understand that the Father is in me and I am in the Father. I tell you now that I and the Father are one."

"How can you be one with God?"

"Ha! Did you hear that? This proves the fellow is crazy!"

"You deserve to be stoned for such a claim!"

Jesus interrupted the outburst. "I have shown you many good works. For which of them do you wish to stone me?"

"It is not for works that you should be stoned, but for blasphemy because you, being a man, make yourself God!"

"Yes! Your arrogant claims cannot be allowed to stand!"

"Do not listen to this imposter!"

"All of you who tolerate this blasphemy, be warned that action will be taken!"

Jesus's accusers moved off in fury, accompanied by those who feared attracting the extreme antagonism that was developing against this man and his strange teachings. Some who had dared to speak out in support of the Nazarene had been threatened with expulsion from the synagogue, and it seemed that to be associated with Jesus was to court the increasingly dangerous disapproval of influential Jewish leadership.

15

My Peace I Give to You

"BUT THIS MAKES NO sense, Joseph! Surely even you can see that!"

Lucius rubbed a hand over his pale, cropped hair and pushed himself briskly from the padded leather chair, his brow knotted in frustrated disapproval. Joseph patiently watched the broad back of his host while the tribune approached the deep wooden sideboard and topped up his wine. Then Lucius turned back, gesturing with his goblet in irritation.

"You cannot deny that you Jews have suffered, Joseph. Wasn't your nation enslaved for hundreds of years by the Egyptians? And look at your present plight—you continue to strike out at us, and we in turn continue to pound you back into the ground! If your god really is all-powerful and loves your nation as you claim, why does he not use his power to drive us out and restore your land to you? Answer me that. Has he wandered off, perhaps? Is he sleeping for a thousand years? How can you people hold on to this blind belief that he loves you?"

Lucius retook his seat, resting an elbow on one knee as he leaned forward to make his point. "The fickle gods often desert us when it suits them, and we don't expect anything else, which is why we must continually propitiate them with gifts and prayers. We are certainly not so arrogant as to believe they *love* us! That is an absurdly foolish belief, Joseph! Nothing you have said makes sense to me. Or to any sane man, for that matter."

Joseph responded pensively. "There is no doubt, Tribune, that on this issue we stand at points that are exceedingly far apart. You Romans and Greeks have gods *of* love, which are dedicated *to* the art of love, but you do not have any god that *is* love."

Lucius nodded firmly and sat back. "Precisely!" he said with grim satisfaction, raising his goblet in mock salute. "Well put! I could not agree more. And this is because of one simple fact, Joseph: gods cannot love mankind any more than we can love a . . . a nest of ants! I state categorically that no god loves humanity for its own sake. We hear about gods and goddesses falling in love with a particular human being, but this usually ends in disaster." Lucius pulled a wry face. "In this regard the gods are much like us: they might be obsessed with a human being for a while, but if the relationship is threatened they usually destroy the hapless mortal! This we can understand. But a god who continues to offer love in the face of repeated disloyalty—this I cannot accept. You tell me that your people have often turned their back on your "One God" and worshiped other gods, is that not so?"

As Joseph nodded slowly in confirmation, Lucius gave a scoffing laugh and continued. "Then I despise your weak god if he continues to regard you as his people! Or I am not surprised that he has deserted you!"

"Oh, no, Tribune. This is where you stray far from the truth. For God is not as we humans are. Unlike us, He does not love for what He can gain. No, His love is freely offered for our sake and remains eternally unchanged whether we accept or reject Him. What does change, however, is how He expresses this love. As His people, we will either experience the grace of His love or the righteous wrath of His love, depending on which path we choose. Our God is a compassionate and righteous Husband, and He will not forsake us. However, we will be corrected in times of disloyalty."

Lucius merely grunted again and rubbed his creased forehead.

"So tell me," he asked after a short silence, "when did this trouble with your god start?"

Joseph angled his head slightly as he searched for the right words.

"To answer this, I must reach back to the beginning, Tribune. When God formed creation, there was no suffering. There was only peace and harmony, which God declared to be very good. Then he created the man Adam and placed him in the Garden of Eden to cultivate it and be *shomer* over it—an important word, Tribune, which means to guard and preserve. This same word is used when we are instructed to preserve God's commandments and his covenant. The first man therefore had a crucial role to play in cooperating with God's plans for creation. God warned Adam and the woman Eve not to overreach their intended purpose, and in particular, not to eat from the tree of knowledge of good and evil."

"Ha!" Lucius snorted. "Already your tale makes little sense. Why would a god not want humanity to be wise enough to tell the difference between good and evil? Or is this again something to do with being sheep?"

"Indeed not, worthy Tribune." Joseph's eyes crinkled at the corners. "Our scripture encourages us to seek wisdom, and King Solomon prayed that God would bless him with a discerning heart to distinguish right from wrong. However, Adam and Eve desired far more than merely discerning evil: they wanted to know it and experience it intimately, in the same way that a man is said to 'know' his wife."

"This is surely splitting hairs, like the argument of a sophist," Lucius responded curtly, waving a hand in rejection.

"Perhaps I can explain it like this, Tribune: humanity is indeed expected to exercise wisdom in *choosing* to walk the correct path, but it does not lie with us to *define* the correct path. This must follow solely from God's guidance. We are taught: '*Trust in the Lord with all your heart and lean not on your own understanding. In all your ways acknowledge Him, and He shall direct your paths. Do not be wise in your own eyes.*'"

Lucius shrugged. "Like sheep," he muttered into his glass of wine.

Joseph persevered, ignoring the comment.

"Think about this, Tribune. When God brought the entire cosmos into being, He separated primal opposites: light from darkness, the heavens from the earth, and water from land. His creation, which was very good, presumably existed separately from evil. We were therefore designed to function only within God's good creation. Knowing both good and evil is solely His prerogative, and exposure to it is far more than we are able to bear. I urge you to consider what you see in the world around us: the appalling chaos and violence that results from each of us believing we can forge our own way. We want to taste and experience everything possible, both good and evil, and we believe we are qualified to make moral judgments independent of our Creator. As if we could safely pass through such corrupting experiences. As if we could judge more wisely than our Shepherd."

"Hmm," Lucius sounded unconvinced. "So tell me, what did your Adam and Eve decide to do about this tree of knowledge?"

"They chose to believe the tempter's promise that its knowledge would make them like gods. They defied God's direct instruction and ate from the tree."

Wine sloshed in Lucius's goblet as he let out a blast of laughter. "So the trouble started right at the beginning! I'll bet Eve had a lot to do with it, like the foolish Pandora who opened a jar of the gods to release death and evil."

"Well, this first disobedience in Eden indicates something that still holds sway today: our stubborn rejection of anything that limits our freedom, regardless of the consequences. In rebelling against God's will, we reveal our ultimate intention—to *be* gods."

"So how did your god respond to this flagrant disobedience?"

"Needless to say, Adam and Eve did not achieve the divine autonomy they aspired to. In a typically human reaction, Adam blamed Eve and Eve blamed the tempter, but as God had warned them, they were cast out of His Presence in a form of spiritual death. And this rejection of God's authority called forth His curse upon the earth, so that our alienation from God is now reflected in nature." Joseph nodded mournfully. "Yes, the suffering that afflicts all creatures reveals the profound impact of humanity's separation from God. As rebels against our Creator's will, we now lie in the grip of cosmic powers that have been strengthened by our disobedience—powers that are antagonistic to God, to humanity, and to all of creation."

"Well, that's an entertaining story to explain the turmoil of our world, Joseph," Lucius said lightly. "But we could just as easily blame our own gods or Pandora."

"Yes, Tribune, this is indeed a decision that faces each one of us. But we are taught that in the eyes of God, there is no safe middle ground on this issue. The rebellion in Eden led to exile from God's Presence; only those within Noah's ark survived the great flood; in Egypt, the Angel of Death only passed over those who were protected by the blood of the sacrificial lamb. We must each of us choose to be for or against God's will and to be under His merciful protection or exposed to His wrath."

"Well," Lucius responded sardonically, "this is exactly why we hedge our bets by including many powerful gods within our pantheon. But even this does not prevent us from experiencing problems."

"In our belief, Tribune, some suffering provides a call to repentance. Hear God's words through his prophet Amos:

> *I blasted you with blight and mildew,*
> *yet you have not returned to Me.*
> *I sent among you a plague,*
> *yet you have not returned to Me.*
> *Therefore prepare to meet your God, O Israel!*

You claim that we would not suffer if an omnipotent God loved us, Tribune." Joseph's eyes gleamed intensely as he held out a hand in appeal. "But this argument mistakenly imagines that God's love is a sentimental wish for us to be comfortable in this world. No, His love is not a weak emotion but a holy, uncompromising force. It is the love of His Glory that He chooses to share with us and which must involve correction to bring us to perfection. God warns: '*I will be his Father, and he shall be My son. If he commits iniquity, I will chasten him with the rod of men.*' With God, there can be no mercy without wrath. However, He does offer His holy grace to all who repent."

Lucius again stood abruptly, this time gesturing to the guard to indicate that the session was over. His eyebrows drew closer in barely concealed exasperation as he stated his adamant conclusion. "I still say, Joseph, that it makes no sense to talk about a god who is all-powerful and all-loving and yet allows you to suffer."

Joseph also rose and gently laid a hand on the Roman's brawny forearm. "We do not deny our suffering, Tribune," he said calmly. "But we have a different interpretation of our plight. We know with certainty that the all-powerful God is able to end suffering and that He does desire to end it. Therefore, the fact that we still suffer indicates this simple conclusion: God's plan for His creation is not yet completed."

"The Son of Man must yet suffer many things."

The grey-white sky stretched overhead, brittle and chilled like a vast slab of scored ice. Pale winter mist drifted across the hills, scattering the dim morning light in all directions and wrapping the groves in eerie winding sheets. Spectral trees dripped rainwater from dark leaves, and the bleak atmosphere lent a sharp poignancy to Jesus's words. He had stopped in a damp clearing on their way across the Mount of Olives, and his close followers now stood forlornly around him as he forced them to hear hard truths.

"While we were yet in Galilee, I taught you that the Son of Man must be delivered up to the chief priests and teachers who will mock and condemn him and hand him over to the Gentiles to be scourged and killed. But after three days he will rise."

The disciples had by now heard this warning more than once, but they still did not know how to interpret the strange words. And they were reluctant to ask for an explanation. After all, when Peter had rejected Jesus's first prediction of his suffering, their teacher had compared his response to the temptations of the devil! Jesus now walked among the small group, spreading reassurance and fortitude through his firm touch.

"These things," he said gently, "have filled your hearts with sorrow. But I tell you this so you will be strengthened and not stumble during the trials that lie ahead. For whoever wishes to be my disciple must deny themselves and take up their cross and follow me. Whoever wants to save their life will lose it, but whoever loses their life for my sake will save it. After all, what does it profit to gain the whole world but forfeit your soul?"

The mournful call of a dove echoed hauntingly through the shrouded woods.

"I send you out as sheep among wolves, for the good news must be preached to all nations.[41] But you will be hated for my name's sake, and the time is coming when they will beat you and put you out of the synagogues. A servant is not greater than his lord, so if they accuse me of being a master of the house of Beelzebul, how much more will they accuse you! Yes, those who kill you will even believe they serve God because they have not known the Father or me."

A few of the women wiped away tears of dread as Jesus tried to soften the impact of his appalling message.

"But remember, are not two sparrows sold for a pittance? And yet not one of them falls to the ground apart from your Father's will. Therefore do not be afraid. You are of more value than many sparrows. And everyone who confesses me before men, I will also confess them before my Father in heaven. Be assured that the Father will honor anyone who chooses to serve me. So do not be afraid of those who kill the body but are not able to kill the soul."

John wrapped an arm around James's shoulder in a gesture meant to strengthen them both as they listened intently to their master's disturbing words.

"You know that in this world everyone experiences trouble and pain. After all, those eighteen who died when the tower in Siloam fell on them—do you think they were worse offenders than all others in Jerusalem? And when Pilate's soldiers mingled Galilean blood with the Temple sacrifices, were these men worse sinners than others? No. But you must take heart because I have overcome the world! You believe in God—believe also in me, for he who endures to the end will be saved."

The urgency in Jesus's voice intensified his followers' anxiety. Sensing their deep unease, he raised his hands toward them, palms down in blessing, and his voice reverberated among the dark sentinels of silent oaks.

"I am the Way, the Truth, and the Life. No one comes to the Father, except through me."

As the lone dove called again, Jesus lowered his arms and bathed his loyal disciples with a reassuring smile that somehow eased the tightness in their chests despite their chilling fear.

"My peace I give to you—not as the world gives, but my peace. So do not let your heart be troubled, neither let it be fearful. Anyone who loves me will obey my teaching. Then my Father will love them, and we will come to them and make our home with them."

It seemed the disciples would have to be satisfied with this obscure promise. As the sun started to burn away the morning mist, the subdued company followed their teacher who had turned from them to continue his descent into the Kidron valley.

16

Today Salvation Has Come to This House

A HAND TWITCHED, FLINGING a distorted claw of shadow across the wall. On a crude stone shelf protruding from the wall, an oil lamp sputtered and continued to burn through the night. Rachel moaned softly, her dreams swirling with fluid images that haunted her restless sleep. A shadowy figure moved through murky mist—Daniel was in terrible danger! Violent Romans with glinting swords were hunting him down for plotting insurrection, but he was unaware and vulnerable. As his smiling face turned away from her, she shouted an urgent warning, desperately trying to reach out her hands to save him. But her arms were frozen by her side, and Daniel could not hear her frantic calls as he slowly faded away. A muffled sob escaped Rachel's lips and her hand convulsed again.

But now she was on a mission to find something important, moving through the familiar maze of dusty streets. Assailed by pungent odors of perfumes and spices, she drifted effortlessly along Small Market Street, past a potter, a tailor, a metalworker bent industriously over their work while day laborers called for work and merchants stridently showed off their wares. The crowded, colorful bazaar flowed alongside her, its shelves crammed with clay pots, swathes of bright cloth, dates from Jericho, amphorae of fish sauce, wine from Samaria, frankincense from Arabia, and aromatic spikenard. But her basket was empty.

Now the streets were widening as she ascended into the Upper City, drawn toward the area near Herod's Palace, with the Temple Mount towering on her right. She was on an important quest.

Then suddenly she was inside a gracious, high-roofed atrium. Rachel's closed eyelids flickered and she moaned again as vivid memories flooded her sleeping consciousness. She had visited this home a few times to deliver messages and scrolls for her Abba, but on this occasion, Benjamin's luminous eyes shone down as he drew her gently against him. She could smell the deep male warmth of his body. She could see where soft dark hairs sprung from his cheeks and around his full lips. Then she heard a lilting, sneering voice: "*At least you have your many little scrolls and your old scriptures.*" An acrid taste filled Rachel's mouth and bitter desire surged within her. She wanted to hurt someone. Hurt her husband Zebediah for abandoning her. Hurt all the women who scorned her as *agunah*. Hurt elegant, derisive Abigail. Hurt Benjamin for his privilege and brash confidence. Hurt even herself.

Benjamin's face drew closer and Rachel groaned and half-turned in her sleep as her body flooded with urgent need. Then she surrendered to the sensation of being desired, lost in the heady memory of sharing her aching body.

But now she was falling, falling . . . Icy air roared wildly in her ears and buffeted her body as she grasped frantically at cords and ropes that flew past her, offering false hope. For as she gripped them, each one snapped, snapped, snapped, leaving her hurtling helplessly through space. Her limbs grew numb and she knew that the rising ground would soon shatter her into pieces. Her Abba's voice sounded gravely in her ears: "*The summer is ended and we are not saved . . . We are not saved . . . We are not saved . . .*" The words echoed relentlessly as she plummeted in frozen terror.

Then sun-bronzed arms reached out of the darkness and held her fast, halting the stomach-lurching fall. She was securely cradled—cupped in an enormous palm and protected from harm. With a deep sigh, she surrendered to the glorious sensation of being loved.

When the first cock crowed, Rachel awoke sweating and weeping. Whether from despair or joy, she could not tell.

Knowing that his time was not yet come, Jesus had withdrawn from the intensifying threats on his life in Jerusalem. He and his closest disciples had traveled east across the Jordan River to work in Perea during the winter months, where many more had come to believe his teachings.

Now, with the approach of yet another spring, they had re-crossed the Jordan at the fords of Bethabara and were heading back toward Jerusalem for the week of *Pesach*.

The group plodded patiently through the bleak, arid Jordan valley with its eye-searing outcrops of brilliant white quartz and swathes of black basalt where lone hermits could be spotted outside the scooped hollows of their elevated caves. Their path meandered between abrupt granite cliffs, along narrow trails only broad enough for a laden camel, through rugged landscapes of gravel and flint, and across vast stretches of tumbling rock that surged ahead like petrified waves. Their sandals scrunched across silent sandy expanses where palm trees rose like ship masts above becalmed water and nomads clustered around pale tents with dusty mules tethered beneath the sparse shade of thorny acacias. At a small well, they gratefully bought fresh quail meat from a goatherd who told unsettling tales of hungry wolves. And always within sight, the Jordan River laid down a snaking swathe of luxurious vegetation that contrasted sharply with the rocky slopes and peaks.

Finally, Jesus and his weary followers descended a limestone hill toward the bustling city of Jericho that nestled in the depression like the center of a vast amphitheater. The region was a furnace in summer, but its tropical climate was a pleasure in these cooler months. Abundant underground springs created a sea of green in the barren desert, and lush oases sprang up around the precious blue gems of water holes.

The disciples' hearts lifted as they approached the famous City of Palms. They walked more briskly alongside flourishing rose gardens, aromatic balsam plantations, and palm groves where workers in light tunics bent to pack young roots with ash and salt and climbed to lop off the lowest leaves of mature trees, using the stumps for footholds. The path led beside a spring of cool, sweet water that gurgled from beneath a boulder to fill a large clear pool fringed with tamarisks and oleanders. Gratefully stooping to fill their water skins, the disciples drank heartily alongside sweating herders who poured water into a trough of hewn stone while their thirsty goats butted each other and bleated urgently.

At the gates of Jericho, women flourished their baskets and called out enticingly to attract sales, offering skins filled with carob juice, vials of valuable balsam sap, medicinal oil from the Jericho plumtree, and sweet moist cakes from the minced fruit of the Nebek shrub.

Then Jesus healed blind bar-Timaeus and all sense of peace evaporated. News of the miracle exploded through the community—the controversial Galilean miracle worker had arrived! The city was now abuzz with excitement, and people thronged around Jesus, making progress increasingly difficult through the narrow streets.

"Jesus, heal my hand!"

"Son of David! Have mercy on me!"

"My eyes! Jesus!"

"Bless my child, master!"

But amid the swarming chaos, Jesus seemed to have a clear idea of where he was heading. While blessing and healing those who clamored around him, he made steady progress westward. Then he stopped, lifted his head, and called out, "Zacchaeus!" The churning crowd halted, their eyes following the line of Jesus's contemplative stare.

"Zacchaeus, come down immediately."

A collective laugh rippled through the gathering as they spotted a figure perched precariously in a gnarled sycamore-fig. Flushing slightly the man started his cautious descent, mortified at having been spotted in his awkward vantage position. Being short of stature, this had seemed the ideal way for him to catch a glimpse of the visiting teacher, but he was now discomfited by the indignity of the maneuver. As chief administrator of Roman taxation in the area, Zacchaeus knew all too well how he was perceived by his fellow Jews. But he had long ago learned to bear the consequence of his wealthy lifestyle, and when he reached the ground, he raised his head in proud defiance, ignoring the condemnatory expressions and derisive whispers.

Yet when Jesus beckoned him forward, Zacchaeus found himself wishing he had remained safely at home. He approached reluctantly, trying not to betray his nervousness. Then all trepidation evaporated as Jesus took his trembling hands firmly between his and smiled down at him kindly.

"Zacchaeus. Today I must stay at your house."

A surprised mutter spread rapidly through the crush of people. Why was this teacher singling out a tax collector for special recognition? A Pharisee in a decorative mantle pushed forward boldly and gestured to the group behind him.

"Rabbi," he said authoritatively, "as fellow teachers we have made arrangements for you to dine with us. You have no need to enter the home of this sinner who is ritually impure."

But the man's confident expression grew dark as Jesus shook his head and responded firmly. "Why would I come to break bread with you?

Do the healthy need a doctor? No, those who are sick need a doctor. In the same way, I have not come to call the righteous, but sinners."

The Pharisee raised a hand and started to protest, but Jesus turned abruptly from him to address the crowd. "I speak now to all who treasure their own righteousness. He who has ears to hear, let him hear!" Ears did indeed prick up at the promise of a parable. "Two men went up to the temple to pray, one a Pharisee and the other a tax collector. The Pharisee stood by himself and prayed, 'God, I fast twice a week and give a tenth of all I get. I thank you that I am not like other men—robbers, evildoers, adulterers, and even this tax collector.' But the tax collector did not dare to lift his eyes to heaven and only beat his breast, saying, 'God, have mercy on me, a sinner.' How do you think these two men appeared in God's eyes?"

No one offered an answer.

"I tell you," Jesus concluded in an uncompromising tone, "that the tax collector went home justified before God—but not the Pharisee!"

The crowd turned wide eyes toward the man who had invited Jesus. How would he react to the insult? The Pharisee stiffened with indignation and his face turned a mottled red as he sucked his lips in agitation. Reluctant to show weakness, he maintained a stony silence then turned on his heel and stalked off, followed by his shocked companions. Jesus raised his voice for the departing group to hear.

"Be certain of this: he who says he is without sin has no understanding. And those who exalt themselves will be humbled, while only those who humble themselves will be exalted!"[42]

But the people were too excited to give attention to any serious message. Cheering enthusiastically, they swept the popular teacher toward the home of the wealthy Zacchaeus, who had hurried ahead to make hasty arrangements for the privileged visit. The gathering developed a festive air, and children ran between their elders, laughing and ducking beneath elbows in merriment until Jesus and his disciples were directed into a high, cool atrium centered on the soothing trickle of a lavish fountain.

The stately mansion was a hubbub of activity. As the guests cleansed their hands in large limestone jars, some servants knelt to remove sandals and wash feet while others bustled to and fro, carrying savory food to a long table laden with golden lampstands. Inquisitive faces peered around corners to catch a glimpse of the newcomers, and Jesus managed to bestow an affectionate smile on a solemn, doe-eyed boy before a servant snatched the child away with clucking disapproval.

Finally, Jesus pronounced the benediction over the meal, and the guests reclined comfortably on low, decorated couches covered with cushions and costly tapestries. They drank from burnished metal goblets and dipped hot bread into steaming bowls while their host beamed blissfully. Other Jews might reject him as a traitor, but this famous healer had blessed him by entering his home to break bread. Zacchaeus could not find adequate words to express his humble delight, and he pressed choice morsels on Jesus while absorbing every word he spoke.

Then during the gaiety, Jesus sat up straight and gave his host such a piercing stare that the small man's hand froze midway to his mouth. The teacher's penetrating voice delivered a challenging question.

"And what about the meaning of your name, Zacchaeus? Are you indeed an 'innocent one'?"

Heads turned as Zacchaeus slowly lowered his hand and stared down at the table, his mind racing to find the most suitable response. Jericho was a major center for the collection of tax and custom, situated at a strategic hub in the vast network of roads, and Zacchaeus had thought it worth bidding a high price for the position of tax administrator. He had undeniably gathered much income from the post, but was wealth not an indication of God's blessing? Surely this did not in itself make him guilty of anything.

"Well," he mumbled, still looking down as he nodding thoughtfully, searching carefully for the correct words. "I . . . I follow Moses's commandments. I pray, I read Torah, I go regularly to the Temple . . . and I . . . I pay the Temple tax. I do not beat my servants more than is just. Yes, I also—"

Zacchaeus was warming to his theme, but as he looked up into Jesus's eyes, his flow of words dried out. A sharp pain struck his chest—an acute heartache that matched his sudden, vivid awareness of the terrible suffering that his exorbitant taxes had inflicted on others. He felt the degrading humiliation of imprisonment, the agony of flogging, the devastating loss of family homes and lands. Standard defenses leaped immediately to his mind: someone had to collect the taxes; he didn't write the legislation; he had to make a living somehow . . . But as he opened his mouth to make these justifications, Jesus raised an eyebrow and held his eyes in a steely gaze that seemed to swallow time and thought. Zacchaeus exhaled heavily and his chest collapsed. He wanted to weep as a black, devastating sense of guilt assailed him with a power that threatened to overwhelm him. Again, he struggled to frame logical excuses. Then without warning he was on his feet and words tumbled out of him.

"Behold, Lord! Before all these people, I vow to commit half of my goods to the poor! And if I have wrongfully exacted any payment, I will restore four times as much to that person!"

A buoyant sense of relief flooded the diminutive tax collector as he collapsed into his chair with a deep sigh, not caring where the words had come from or why he had made such rash promises. Among the buzz of astonished whispers, Jesus reclined again on his side, smiling warmly as he swept his arm around the room.

"Hear this that I say to you all," he called out joyfully. "Today salvation has come to this house! For our brother is a son of Abraham, and the Son of Man has come to seek and save those who are lost."

There were cries of celebration around the table, but Zacchaeus's voice caught in his throat as he was struck by the significance of his guest's Aramaic name, Yeshua. As an abbreviation of Yehoshua, it meant—God saves.

17

The Lord You Are Seeking Will Come to His Temple

LUCIUS STARED DOWN INTENTLY from his balcony onto the fortress grounds below. The troops needed to be thoroughly prepared for the volatile Passover week, and soldiers were drilling and practicing formation maneuvers in the gusty spring drizzle. Lucius stretched a shoulder and rubbed the side of his neck. The stress of this period was taking its toll, and he looked forward to the distraction of debating Joseph's strange doctrines. He did not have long to wait before he heard the familiar gentle voice from behind him.

"*Shalom*, Tribune."

Lucius strode back into his room to return the salutation, and his visitor spoke up as they both took their usual seats.

"Today, Tribune, I hope to take the initiative if this is acceptable to you. For it lies on my heart to speak of God's faithfulness and compassion."

"Well, I think in our last discussion we agreed that your god is certainly one to keep on the right side of," Lucius commented wryly. But the light-hearted quip did not raise an answering smile.

"Indeed," Joseph responded gravely. "We spoke about the sufferings of faithless Israel who repeatedly ran after foreign gods in the manner of an adulterous wife. And yet, Tribune—and this is my theme for today—God ultimately desires mercy. He repeatedly pleads for his people to repent and return to Him. I would like you to hear how His voice of appeal has spoken consistently through His prophets over many centuries."

Recognizing the faraway look that was seeping into his guest's eyes, Lucius settled himself comfortably in preparation for the coming verses.

"Listen, Tribune, to God's plea through the prophet Ezekiel:

Cast away from you all the transgressions which you have committed,
and get yourselves a new heart and a new spirit.
For why should you die, O house of Israel?
I have no pleasure in the death of one who dies.
Therefore turn and live!

And here is His promise through Isaiah:

Seek justice, rebuke the oppressor;
defend the fatherless, plead for the widow.
Come now, and let us reason together.
If you are willing and obedient,
you shall eat the good of the land.

Yes, it is God's wish that He will not be required to correct His people, as He informs us through Jeremiah:

It may be that the house of Judah will hear
all the adversities which I purpose to bring upon them,
that every one may turn from his evil way,
that I may forgive their iniquity and their sin.

So you see, Tribune, we know that God yearns to bless His children and mourns our suffering. Through Hosea, God cries out, '*How can I hand you over, Israel? My heart churns within Me. My sympathy is stirred.*'"

"These are moving words indeed, Joseph, if this is truly how you think your god feels about you."

"This is what we are taught by God, Tribune, and this is what we believe. Hear for yourself God's cry of distress for His rebellious nation:

But My people would not heed My voice,
and Israel would have none of Me.
So I gave them over to their own stubborn heart,
to walk in their own counsels.
Oh, that My people would listen to Me,
that Israel would walk in My ways!

God has such passion for His people, Tribune!"

Lucius lifted one shoulder and nodded. "I can certainly hear a note of frustration."

"But more than frustration, Tribune: our repeated rebellion leads to God's condemnation. Listen to His words through Zechariah:

> *The flock detested me,*
> *and I grew weary of them and said,*
> *'I will not be your shepherd.*
> *Let the dying die, and the perishing perish!'*

Yes, Tribune, God has warned us:

> *I will hide my face from them.*
> *I will see what their end shall be;*
> *for they are a perverse generation,*
> *children in whom there is no faithfulness.*

Because of our stubborn infidelity, we have been deprived of the presence and guidance of God, left to wallow in our iniquity." Joseph shook his head in sorrow. "In a vision, the prophet Ezekiel saw the *Shekinah* Glory of God depart from His Temple through the eastern gate and rest above the Mount of Olives."

Joseph sighed and sank his chin onto his steepled hands. Then he raised his head and smiled faintly. "And yet," he explained, "our compassionate God has provided us with a powerful message of hope and encouragement:

> *In overflowing wrath,*
> *I hid my face from you for a moment;*
> *but with everlasting loving-kindness,*
> *I will have mercy on you.*

Isaiah assures us that God's plan for us will not be thwarted. It is written:

> *He has swallowed up death forever!*
> *The Lord God will wipe away tears from off all faces.*
> *He will take the reproach of his people away from off all the earth.*

And this promised redemption involves the Messiah who you often inquire about, Tribune. God's Chosen One will be our king and our shepherd, and he will restore us to God's grace.[43] Hear Zechariah's prophecy." Joseph's warm vibrant voice filled the room:

Rejoice greatly, Daughter Zion!
Shout, Daughter Jerusalem!
See, your king comes to you,
Righteous and victorious,
Lowly and riding on a donkey.[44]
The Lord their God will save his people on that day
As a shepherd saves his flock—

"Ha!" Lucius's sharp laugh stemmed the flow of words. "How victorious can your king be if he will arrive on a donkey? Surely you expect your promised liberator to straddle a mighty steed, like Alexander the Great?"

But Joseph resumed without acknowledging the interruption. "Through Zechariah, we are told that on that great day of the Lord, '*a fountain shall be opened for the house of David and for the inhabitants of Jerusalem, for sin and for uncleanness*.' But hear God's warning through the same prophet." Joseph's solemn voice rose again:

"Awake, sword, against my shepherd,
Against the man who is close to me!"
Declares the Lord Almighty.
"Strike the shepherd,
And the sheep will be scattered!"

"Be careful, Joseph." Lucius automatically raised a cautionary hand at the mention of swords. "We might have developed a certain level of mutual respect, but even I cannot protect you if you speak incautiously about violent messianic expectations."

Joseph dipped his head slightly. "God's sending of His Messiah will not be advanced or delayed by any person, Tribune. But those of us who await the arrival of God's kingdom have a far greater vision than merely replacing one earthly ruler with another. God has made us the glorious promise that one day He will return to His people. Hear God's stirring words:

Behold, the Lord is coming out of His place
He will come down and tread on the high places of the earth.

Sing and rejoice, O daughter of Zion!
For behold, I am coming and I will dwell in your midst.[45]

Yes, we are assured that God will return to us, a pledge that sustains us through times of oppression and difficulty. And it is tied to God's promised messenger. Hear these words, Tribune, the faithful and true words of the Lord God Almighty."

Joseph leaned back, smiling confidently as he provided the precious verses:

I will send my messenger, who will prepare the way before me.
Then suddenly the Lord you are seeking will come to his temple;
the messenger of the covenant, whom you desire, will come!

"*Hoshiana!*"
Blessed is he who comes in the name of the Lord!"

The jubilant voices of Jesus's disciples mingled with those of other pilgrims as the traditional praise psalm vibrated in the cool morning air, sending pigeons clattering through date palms. The festive group flourished branches and sang joyfully as they followed the road that wound around the southern shoulder of the Mount of Olives. Amid the good-natured jostling, Jesus made steady progress toward Jerusalem, mounted on a donkey.

The rounded knolls of the hillside offered ever-changing vistas, and when the city came into view, rearing above the Kidron Valley, Jesus nudged his placid beast to a vantage point and dismounted as excited pilgrims flowed past in their haste to reach the Temple. Raising a hand against the sun, he stared out across the valley where scattered sepulchers had been newly whitewashed to alert pilgrims against accidental defilement. Then his gaze ranged slowly over three prominent buildings that lay in sight: God's Holy Temple, the Roman-occupied fortress of Antonia, and the palace of the high priest in the Upper City—three significant structures that symbolized powerful but conflicting desires. Jesus's disciples waited patiently while their teacher lifted his arms in prayer. Then he remounted and urged the donkey forward, continuing down and across the Kidron valley.

It was the tenth day of Nisan, and according to God's instructions Jewish families were carefully selecting unblemished male lambs in preparation for the ritual *Pesach* sacrifice on the fourteenth day.[46] On this significant morning, Jesus entered Jerusalem surrounded by exuberant pilgrims who chanted and spread palm fronds and cloaks in his path, in the traditional welcome for a king. Curious bystanders asked, "Who is this man who you celebrate in this manner?" And they were told: "This is Jesus, the prophet from Nazareth in Galilee."

The high-spirited procession then made its way through the Lower City and up toward the Temple while people around them shopped and bargained, sold and bought food from enormous steaming pots, and drove bleating, lowing sacrificial animals along the narrow roads. When Jesus reached the Temple Mount, he dismounted and entered the plaza area among the triumphant cries of his supporters, while the blind and lame called out for healing. People around him sang, "Blessed is the king who comes in the name of the Lord! Peace in heaven and glory in the highest!"

But offended priests and teachers wore dark expressions of disapproval at the unrestrained outpouring of adoration. They muttered bitterly, "See how our efforts have failed. The whole world goes after this man!" Some elegantly turbaned Pharisees elbowed their way roughly toward Jesus, shouting in anger.

"Teacher, teacher! You must rebuke your disciples!"

But Jesus shook his head. "I tell you," he replied firmly, "if these people kept quiet, the very stones would cry out!"

And the antagonistic glowering intensified.

From the height of the Antonia fortress, wary Roman soldiers surveyed the plaza below with their own disapproval and foreboding. Any excitement around the time of a Jewish festival could precipitate violence. As sunlight gleamed off burnished helmets, they stood at tense attention with hands on sword hilts, ready to respond immediately and ruthlessly to the first hint of rebellion. But so far, the mood of the swarming mass seemed harmless enough, characterized by spontaneous singing and clapping of hands.

Amid the celebration, some of Jesus's disciples stared in awe at the dazzling splendor of the Temple. "Look, Lord!" gushed Mary, who hailed from the Galilean fishing town of Magdala. "See all this gold and marble and the beautiful stones of the Temple!"

But Jesus's response was somber. "You might admire this now, Mary. But as for what you see here, its time of destruction is coming. Truly, I tell you, the days will come when not one stone of this Temple will be left upon another. Every last one of them will be thrown down."

The wide eyes and pursed lips of the disciples indicated their skepticism. All Jews prayed toward Jerusalem as the center of their history and the root of their spiritual hope; it was unthinkable that its Temple would be destroyed in their lifetime. Then the group watched, bewildered, as tears welled up in the eyes of their beloved teacher. Jesus gazed around at the swarming pilgrims and beyond to the city below then released a deep, shuddering sigh.

"Ah, Jerusalem, Jerusalem," he murmured mournfully, "you who kill the prophets and stone those sent to you, how I have longed to gather your children together, as a hen gathers her chicks under her wings.[47] But you were not willing. No, you were not willing." The gathering tears started to roll down his cheeks. "If only you had known what would bring you peace. But now it is hidden from your eyes. And the days are coming when your enemies will surround you and throw up a barricade. They will dash you and your children to the ground, and they will not leave one stone upon another."

An awkward silence followed, and the disciples exchanged puzzled looks. John pulled a wry face at the others and put his hand reassuringly on Jesus's shoulder. "Let us not dwell on needless fears, Lord," he said lightly. "This is surely not the time for gloomy predictions. We should rather—"

But the words died in his throat as Jesus turned and fixed him with an intense stare. Light exploded behind John's eyes and myriad images of nightmarish terror flooded his horrified mind.[48] A man yelled in pain and fear as he was knifed for a scrap of food. A sobbing woman ate the boiled flesh of a child. Agonized howls merged with wild crackling as ferocious fire engulfed writhing figures and sent others plummeting from roofs to escape its red maw. Soldiers swarmed the Jerusalem streets with swords and knives, butchering screaming women and children. Swarms of flies blackened the bloated dead that lay where they had fallen, infants were tossed wailing from the city walls, and wild shrieks rent the air as thousands were crucified in excruciating positions. Palls of dark smoke billowed over the Temple as its walls crumbled away and the holy things were looted. Multitudes of Jews were dragged away in the chains of slavery, the city was reduced to a heap of smoldering rubble, and a temple to the pagan god Jupiter reared up into the blackened sky—standing on the site of God's Holy Temple.

John stopped breathing. As the horrendous vision faded into blackness, he heard God's warning through the prophet Isaiah:

What more could have been done to My vineyard
That I have not done in it?
Why then, when I expected it to bring forth good grapes,
Did it bring forth wild grapes?
And now, please let Me tell you what I will do to My vineyard:
I will take away its hedge, and it shall be burned;
And break down its wall, and it shall be trampled down.
I will lay it waste!

The disciples knelt in concern.

"John! John!"

But he was slumped over, unconscious. Jesus's head drooped forward, and his tears made small splashes on the dusty tiles. His words were barely audible.

"Oh, Jerusalem, Jerusalem. Look, your house is left to you desolate."

18

I Myself Will Judge between the Fat Sheep and the Lean Sheep

RACHEL STOOD IN THE low doorway of her Abba's home, lifting her face to savor the fresh spring air that was melodious with birdsongs trilling the promise of new life. But as the smell of baking bread spread through the sweet pollen-laden air, she sat down heavily on the threshold stone, her stomach roiling.

Her thoughts were again on Daniel. He had been in her prayers and her haunted dreams since her shocking discovery during *Sukkot*. After the festivities that followed the water libation ceremony, she had again caught sight of his reddish hair in the crowd and trailed him from a distance. She had enjoyed a mischievous delight in secretly following him as the sun went down, but more importantly, he was sure to join a group to discuss the significance of the *Sukkot* rituals.

Daniel had indeed met up with other men and entered a small room, and Rachel had hastily slipped behind a leafy bush outside the window, silently squatting in her familiar position as ardent eavesdropper. But to her growing alarm, the occasional raised voices that she could hear were not talking about festival traditions but about rebelling against Roman authority! In the name of Jesus! Terrified that she might be spotted by the guard posted at the door, Rachel had remained huddled in the deepening darkness until the meeting finally disbanded and all had left. The closing words of that night still rang ominously in her head: "Death to all Romans!"

She was certain that Daniel was heading down a dangerous path. Should she speak to him? Should she ask her Abba for advice? Although she envied and resented Daniel's male privileges, they had known each other since they were children, and she could not bear the thought of him being harmed. What if his treasonous involvement was discovered and the Romans crucified him! A ghastly, nightmarish image from Rachel's childhood rose before her—a scavenging crow pecked at the eyes of an inhuman, blackened body nailed to a cross with its limbs twisted like those of a broken doll. The thought of this happening to Daniel made her nauseous, and prayer flowed spontaneously through her mind.

> *Almighty God, spare Daniel! Please, Lord, have mercy on him and keep him from harm. El Shaddai, show me how to act if I can protect Daniel in any way.*

Yet what could a woman achieve when she knew so little about politics? And maybe these men were correct after all. Perhaps it was their duty to serve God by resisting heathen rule. But Rachel was confused because from what she had heard, Jesus did not preach rebellion or any form of violence. How could they use him as a rallying point for riots and aggression? She longed to discuss this with her Abba, but he would not tolerate any mention of that name. Rachel sighed. Life seemed to be getting increasingly complicated, and as *Pesach* approached, the tension in the city was becoming palpable. Once again, she appealed to God.

> *El Elyon, I pray for your guidance. If it is your will, use me some-how to protect Daniel. El Shaddai, show me—*

"Rachel! Rachel!"

Abba sounded querulous this morning. Closing her eyes briefly, Rachel reluctantly pushed herself to her feet and entered the house. Seated on his bench, Hilkiah waved her over to the table.

"I have need of your scribing, my child," he said urgently. "There is still much that churns in my mind. So many of our scriptures have been neglected, and they must be gathered together for others to consider. Although," he grumbled, "I do indeed regret having had no visit from young Benjamin these past few months. He was so zealous to study the prophecies about the coming Messiah, but these days the youth seem quick to decide they have learned all they can from their elders. So be it. The others will discuss my work when they come. But you look unwell, my child. Do you have a chill?"

"No, Abba, thank you. I am quite well."

Rachel wiped her clammy, pallid face and settled on the mat, dipping her pen in readiness.

"Today, Rachel, the scroll of Daniel is on my mind. This predicts a Coming One who will be brought before God to inaugurate the eternal kingdom. Write down what appeared in this vision." Rachel scribed carefully as the rabbi's voice rang out:

> There before me was one like a son of man, coming with the clouds of heaven. He approached the Ancient of Days and was led into his presence.[49] He was given authority, glory and sovereign power; all nations and peoples of every language worshiped him.

In accompaniment to the scratching of her reed pen, Rachel slowly quoted the next verse from memory:

> His dominion is an everlasting dominion that will not pass away, and his kingdom is one that will never be destroyed.

"Indeed," Hilkiah mused, slowly rubbing his papery hands. "A kingdom that will never be destroyed, Rachel. So who is this significant figure who will arrive on divine clouds to inaugurate God's kingdom and receive worship, yet is not named and is merely described as a son of man? What are we to make of this prophecy? And what about Zechariah's words about these promised end times?" Hilkiah tilted his head and allowed the words to flow:

> A day of the Lord is coming, Jerusalem, when your possessions will be plundered and divided up within your very walls. Then the Lord my God will come, and all the holy ones with him, and the Lord will be king over the whole earth.

Rachel's pen slowly captured the precious verses. Then trumpets blared out, signaling the time for the morning sacrifice as they blended with Hilkiah's grave voice.

"Yes, at these end times, God will judge between the righteous and the unrighteous. As He says through Ezekiel, '*See, I myself will judge between the fat sheep and the lean sheep.*' Let us pray that in those days, Rachel, we will find ourselves standing safely on God's right hand among His chosen sheep."

"By what authority do you do these things?"

Since his arrival in preparation for the coming *Pesach* week, Jesus had been teaching daily in the Temple courts, where people gathered from early morning to hear him. Then each evening, he and his close disciples would walk two miles to sleep in Bethany on the southeast slope of the Mount of Olives.

Jesus's popularity was growing rapidly. His followers now included even learned scribes who taught the law,[50] and the Temple priests and Pharisees were desperate to find an accusation that would condemn the Nazarene in the eyes of the people. During this notoriously unstable period, there was no telling what the flourishing Jesus-movement might develop into as pilgrims poured into the city to celebrate liberation from Egyptian slavery. It would not take much to inflame the simmering resentment against Roman occupation and taxation. Many of the Jewish leaders agreed that this dangerous preacher had to be silenced. And silenced soon.

Today the air within the temple colonnades was unseasonably hot, tinged blueish-grey by a sandy wind driving in from the eastern desert. A teacher of the law repeated his challenge to Jesus as he squinted against the gritty gusts that flipped his shawl.

"I ask again, who gave you authority to teach as you do? You do not belong to any Torah school. Why should anyone accept your words as true?"

"Indeed!" called another elegantly groomed scribe. "God has taught us: '*You shall observe My judgments and keep My ordinances.*' Yet you encourage your followers to listen to your own instructions!"

"Yes," Jesus answered calmly. "To those who have ears to hear, I say this: if you love me, you will obey my commandments."

"This is sacrilege! Why do you listen to this man?"

A priest stepped forward and gestured authoritatively. "We have also heard that you claim the right to judge us. What is the basis for your outrageous declaration? All who stand here know perfectly well that God is the only judge of His people and the nations. Is this not so?" He turned to those around him and received firm nods of agreement. "Therefore, I say that you speak falsely when you threaten to judge us! Not even the *Kohen HaGadol* himself would dare to make such an offensive and blasphemous claim."

"And yet, I tell you this," Jesus replied insistently. "The Father has given me authority to judge. And the Son of Man will come in clouds with great power and glory. He will send out his angels and gather his chosen ones from the ends of the earth, and he will judge all people according to their deeds!"

There was a loud buzz of shocked disapproval. No prophet or teacher had ever dared to make such a radical statement, claiming God's divine right of judgment!

"When the Son of Man comes," Jesus stated firmly, "he will sit on his glorious throne. All nations will be gathered before him, and he will separate the people as a shepherd separates the sheep from the goats. He will set the sheep on his right hand and the goats on his left. Then the King will say to those on his right, 'Come, you who are blessed by my Father, inherit the kingdom prepared for you from the foundation of the world!'"

The priest raised both arms and appealed to the bystanders.

"Do you hear this?" he cried out triumphantly. "You are witness to the blasphemy from this man's own lips! Now you can all see that this false teacher is worthy of death!"

19

Come to the Wedding Feast!

WHAT WAS THIS DISTURBANCE about now? Lucius glowered down at the Temple grounds. Was there never a moment of rest among this troublesome, aggressive people? Some fellow in a striped cloak was striding around the Royal Stoa, upturning tables, sending coins flying, and setting money-changers yelling. What in the name of Jupiter was this about? With only days before the start of the emotionally charged Passover week, the slightest spark could inflame a riot. But not on his watch.

"Should we send a unit, sir?" asked Stolo at his shoulder.

Folding his arms, the tribune responded with an almost imperceptible shake of the head as he rapidly assessed his options. He was reluctant to risk precipitating a violent clash because the Jews had already complained to the emperor about Pilate's conduct as Prefect of Judea.[51] When Pilate took up his prefecture only a few years ago, Roman soldiers had erected standards in Jerusalem displaying the emperor's image, and a large number of Jews had prostrated themselves for days outside the prefect's palace in Caesarea. Pilate had finally called a public tribunal on the pretext of listening to their complaints, but at his signal the disguised Roman soldiers in the crowd had drawn their swords and threatened to cut everyone down. Lucius remembered all too well that these fanatical Jews had been prepared to die rather than allow their extreme superstition to be transgressed, so Pilate was forced to capitulate and remove the standards. The prefect faced a second protest when he hung shields dedicated to the emperor in Herod's Jerusalem Palace. In response, Herod's sons had written an official letter of protest to Emperor Tiberius, who had firmly instructed Pilate to take down the shields and refrain from offending the Jews any further. Lucius was therefore keenly aware that Pilate wished to avoid unnecessary confrontation, and given the history of these intractable Jews there was no knowing how the excited pilgrims below might react to an armed Roman troop in the Temple grounds.

The tribune therefore silently raised two fingers, and Stolo signaled for two scouts to be sent down to the Temple Mount. Fortunately, the noisy altercation seemed to be subsiding, and the troublemaker was already heading for the plaza gates, accompanied by a small band of supporters. Lucius pensively ran a hand along the raised line of his scar. Was this perhaps the same man who had recently entered the city on a donkey, hailed as a king? Could this be the popular preacher from the north who the Temple priests were continually complaining about to Pilate? The tribune gestured for Stolo to remain vigilant over the Temple Mount and returned to his rooms, impatient to gather relevant information from Joseph of Arimathea.

When Lucius entered his rooms, his greeting to the waiting guest was unusually terse, and for a while he sat without speaking, brooding over the possibility of revolt during the hazardous Passover week that crept ever nearer. He needed specific information today, not vague promises from some invisible god. Quickly noting the strained mood of his host, Joseph waited for his cue. Then Lucius thrust his chin forward.

"Joseph, you say you Jews expect a time when your land will be returned to your control. This is to be the work of your promised messiah, correct?"

Joseph replied cautiously, trying to discern the motive behind the crisp, interrogative tone. "This is indeed our belief, Tribune. And through the Messiah, Israel will be restored to God in a marriage relationship: '*In that day, you will call Me: My Husband, and will no longer call Me: My Master.*'"

The tribune nodded briefly but offered no response. After moments of silence, Joseph continued. "You might remember me telling you, Tribune, that after the rebellion in Eden, God declared hostility between the seed of His enemy and the seed of Eve: '*I will put enmity between you and the woman, and between your seed and her seed; he shall bruise your head, and you shall bruise his heel.*' We are taught that the work of the Messiah will finally resolve this ancient conflict: we are told that 'they shall make a remedy for the heel in the days of the King Messiah.'"[52]

"Hmm." The distracted Roman seemed little interested in Jewish expectations of redemption. "And these messianic expectations," he asked brusquely, "what are the latest rumors? What about the popular teacher from Galilee?"

"Jesus of Nazareth?"

"Yes, that's the one. Some of your leaders have brought complaints about him to Prefect Pilate. They accuse him of inciting rebellion and claiming to be king of the Jews, and they insist that Pilate must bring him to trial. Are they correct? Does this preacher claim to be a messiah? Or a king? What exactly does he teach his followers? Does he have political aspirations?"

Joseph sat patiently as his host punched out each question. Then he answered thoughtfully, "This is a trickier question than you might imagine, Tribune."

Lucius again thrust his chin forward impatiently. "Because . . . ?"

"Well, from what I have heard, both directly and indirectly, Jesus does indeed preach the coming of a new kingdom. And his parables seem to imply that he will be king of this kingdom, or at the very least, the only son of the king. Some interpret this as a possible messianic claim to the throne of David, which would threaten rulers such as Herod Antipas who are appointed by your empire."

Lucius did not like the sound of this. Perhaps the Jewish leaders were correct about the danger this teacher posed. His expression darkened, and he tapped a finger on one knee.

"However," Joseph continued, "Jesus does not preach a political message. He challenges some of our traditions that are not found in scripture, which has made him highly unpopular with our leaders, but he has never advocated violence against the Temple, our religious teachers, or imperial rule. His consistent message is that we should always act with love—even toward our enemies."

Joseph smiled as Lucius pulled a wry face of skepticism.

"Yes, I know. This is a strange concept for us, too, Tribune.[53] But I confess, I like to imagine what the world would be like if we all followed this simple injunction. And it is certainly in accordance with God's promise to instill a perfect spirit in His people: '*I will give them an undivided heart and put a new spirit in them.*'"

But the conversation was veering further from Lucius's immediate concern. He indicated his impatience with a brief shake of a hand as he spoke. "Well, my informants tell me the Galilean declares that he brings a sword and promises to kindle fire on the earth! Tell me honestly, what do you think about this man from the north and his teachings?"

To Lucius's surprise, his guest stood up, something he had not done in previous sessions, and walked with measured tread to look meditatively through an arched window as wispy clouds blew past. Joseph nodded slowly, still looking ahead as he murmured, "Indeed, God made a similar prediction through His prophet Ezekiel: '*Behold, I will kindle a fire in you, and it will devour every green tree in you, and every dry tree.*'"

Then Joseph turned and addressed his host in a musing tone, lines of thought puckering his forehead. "To tell you the truth, Tribune, this man Jesus baffles me. He speaks with a strangely persuasive authority. And none of our highly trained scribes or priests has been able to defeat him in a debate of scripture or tradition, although to our knowledge, he has received no formal instruction. But he also makes wild, outlandish claims that we have never heard from any prophet or teacher. For example, he claims to be the unique Son of God and says that to see him is to see God Himself! Of course, no man can be the very Presence of God, so these must be the declarations of a deluded maniac or a vile, blaspheming charlatan. However—and this is what puzzles me, Tribune—his words sound nothing like the smooth patter of a trickster or the ravings of a madman. Instead, they resonate with profound wisdom and compassion. I have also personally heard testimony from a couple whose blind son received sight from Jesus, and I know a man who was healed at the pool of Bethesda—"[54]

"The Galilean's deceptions are of no interest to me," Lucius interrupted, narrowing his eyes and again shaking a hand in dismissal. "The important question is whether your leaders are correct to be wary of his intentions. Tell me finally: does Jesus threaten the political status quo?"

"In my opinion, Tribune—no, not directly. Jesus does not preach revolution in a political sense. His revolution is one of the heart, mind, and spirit, and he consistently urges his followers to love God and their fellow men and to practice forgiveness."

Lucius slumped in his chair with a welcome sense of relief. But Joseph turned back to the window and muttered, "And yet . . ." The tribune looked up as Joseph murmured pensively. "While Jesus does not preach violence, this does not mean he will not precipitate it. Whoever this man might be, he stands at the center of a growing tempest. Forces of tremendous passion are escalating against him. And I cannot envisage a peaceful outcome."

⊰◈⊱

The Court of Gentiles was humming with activity. Beggars clamored for coins, visitors excitedly pointed out impressive features of the Temple, and well-versed scribes debated fine points of the law. Within the Royal Stoa, a confrontation was becoming increasingly strident.

"I said *lamb*, you idiot," spat the red-faced Peter, fingering the coins in his hand. "*Lamb!* You know very well that I wish to buy a lamb for sacrifice, not wool to wear! Why would I want to buy wool here? Are you trying to provoke me?"

Peter glared threateningly at the turbaned merchant behind the money table, who responded by adopting an exaggerated expression of apology, pulling down the corners of his mouth and widening his eyes innocently as he spread out his hands and waggled his head.

"My sincere apologies to my friend from the north country," he said in a mocking sing-song voice. "But can it be considered *my* fault if you Galileans don't know how to pronounce simple words? Hey? Listen carefully, fellow, and learn the correct pronunciations for lamb, wool, wine, and donkey: *im*ar, *am*ar, *ha*mar, and *ha*mor.[55] Do you get it now? I know you lot struggle with this, but perhaps my three-year-old son could give you some speech lessons."

Peter bristled with indignation and glared around resentfully as amused titters emboldened the arrogant trader to continue. "Who indeed is the idiot, you country bumpkin! How is it my problem if you cannot speak decent Hebrew or Aramaic? Perhaps you should rather try Greek! Move along now, instead of wasting my time."

Sensing an escalation of the quarrel, Judas Iscariot quickly stepped forward, unceremoniously nudging Peter out of the way as he offered words of conciliation. The merchant looked relieved to hear a familiar Judean accent, and as the two entered into negotiations, the fuming Peter spun on his heel and barged through the swarm to find their teacher. Stomping up some steps, he used the elevation to look around the plaza area and glimpsed Jesus surrounded by attentive listeners with one arm extended in a familiar gesture. As Peter approached, he could hear that the parable of the wedding feast was being taught.

"The kingdom of heaven is like a great king who planned a wedding feast for his son. He sent out his servants, saying, 'Tell those who are invited that the cattle are killed and all things are made ready. Come to the wedding feast!' But the invited guests rejected their king and made excuses. 'I have bought a field and must go see it,' said one. 'I have bought five yoke of oxen and must try them out,' said another. Yet another said, 'I have married a wife and therefore I cannot come.'"

There was some ribald laughter at this excuse but Jesus continued. "Some guests caught hold of the king's servants, treated them shamefully, and even killed them."

"Not a wise move!" called out a cheerful voice.

"No, indeed," agreed Jesus with a nod. "The enraged king sent out his armies to destroy those murderers."

"What about the feast?" called out another. "What did the king do about that?"

"Well," Jesus responded, "the king said to his servants, 'The wedding feast is indeed ready, but those who were invited were not worthy. Go therefore to the intersections of the highways, into the streets and lanes of the city, among the fields and hedges, and gather as many as you can find, both bad and good. Bring in even the poor, maimed, blind, and lame. Invite them all to the great wedding feast of the king's son! Let my house be filled with celebration. But I tell you that none of those men who were first invited will taste of my banquet!'"

The parable was over. As so often happened after Jesus's teaching, there was animated debate about the meaning of the story. Who was the king? What groups were supposed to be represented by the first guests and the later guests? Glowering priests and scribes muttered darkly, suspecting a slight against themselves.

Sitting at Jesus's feet in quiet contemplation, John absently ran one end of his rope girdle through his fingers. The excuses of the first guests in the parable reminded him of the pretexts that some men offered when Jesus called them to follow him. One young man had asked if he could first put his affairs and his relationships in order, while another requested time to bury his father and claim his inheritance. But Jesus did not wait for these men and instead described them as those who look behind when they put their hand to the plow, thus digging a crooked furrow. By contrast, John and others had answered Jesus's call by leaving everything and following him. The more John was in the company of this unique teacher, the more he became convinced that Jesus was not offering to *add* wisdom to their lives but to *be* their new life.

The disciple's reverie was interrupted by raised voices, and heads turned at the growing commotion. A large and voluble crowd was approaching, barging its way forcefully across the busy plaza. Jesus's followers moved aside as the group drew up in front of him, and one of the arriving Pharisees roughly flung down a disheveled, weeping woman. Her torn headscarf dangled over her back, shamefully exposing her tousled hair.

"Teacher!" the Pharisee challenged, gesturing dramatically to the drooping figure on the ground. "This woman is guilty of adultery, and our law commands that such a one must die! What do you say in this matter? Do you support or defy our laws?"

The accuser raised his arm and pointed a challenge directly at the teacher from Nazareth, who looked down pensively at the heaving, sobbing bundle. Then Jesus stooped down and gently raised the woman's head, to look directly into the swollen eyes of Rachel bat-Maoz.

20

Neither Do I Condemn You

THE TROUBLE HAD STARTED the day before. Despite her best efforts, Rachel's pregnancy had become suspected. Struck by a sudden surge of nausea, she had vomited in a side street of the market. Weakly pushing herself erect, she had met the shocked expression of guilt and anxiety on the pale face of Benjamin, standing frozen at a corner stall. Even worse, his wife Abigail was beside him, her eyes moving sharply from Benjamin to Rachel as she took in the scene.

Early that following morning, a vengeful Abigail and friends had accosted Rachel in her home and forcefully dragged her to where the elders regularly gathered in the marketplace. The accusation was deadly serious.

"This woman is a slut!" Abigail had screamed. "A whore! I say that she has committed adultery, and we are instructed to condemn her to death! I insist she be examined on this matter!"

Bystanders were intrigued and scandalized. It had been many years since a public allegation of this nature had been made. Was the woman guilty? Who was it? What would happen to her? Speculation spread rapidly, drawing curious people into the open square. Then even more astonishing news was heard: the woman was the niece of the highly respected Rabbi Hilkiah! No! How could that be? Heads wagged wisely. It just went to show that no one should hold themselves holier than others. But was it true? Had she confessed? Had she named the man? Taking advantage of a baker's distracted attention, a young beggar slipped two hot loaves under his tunic and ducked into the swelling crowd. Among the growing hubbub, an elder raised his hand.

"Adultery is a most severe offense!" The excited chatter subsided gradually as his raspy voice traveled across the throng. "Such an accusation is not to be lightly made, and we require more than one to bring testimony in this grave matter. Can the accuser provide evidence? Are there witnesses?"

Quivering with exultant fury, Abigail pointed a shaking hand at Rachel, who knelt subdued in front of the elders.

"We have no need of witnesses!" she screeched. "This woman's shameful condition is its own evidence. If she has any conscience at all, she will confess herself before God and accept her disgrace and punishment. If she denies it, justice will triumph in the course of time!"

Rachel's heart thumped painfully. Abigail was of course correct: in time, the shameful truth of her condition would become undeniable. Where could she turn? What were her options? How had she come to be in this situation, kneeling in public disgrace, when all she had ever wanted was to know and please God? Waves of red-hot humiliation crashed against billowing clouds of black rage as she was violently gripped by a blinding fury against so many things in her life: against the father who plunged her and her mother into poverty and ignominy; against God who tore her mother from her; against the cowardly husband who deserted her; against the man who took advantage of her aching loneliness; against the women who scorned her and rode roughshod over her suffering; against vindictive Abigail who craved her destruction; against the unwanted intruder that drew its strength from her meager resources, growing inside her like a tumor. And against herself for her stupid, stupid, stupid lack of restraint . . .

"Yes! Yes!"

Startled, Rachel realized that the cry had been torn from her own lips. Bitterness poured from her in wild, shuddering gasps.

"Yes! I have lain with a man not my husband! Yes! I am an adulterous woman! Yes! Do with me what—"

But her words were snatched away as Abigail and two friends fell upon her with shrieks of gleeful outrage, ripping off her headdress, scratching at her hair, and ripping her cloak to reveal her under-tunic. The elders watched impassively in cold antipathy as the bruised offender was finally hauled to her feet to face judgment.

"Who is the man?" one demanded harshly. "You must speak up, now, harlot! Who is he?"

Hardly raising her head, Rachel's flickering eyes glimpsed Benjamin in the crowd, white-faced with fear. She knew he would not help her. Her last reserves of defiance were spent, and she sagged, sobbing in the arms of her attackers as despair flooded her. Paralyzed with fear, Benjamin held his breath. He was in terror for Rachel but also dreaded the words she might say next, which could plunge his life into chaos and even destruction. He made a slight move forward but was stopped by the glittering warning in Abigail's eyes. As he wrestled with conflicting emotions, a nearby Pharisee muttered to no one in particular.

"Now she must surely die," he observed philosophically. "Not even the crazy teacher from Nazareth could argue against the outcome."

Benjamin's eyes narrowed as the words seemed to offer a last, desperate hope, like a firefly gleaming in dense darkness. What *would* the Galilean preacher say about this situation? Would he support tradition or apply his own strange teachings about forgiveness? Benjamin sidled closer to the Pharisee.

"Well," he said, clearing his throat and trying to speak casually, "that Jesus fellow would certainly make himself highly unpopular if he did flout our law. Yup, I bet people would not like that at all."

His neighbor furrowed his brow in contemplation and pursed his lips as he responded. "Hmm. Quite right. Not even he could get away with defying this law. That would clearly show him to be an enemy of our revered traditions!"

The man hastily left Benjamin's side and pushed through the buzzing crowd to where the knot of elders stood glaring down at the woman sprawled limply on the ground. He engaged them in brief debate then grinned in triumph as they nodded their heads firmly. This was a perfect opportunity to reveal the Galilean as the subversive influence that he was.

"Teacher!" repeated the Pharisee, towering over Rachel as she knelt in quaking fear. "This is an adulterous woman. What do you say should be done to her? I am sure these good people wish to hear your righteous judgment."

The man opened his arm toward the animated crowd, his eyes fixed on Jesus with a steely look of expectation. But no response was forthcoming. A hush fell over the scene. Then people watched curiously as Jesus stooped down. What was the teacher doing? Heads angled for a better look. He was moving his hand on the ground as if tracing a picture or writing words. Why would he not speak?

"Teacher!" came the insistent challenge. "We are called to judge this harlot! Moses directly taught us God's commandment on this matter. And we now ask—how do you judge such conduct?"

Not a sound was heard as Jesus slowly stood up. The pause seemed to have been all he needed, and he spoke firmly.

"Let any one of you who is without sin, be the first to throw a stone."

Turning from his questioner, Jesus again bent down to trace his finger along the ground. In the swelling silence, Rachel warily raised her bowed head to peer at the teacher, meeting a penetrating gaze that seemed to swallow time and thought. Something shifted inside her, as if she was turning inside out, and she sat back heavily on her heels to steady herself. She slowly surveyed the familiar faces of those who had followed the dramatic procession from market place to Temple, and veil after veil started to fall from her eyes.

Never before had she seen so clearly. Staring intently at Benjamin's chalky face, she felt a welling up of immense love for him—not an emotion or passion but deep *com*passion. She suddenly realized that despite his confidence and privileged learning, he was as vulnerable as her, also yearning for meaningful intimacy but now haunted by remorse and guilt. And beneath her smug self-righteousness, his wife Abigail suffered cruelly in the relentless clutches of jealousy, terrified at the thought of losing her husband and her security to a more educated woman.

Even her Abba, who now glared at her in appalled dismay, was not freely choosing to close his heart to her. As he hurtfully turned his shoulder toward her in formal condemnation and rejection, Rachel understood that he was also a victim of their culture, trapped by its norms and expectations. She knew that in the conflict between supporting her or their traditions, he was not strong enough to sacrifice his hard-earned reputation. Without his status in the community, he would be merely another frail old man.

As Rachel's insight grew, she was shaken by the revelation that no one around her was fundamentally different from herself. Like her, each was seeking love and acceptance, anxious to avoid the ever-present threat of isolation and judgment. But why had she never realized this? Why had she always regarded people's words and acts as being about her? Where did this liberating perception come from? As she looked wonderingly back at Jesus, the answer struck her as a powerful truth—she was sharing the teacher's thoughts! This was how the Nazarene saw each one of them: frail, vulnerable, and lovable even in their unloveliness.

Then the last veil fell away as images from her life flashed into her mind: her husband's warm affection gradually giving way to a thin line of bitterness as she repeatedly repulsed him; women's welcoming smiles fading as she coldly turned her back on them to sit alone, and their hurt looks when she flaunted her learning to intimidate them; her Abba's expectant expression falling into lines of disappointment when she rebuffed his invitations to participate in discussions with his students. For the first time, Rachel understood that she was largely responsible for her isolation. In her iron determination to need nothing from anyone, she had erected a barrier of superiority and self-reliance. With merciless clarity, she perceived that her pride, suspicion, and resentment had formed a brittle layer over her aching loneliness. And her new comprehension was like a dawning light that dispelled the darkness of anger and bitterness.

"Woman," came the gentle voice.

Rachel peered up vaguely.

"Woman," Jesus repeated. "Where are they? Has no one remained to accuse you?"

Rachel turned her head in growing wonder. The furious women, the scowling elders, the self-righteous priests—all had melted away, leaving only herself and the teacher in the open space. With growing relief and elation, she answered with a sob.

"No one is left, Lord. There is no one to condemn me."

"Neither do I condemn you," Jesus declared. "You are forgiven. Go now and sin no more."

Something seemed to crack open inside Rachel, and a strange sensation arose—that she was somehow broken and yet somehow healed. And her soul was set singing. A peddler had once struck a copper gong and held it to her ear, sending deep tones thrilling through her body. Now her whole being felt like a freshly rung gong, vibrating in jubilation and sending out reverberations of love and forgiveness. Filled by an extraordinary sense of buoyancy, she slowly rose to her feet without seeming to flex a muscle, released from every negative emotion and flooded by a sweet peace she had never before known. Weeping, she surrendered to the liberating experience of unconditional love.

21

Whoever Believes in Him
Is Not Condemned

THE WEATHER WAS UNSEASONABLY gloomy. Bruised masses of cloud marshaled ominously across the horizon and deep growls of thunder rumbled slowly across the shadowed hills. Lucius found the darkness strangely oppressive, and he turned from the arched window, gesturing for his wine cup to be filled.

"I apologize, Joseph. What were you saying about covenants?"

Joseph tugged thoughtfully at his earlobe. His host was clearly preoccupied today.

"I was speaking about God's promise that despite our stiff-necked pride and repeated fickleness, He will provide for us a final atonement. This great act will restore us to Him forever by establishing a covenant that cannot be broken. Hear God's words through the prophet Jeremiah."

As the tribune swirled his wine and stared moodily out at the somber skies, Joseph's eyes closed and his voice rose enthusiastically:

> *The days are coming when I will make a new covenant*
> *with the people of Israel and with the people of Judah.*
> *It will not be like the covenant I made with their ancestors*
> *when I took them by the hand to lead them out of Egypt,*
> *because they broke my covenant, though I was a husband to them.*

Joseph turned toward his host. "You might know, Tribune, that in our culture the number seven symbolizes perfection. We have seven holy feasts, there are seven weeks from *Pesach* to Pentecost, our great Day of Atonement occurs in the seventh month, *Pesach* and *Sukkot* each last seven days, and so on. But our word for seven—*sheba*—also means oath or covenant. God has so far instituted six covenants with His people." Trying to draw the tribune's attention, Joseph counted the instances on raised hands. "God's six covenants were established through Adam, Noah, Abraham, Moses, the nation of Israel, and King David.[56] God's people broke these holy accords, but His seventh covenant will be the last and perfect one, an eternal covenant that humankind cannot break! Hear God's assurance through Ezekiel:

> I will establish an everlasting covenant with you.
> Then you shall know that I am the Lord,
> that you may remember and be ashamed,
> and never open your mouth anymore because of your shame,
> when I provide you an atonement for all you have done.

This is a tremendous source of joy and hope to us, Tribune. Although we are too weak to overcome our iniquity, God will Himself redeem us from sin and guilt. The prophet Isaiah also shared God's glorious promise of forgiveness: 'I, even I, am He who blots out your transgressions for My own sake; and I will not remember your sins.'"

Lucius nodded vaguely and drank deeply from his goblet, one hand habitually following the line of his scar as his guest persevered.

"Because of our transgressions God instituted ritual sacrifices, and on our annual Day of Atonement the *Kohen HaGadol* sprinkled the blood of sacrifice seven times before the mercy seat of the Ark of Testimony to atone for Israel's sins. But God's final act of atonement will replace all of these temporary blood-sacrifices that have been repeated for so many hundreds of years. At last there will be one final, perfect atonement!"

Lucius raised his eyes from his wine with little expression of interest as Joseph pressed on.

"And this is not all, Tribune. God has promised that he will restore His entire creation to Himself—not only His chosen people but all nations! You were in the city during our recent Feast of *Sukkot*, were you not? Are you aware of its symbolic sacrifice? Thirteen bulls are sacrificed on the first day, twelve on the second, eleven on the third, and so on, down to seven on the seventh day. The significant total of seventy represents the Gentile nations, and Zechariah prophesied that *Sukkot* will be the only feast that the gathered nations observe with God at the end times." Joseph paused and looked quizzically at his silent host. "You are unusually quiet today, Tribune. You have no questions? No challenges to these beliefs and teachings?"

But Lucius was distracted by a lingering unease that he could not shake. And his guest's words set something jangling in his inner being that he also could not identify or respond to. Shifting restlessly in his chair, he shrugged slightly and tilted his goblet toward his guest as he responded half-heartedly to the question.

"All right, Joseph, your god apparently plans to somehow put right all your disloyal behavior, provide atonement for all your transgressions, and draw in all nations. But how does he intend to do this?"

Steel-grey clouds tore apart briefly and a sliver of sunlight lanced through the window, deepening Joseph's pensive expression as he spoke softly, almost to himself.

"This is indeed a crucial question, Tribune. *How* will God provide atonement for our faithlessness? What single act could possibly cover so many centuries of repeated infidelity? Some of us believe it is significant that through the prophet Zechariah, God has linked His redemption to an unnamed figure of suffering. Here is His promise:

> *I will pour out on the house of David and the inhabitants of Jerusalem*
> *a spirit of compassion and supplication, so that,*
> *when they look on him whom they have pierced,*
> *they shall mourn for him, as one mourns for an only child,*
> *and weep bitterly over him, as one weeps over a first-born son.*[57]

But we are uncertain about the meaning of this prophecy. Who is this pierced figure? And what part will he play in God's plan of redemption?"

After a moment of silent musing, Joseph looked across at his host and continued. "We expect that the Messiah will first be sent to us, and God will later institute *Olam Habbah*, the perfect World to Come.[58] This is like the two stages of a traditional Jewish wedding: in the betrothal period, the husband offers a bride price to dedicate the couple to one another and then goes away to prepare a home for them; in the second stage, he returns to bring the bride to the new place where they will live together as husband and wife. But as to your question about precisely how God intends to cover our sin and provide the forgiveness that will make this marriage relationship possible . . ."

Thunder rolled menacingly across the darkened sky as Joseph held out two hands with palms facing the roof.

"The truth is, Tribune—we do not know."

Plump sand-colored partridges darted among dandelion weeds and gnarled roots, scratching at the earth and pecking eagerly at fallen seeds and scurrying insects. Then they jerked their heads up in sudden alarm as a breeze carried the sound of voices toward them. Approaching feet crunched along the stony path and some of the birds scurried off into the long grass while others made awkward little flurries of flight, expressing their disapproval with an offended ku-ku-ku. They were gone by the time Jesus and his followers crested the rise.

The advancing influence of spring was everywhere evident in the Jerusalem countryside: in the swirling, turbulent streams swollen by highland snowmelts; in bright yellow and green crops that carpeted the broad terraces; in the exuberant shouts of boys as they chased swooping birds from the gay buds of peach, almond, and mulberry. But Jesus's small group was immune to the glories of the balmy day, their hearts heavy with apprehension after his most recent warning about the danger that drew relentlessly nearer. They had heard the direct threats from the Temple leadership and were only too aware of rumored plots against their teacher's life. Would his enemies act against him soon? If so, what form would this action take? With *Pesach* commencing tomorrow, were their own lives also in peril? Jerusalem, the city that once filled them with patriotic delight, was now fraught with menace.

Jesus was clearly trying to strengthen them for the coming trials, but they ardently wanted to reject his prediction that he would soon be delivered up to be scourged and killed. They murmured anxiously among themselves, and disciples who spoke only Greek remained close to Philip to hear his translation of Jesus's Aramaic teachings.[59] Meanwhile, their teacher gazed pensively across the rolling fields and orchards patterned with pale, wavering paths that had borne millennia of patient feet rising and falling . . . rising and falling . . . as they trod the relentless cycle of life and death.

Finally Peter mustered courage to speak, breaking the tense silence. "Lord, explain to us again about the bronze serpent that Moses held up in the desert. Those who were poisoned by serpents were healed when they looked at it, but what does this signify to us?"

The disciples waited in keen anticipation. Perhaps their teacher would deliver a much-needed message of hope and healing at this uncertain time. But as so often happened, Jesus's response raised more questions than it answered.

"Now is come the judgment of this world," he responded gravely. "Now the prince of this world will be cast out. And I, if I am lifted up from the earth, will draw all people to myself."

Puzzled expressions flitted across anxious faces. How would their teacher be lifted up? How could he draw people to him?

"Just as Moses lifted up the serpent in the wilderness," Jesus taught patiently, "even so must the Son of Man be lifted up, that whoever believes in him is not condemned but will have eternal life."

"Eternal life" sounded reassuring, and frowns eased slightly. Then Jesus's outstretched arm gestured to the ripening crops that bowed and swayed in smooth ripples.

"The time is nigh for the Son of Man to be handed over," he said somberly. "Truly I tell you, unless a seed of wheat falls to the earth, it remains by itself alone. But if it falls and dies, it bears much fruit."

John's eyes narrowed in concentration as he struggled to interpret these words. Fragments of Jesus's previous teachings raced through the apostle's mind, particularly the seed image: the word of God was like seed that could fall futilely upon stony soil or else bear fruit; God's kingdom would spread rapidly in the way that a mustard seed grows into a large tree; the seed of weeds had been planted among God's good wheat; now, the seed was Jesus himself, falling and dying in order to give rise to a greater harvest. But in what way could his death bring an increased harvest to God? This was not part of messianic expectation, and John frowned, exasperated by his lack of comprehension.[60]

Then his attention was drawn back to their teacher as Jesus dropped his arm and murmured, "Now my soul is troubled. What shall I say: 'Father, save me from this time?' But for this very reason I came."

Jesus closed his eyes briefly then turned to face the fear and trepidation written so clearly across the faces of his followers. He opened one hand in a gentle gesture of reassurance, and his compassionate voice flowed like a balm through their troubled souls.

"Yet a little while and the light is still with you. Walk while you have the light, so you may become children of light. For God so loved the world that he gave his only Son, that whoever believes in him shall not perish. For this is the verdict: light has indeed come into the world, but people love the darkness because their deeds are evil. But whoever lives by the truth will walk in the light."

Philip muttered a brief translation to his Greek group and everyone nodded fervently. They all longed to be certain they were indeed walking in God's light. But they remained deeply apprehensive about where this might lead.

"Do not let your hearts be troubled," Jesus encouraged them gently. "You believe in God: believe also in me. And now I give you a commandment to guide you in going forward."

Ears pricked up. John nudged his brother James in expectation: finally, they might be told how to act against their enemies and perhaps how to protect their teacher. Judas and Simon the Zealot eyed each other furtively, hoping to at last receive instructions for action against the Romans. But all were disappointed with Jesus's advice.

"A new command I give you: as I have loved you, so must you love one another. By this, the world will know that you are my disciples."

Was that all? Foreheads furrowed in frustration and concern. Was that the only counsel they were to receive at this perilous time? To love each other? Peter took a breath in readiness to blurt out a response, but Jesus allowed no opportunity.

"Greater love has no one than this," he said firmly, "that he lay down his life for his friends. I call you my friends, for everything I heard from my Father I have made known to you. You did not choose me, but I chose and appointed you, that you might go and bear fruit."

Jesus laid two reassuring hands on the shoulders nearest to him. This was clearly all the guidance their teacher would provide at this time, and his disciples watched in subdued silence as he turned from them and made his way alone up the rocky path, following the fence of stone and thorns.

22

This Is the Gate of the Lord

MISSHAPEN SHADOWS SURGED AND quivered on the rough walls as the oil lamp sputtered into life. Hoarse whispers sounded in the small room.

"We will not submit to the Roman yoke of tyranny!"

"We do not fear death!"

"Everyone who spills the blood of a pagan is like one who brings a sacrifice to the Temple!"

As Caleb and his fellow conspirators lowered their raised fists, Simon Zealotes took the lead, speaking in muted tones to the tense group.

"I thank you all for answering my call on this critical day before the arrival of *Pesach*. I am pleased to report that Judas Iscariot's interaction with the Temple leaders has borne fruit." Simon smiled grimly. "He has convinced them that he is disillusioned with Jesus's teachings, and they have offered him payment in return for information about the teacher's plans. Caiaphas had hoped to avoid direct conflict at this volatile time, with so many of Jesus's supporters in the city. But Judas has convinced them that if they do not take preemptive action, Jesus will openly declare himself to be the Messiah on the *Pesach* day of Firstfruits and incite a violent revolt."

"Well," Caleb said thoughtfully, "the Firstfruits festival is the day after Shabbat, on the first day of the new week, so it would certainly be a significant time for a rebellion."

"No, Caleb," Simon responded firmly, shaking his head as he held up a hand. "Judas has already laid a careful plan of action."

The room fell into deep silence as the men waited expectantly.

"Tomorrow evening," Simon explained in suppressed excitement, "Jesus will celebrate the *Pesach* supper in the city with us twelve.[61] After the meal, we will walk back across the Mount of Olives to Bethany. But Judas will leave the meal early so that he can lead priests and Temple guards to Gethsemane, where we usually break our return journey. They will arrest Jesus there, far from the unpredictable crowds."

"And that is where we will be waiting to attack?" Gideon suggested eagerly.

"Not yet. Our revolution must strike at the heart of Roman control, and it will require the involvement of our supporters in the city."

"But what if the Temple leaders kill Jesus when they arrest him?" Daniel asked anxiously. "Our venture will come to nothing without him!"

"Do not fear, Daniel," Simon assured him. "That is not their plan. Pilate is residing in Herod's Palace to monitor the city during *Pesach*, and the priests intend to take Jesus to appear before him. Caiaphas has alerted the prefect to the serious risk of an uprising under the popular preacher, and they are confident that they can pressurize him to condemn Jesus to death for stoking fires of insurrection."

"But that's ridiculous!" Daniel blurted out. "I know for a fact that Jesus does not preach violence or resistance against Roman occupation!"

"That may be, Daniel. But Pilate cannot be certain of this." Simon's wolfish grin shifted eerily in the wavering lamplight. "All of you here, along with many others who have been alerted, will be part of the crowd that gathers on the morning after *Pesach* to hear Pilate's verdict about Jesus. And *this* will be our time to strike!"

Simon patted his hands hastily in the air to tamp down the exuberant burst of cheering. "And a further important detail has come to our attention, which could be the key to our success." The men leaned forward as Simon dropped his voice even lower. "One of Judas's spies in Herod's Palace has learned that Pilate is uncertain about how to respond to the furor that has developed around Jesus. He is caught between the accusations of the priests and the lack of evidence that Jesus is plotting against Rome. The prefect has therefore devised a shrewd tactic: he will offer to release one prisoner as a symbol of Roman good faith during our *Pesach* commemoration of liberty.[62] When he makes this announcement, we will all call on him to free Jesus, and when he agrees, it will seem as though the crisis has been resolved. And *this* will be the ideal opportunity for us to act!"

There was a restrained buzz of approval.

"While the distracted palace guards are busy removing Jesus's chains," Simon explained, "Judas will sound a double trumpet call and all of us in the crowd will draw our weapons and attack the soldiers. Judas and I will be at the front with some selected comrades, and we will cut off the head of the snake—Pontius Pilate will fall. A great blow to mark the start of our uprising!"

Among the excited hum, Gideon spoke up. "But Simon, what about the troops at Herod's Palace and the Antonia fortress?"

"Yes," Simon nodded briefly. "It is crucial that Roman military response be curtailed as much as possible. For this reason, Judas and I have arranged that the double trumpet signal will simultaneously set three other events in motion."

The howling of jackals sounded across the hills as Simon detailed the plan. "One: some of our men will be waiting in the street outside Herod's Palace. When they hear the trumpet call, they will run through the city and spread the message for our supporters to slay all Roman soldiers in the streets. Two: a large and secretly armed group of pilgrims on the Temple Mount will attack any soldiers dispatched from the Antonia and also fight their way in to plunder the fortress's armory. Three: a smaller strike will be directed at disrupting the Roman chain of command and throwing the troops into confusion—other prominent leaders must quickly fall."

Simon paused and glanced meaningfully at Daniel and Caleb who nodded solemnly.

"There is no doubt," he continued, "that many more will then join our uprising. We will rally our cause around the figure of Messiah King Jesus and overthrow the despised heathen! As in the days of the Maccabees, many of us will fall. But we do not fear death!"

"We do not fear death!" came the united response.

"Death to all Romans!"

"*Hallelujah!*"

Voices then rang out loudly in unison, chanting from a praise psalm that was always sung at the great and holy festivals:

All the nations surrounded me,
But in the name of the Lord I cut them down!
Shouts of joy and victory
Resound in the tents of the righteous.
This is the gate of the Lord
Through which the righteous may enter!
I will give you thanks, for you answered me;
You have become my salvation.
Lord, save us!
Lord, grant us success!

Voices lifted into the still night as Jesus and eleven apostles trod the familiar path around the Mount of Olives toward Bethany, singing a psalm of the holy feasts:

This is the gate of the Lord
Through which the righteous may enter!
I will give you thanks, for you answered me;
You have become my salvation.
The stone the builders rejected
Has become the cornerstone.
The Lord has done it this very day;
Let us rejoice today and be glad.

But despite the triumphant words, voices were muted and expressions were apprehensive. The stark moonlight splashed inky pools beneath dark trees that loomed overhead, swallowing the sounds of their footsteps. What should have been a joyful *Pesach* meal had been deeply overshadowed by Jesus's warning that his betrayal was now imminent, and while he strode ahead purposefully, his followers walked huddled together for comfort. They were haunted by their teacher's actions at supper—tearing bread to represent his precious body somehow broken and fractured, and pouring out red wine as a symbol of his blood that would be shed for them. He taught that the wine represented a new covenant that would be sealed through his blood, but they had no desire for any covenant that required his death and instead longed desperately to be reassured that they could forever rest in the warmth of his presence.

During the meal Jesus had said sadly, "I will only be with you a little while longer."

"Lord, where are you going?" Peter had immediately asked. "Wherever it is, we will certainly follow you!"

But Jesus's answer was not encouraging. "No, Peter. Where I am going, you cannot follow now. But you will follow afterward."

They had all boldly declared their intention to stay with their teacher, and Peter now muttered again to John that he would most certainly remain by Jesus's side regardless of what might happen. He rejected Jesus's prediction that they would be scattered like sheep without a shepherd, that they would all fall away and disown him. The stalwart fisherman was almost violently confident that at least he would stand firm and loyal, no matter the threat.

A large white owl swooped noiselessly across the black sky as the small group reached their customary resting place on their return journey—the gardened area known as *Gethsemane* or oil-press. Jesus turned to his downcast apostles and gestured for them to sit on the grey slabs of moonlit rock.

"In my Father's house," he told them earnestly, "are many rooms. I go to prepare a place for you. Then when I come again, I will receive you to myself, that where I am, you may be there also. And I will not leave you as orphans but will come to you. Yet a little while and the world will see me no more, but you will see me. The Counselor, the Holy Spirit, whom the Father will send in my name, will teach you all things and remind you of everything I have said to you. I will not say much more to you, for the prince of this world is coming. He has no hold over me, but he comes so the world may learn that I love the Father and do exactly as He has commanded me . . ."

Jesus's voice cracked. He turned his head and murmured, "Sit here and wait. For I must needs pray."

With a glance and a slight gesture of his head, he indicated for Peter and the two Zebedee brothers to join him, and they moved off together while the others remained behind, murmuring uncertainly. After a short walk, Jesus turned to address the three.

"My soul is exceedingly sorrowful, even unto death," he confessed to them, his forehead furrowed and his voice unusually strained. "I ask that you stay close and watch with me. And pray for yourselves, that you might not enter into temptation. For the spirit is willing, but the flesh is weak."

Deeply concerned, the men watched anxiously as Jesus moved ahead. Then they inhaled sharply as he sank to his knees and fell forward, laying his forehead to the ground. They had never before seen their adored teacher so distressed, and they stared at each other in icy apprehension. In the still night air, they could hear fragments of Jesus's urgently whispered prayer.

"Abba, Father . . . All things are possible to you . . . If you are willing, remove this cup from me . . ."

To their horror, the sweat that dripped from his face appeared as dark as blood in the harsh moonlight. Trying to remain calm, they eased themselves onto the bedewed grass, drawing their cloaks around them as they prepared to wait.

Gnarled, grasping branches cast a shadowy net over the lone kneeling figure as Jesus prayed in agonized desperation, blinking through bloody sweat.[63] He poured out his heart to his Father, urgently reaching for strength and resilience. But he struggled to focus, assailed by vivid visions of the appalling suffering to come. He shuddered as flails tipped with metal and bone cut again and again and again into his quivering body, stripping flesh down to muscle and bone. Now searing cramps raced up his calves from his shattered feet. His chest heaved—he could not breathe. Agonizing flashes of jagged pain blazed along his arms. He grimaced and sobbed as his shoulder tore from its socket. He frantically took a shallow gulp of air, but now he could not exhale. His dry throat was closing and his heart pounded as if it would burst. He could not breathe. He could not breathe.

Gasping raggedly, he turned his drooping head toward his three chosen apostles. But their eyes and hearts were heavy with weariness and dread, and despite their intentions, they were slowly succumbing to the deep draw of sleep. As they slipped away, Jesus's panted words hung in the brittle night air between heaving gulps.

"Nevertheless . . . not my will . . . but yours . . . be done."

23

I Do Not Know This Man!

SUDDEN GASPS WERE QUICKLY cut off by thin, ruthless ropes that were drawn tighter, ever tighter, cutting into the yielding flesh of two necks, heedless of fingers clawing desperately against the coming darkness. Barely minutes later, legs frantically kicked their way into death. Ashen-faced, Daniel released the rope from his whitened knuckles and collapsed backward on the ground, panting even more from revulsion than effort. Grinning in exhilaration, Caleb thumped his brother on the shoulder.

"Our first two!" he hissed fiercely. "And this is only the beginning!"

Trying to steady his trembling hands, Daniel frantically scrabbled away from the body of the Roman soldier slumped grotesquely across his legs. He had thought he was prepared for this deed, which they had discussed so often with Simon Zealotes, but the appalling reality now trapped him in grisly, nightmarish dread. Two men were dead. Because of him and Caleb. Through their deliberate, intentional actions. Dead. Someone's son, someone's brother, perhaps someone's father. Dead! Murdered in cold blood! He feared he might retch.

"Daniel!"

Caleb shook his brother roughly, trying to jolt the glaze from Daniel's wide eyes.

"Daniel! Do you hear what I say? Strip him before we are discovered! What are you waiting for?"

With numb fingers, Daniel fumbled clumsily with clasps and laces until finally two men in Roman uniforms faced each other and gave a wry salute of glinting knife-blades. But Daniel could not resist a sideways glance at the heap of scraps and stones in the back of the alleyway.

"Focus, Daniel!" Caleb snapped. "This is no time for womanly weakness. Believe me, those two would not have wasted a moment of pity on us Jews! And this is but the first blow," he whispered urgently. "As we speak, Judas's plan unfolds, starting with Jesus's arrest."

Jesus. Jesus, who taught to turn the other cheek. To love even one's enemy. Doubt flooded Daniel's mind. What were they doing? What was *he* doing? But his brother glared at him, holding his eyes in a determined stare.

"Now we fulfil our part, Daniel! Right?" Caleb said harshly, the sound echoing eerily in the small alley. "All aspects of the plan must be carried out perfectly. Remember, we will rise like the Maccabees of old to cast off the despised yoke of these barbaric heathen! Not so? Not so, Daniel!"

Daniel again swallowed the bitter bile that kept rising at the back of his throat and nodded vehemently, struggling to recapture the patriotic joy he had experienced when planning this very moment. Yes, this must be done. Of course, this was the only way! He took a deep, sharp breath and raised his blade again, striking it forcefully against his brother's. Caleb grinned in encouragement and laughed softly.

"Take heart, Daniel!" he hissed. "We can do this! In these uniforms we will be able to follow the tribune wherever he goes until we hear the trumpet signal. If you were not my own brother, I would have to say that I do not know you as a son of Abraham!"

Peter pulled his cloak tighter against his body as he shivered in the chill of the pre-dawn air. Keeping a wary eye on the people around him, he sidled closer to a flaming brazier, stretching out a hand toward the flickering warmth. No one seemed to notice him as shouts and slaps emanated from a room above where Jesus was being interrogated. Peter gritted his teeth, shaken by a powerful combination of rage and fear. As yet, only Jesus had been arrested, but that did not guarantee the safety of his followers, and Peter wondered again at the wisdom of following him this far, into the lower courtyard of Caiaphas's palace.

In the garden of Gethsemane, their teacher had wakened them to warn that his time was now come. They had all instinctively rallied around him when voices and flaming torches had approached and a multitude bustled up, glaring ferociously and brandishing weapons. The disciples had hoped the darkness would keep Jesus's identity hidden, but he had deliberately moved out of their protective circle, and Judas had hastily stepped up to kiss him. This was apparently some sort of signal because four burly guards had immediately pounded up to grab Jesus, tying his hands roughly with thick rope. The disciples had cried out in protest, but Jesus stood firm.

"Have you come out as against a robber with swords and clubs to seize me?" he had asked calmly. "Even though I taught daily in the temple and you did not arrest me there? And do you think that if I now asked my Father, he would not send me more than twelve legions of angels? But all this has happened that the writings of the prophets might be fulfilled."

Peter held out his other hand toward the shimmering heat of the brazier, his heart racing as he recalled the turmoil of distress and anger that had flooded him during the confrontation. He had instinctively pulled out the sword he was carrying for protection, lashing out at the nearest man who yelled in pain and clutched at his ear.

But Jesus had raised his hand. "Put your sword away!" he had instructed firmly. "Shall I not drink the cup the Father has given me?"

When the crowd manhandled Jesus out of the garden, the disciples had fled, terrified that they, too, might be seized. But after crashing blindly through dense undergrowth, Peter had stopped, panting heavily as he tried to master his violent emotions. Finally, desperate to be close to his beloved teacher, he had forced his reluctant feet to retrace their steps. It had been easy to trail the noisy arresting mob from a distance, but the danger of his present situation threatened to overwhelm him, and he pulled his scarf further over a forehead that was wet with the perspiration of intense anxiety. At least his presence seemed to be attracting no attention.

But to his great dismay, a passing maid looked at him curiously, halted, peered even closer, and said loudly, "I recognize you. You're a follower of the Galilean Jesus, aren't you?"

"What?" Peter croaked in panic, pulling his cloak higher around his chin as he turned his back to her. "You talk nonsense, woman!" he said gruffly.

"That's right!" A soldier pointed at Peter who stood motionless with terror, red firelight splashing across his pale face. "I saw this man with Jesus of Nazareth in the garden!"

"And I say I have nothing to do with this Jesus!" Peter spat out hoarsely. "I swear I don't know who you are talking about!"

"Wait a minute!" called another man, pushing closer and gesturing angrily with a fist. "Yes! This is the brute who cut off the ear of my cousin Malchus, Lord Caiaphas's servant! I saw him do it!"

Peter's gaze darted wildly as sweat trickled into his eyes.

"We know you must be one of Jesus's men, fellow," said another curtly, "because your Galilean accent betrays you!"

In growing terror, Peter began to curse and swear. "No! Listen to me!' he hissed, raising both hands in desperate emphasis. "I tell you . . . I do not know the man!"

Then the first cock crow of the day echoed across the Tyropoean valley. Peter froze and held his breath, his heart pounding painfully as an image from the *Pesach* meal flashed into his mind: Jesus looked intently at him, shook his head, and said sadly, "*Before the rooster crows, you will deny me three times.*" Peter's shoulders slumped, and a devastating sense of loss flooded him as the teacher's warning rang in his ears: "*Whosoever denies me before men, I will also deny him before my Father in heaven.*" The Galilean fisherman, called by Jesus to be a fisher of men, pressed his fist to a chest already wracked with painful sobs. Without caring whether he was followed or not, detained or not, he staggered out into the darkness.

24

What Is Truth?

LUCIUS LAID A HAND on the fortress parapet and stared distractedly across the city. A crisp breeze swept down from the hills, fluttering his red cloak like a warning signal and intensifying as it channeled along the narrow streets to swirl loose leaves and scraps into brief flurries. On the horizon, tongues of pink and orange pushed across the lightening sky as the rising sun slowly spread its promise of warmth. But Lucius's mood was morose and the beauty went unnoticed. He turned his head at the crunching sound of nailed boots on flagstones.

"Greetings, Tribune Ocella."

"Greetings, Stolo. Your report?"

"The Galilean Jesus has been arrested, sir."

Lucius nodded once and looked back out across the Temple Mount as Stolo stood rigidly at his side. Many thoughts jostled for attention in the tribune's mind. Family and friends in Rome had no idea how complex the situation in Judea was. He, too, had mistakenly believed that Jews would be relatively simple to control in that they at least had only one god to avoid offending. But tutored by Joseph of Arimathea, Lucius had been surprised by the range of beliefs and attitudes in their various sects.

The tribune had been introduced to many of the aristocratic Sadducean families, who wielded considerable political power by dominating the priesthood and the Sanhedrin council. This group generally had a more cordial relationship with the imperial Roman forces than with their Pharisaic fellow Jews, who sternly opposed foreign culture. And although the Sadducees adhered strictly to Mosaic Law, they rejected many traditions and rituals developed by the Pharisees. Lucius had learned that the two groups argued fiercely over seemingly minor issues.

"Do you know, Stolo," he mused aloud, "these Jews have passionate debates over such trifling matters,"

"Indeed, sir," came the respectful response.

"Yes. For example, they apparently can't agree on the precise starting time of their sabbath, whether they are allowed to light fires in their home on that day, and whether or not to perform their annual water pouring ceremony. Sadducees and Pharisees have been prepared to murder each other over such trivial disputes! And even Pharisaic schools argue among themselves about some practices. Then there's a sect called the Essenes . . ."

Lucius subsided into contemplation. After a period of silence and a sideways glance, Stolo decided to contribute.

"Live mainly around Qumran, sir."

"Who? Essenes? You know much about them?"

"Fourteen years is a long time, sir. You get to know stuff."

"So what makes them different?"

"Well, they reject all the Temple worship we can see down there on the Mount, sir. Say it's been totally corrupted. Most of them live near the Dead Sea. It seems they follow strict purification rituals while waiting for their promised messiah to arrive and lead a final holy war against us heathen oppressors. And against all other Jews, apparently. Not a very tolerant bunch."

"Hmm," Lucius grunted. "And now another major rift has developed," he murmured.

"Sir?"

"Between Jewish leadership and the supporters of this Galilean Jesus. And what information do you have about these pestilential rumors of some imminent revolt? The last thing we need is someone throwing a torch among the hot-headed patriotism of these palm-waving pilgrims!"

"Our spies are trying to identify the main conspirators, sir. They believe they're getting closer—"

"Blast it, you need to do better than 'closer,' man!"

"Of course, sir."

Lucius suppressed an exasperated sigh. There was heightened tension in the city, his soldiers were on edge, and a weight of responsibility and uncertainty seemed to press on the tribune's chest, at times almost constricting his breathing. His recent meeting with Pilate had been uncomfortably strained as the prefect again grilled him about increased security for the

Passover week. And Lucius was frustrated that he was still unable to provide decisive information to Pilate about whether or not the popular Jesus was part of a seditious plot: various spies offered conflicting opinions, and even his discussions with Joseph had not brought final clarity.

Lucius stared down pensively at the courtyard below. Deep channels carried rainwater into underground cisterns, and the enormous paving stones were scarred from rough board games etched over many decades by idle soldiers. Hundreds of years from now, these cisterns and engravings might still exist but what else would remain? After all, towers and temples might rise, but towers and temples also fell. At one time, the Assyrians dominated the political landscape until the Babylonians subjugated them, followed in turn by their own fall to the Persians. Then the young Alexander had enlarged his Greek empire with phenomenal rapidity, and now Rome flexed its muscles and imposed imperial control. But what would the future bring?

"Which do you think will last longer, Stolo?" Lucius mumbled without lifting his gaze. "That Jewish Temple over there or this great fortress, symbol of Roman sovereignty?"

Stolo raised one eyebrow to simulate thought but, deciding the question was probably rhetorical, remained silent.

Lucius shrugged lightly. Did he even care? What was he supposed to achieve here? Somehow, this place was eroding his confidence in simple truths about power and dominance. A tantalizing vision of Alessandra's loving smile filled his mind. Perhaps it was time to return to Rome and settle down, far from the labyrinthine confusion of Jewish disputes and beliefs. The tribune shook his head slightly and brought his thoughts back to immediate considerations.

"So, the Galilean is in chains. Is the Antonia prepared for possible unrest?"

The chin strap of Stolo's helmet disappeared briefly into his thick neck as he bent his head.

"Yes, sir. Extra men have been posted. Entry points are checked. Armory guard doubled. All on the highest state of alert."

Lucius nodded. The Antonia needed no further monitoring, but he must now assess the state of readiness at the barracks near Herod's Palace.

Minutes later, the tribune and two armed soldiers exited the fortress and marched briskly toward the palace in the Upper City. And two uniformed figures peeled unnoticed out of the shadows and trailed behind them.

Heads turned as a ghastly yowl tore through the palace gardens, sounding horribly like the scream of a woman in anguish. But it was only a strutting peacock, calling raucously as it spread its resplendent feathers to display a quivering arch of brilliantly colored eyes. Peahens ignored him and scratched in the rich soil while people turned back to their tasks.

The palace of Herod the Great, the second most important building in Jerusalem, had been Roman property since the client king's death. The imposing structure spread over a vast raised mount that dominated the western wall of the Upper City, its two wings containing large banquet halls, luxurious bathing rooms, and accommodation for hundreds of guests. Three defense towers reared up near its northwest corner, the massive stones so skillfully crafted that each fortification seemed to be carved from one solid block. And the palace grounds boasted lush gardens with stone pathways, covered colonnades, dove-cotes filled with the cooing of pigeons, deep gurgling canals, and huge cisterns decorated with bronze statues that spewed out sweet water.

Inside the royal palace, surrounded by decorative marble columns and intricate mosaics, Pilate of the Pontia family drummed his fingers on one arm of the cold stone chair, trying not to blink from lack of sleep. Caiaphas had personally informed him that they planned to bring the Galilean teacher early that morning for trial, and the prefect had assigned supporting Roman soldiers to ensure that his arrest would be without incident.

Throughout the night, Pilate's mind had churned furiously over the options available to him. And he had hardly been aware of anything else during his pre-dawn rituals: when his servant brought him the brass pot for relief, carefully drew the grooming blade over his stubbled cheeks, and laced his sandals around his ankles; when he donned his purple-striped tunic and draped his toga over it; when his wife greeted him gently, fully aware of his dilemma; when his hand mechanically transferred food into his mouth; even when he prayed in front of the statuette of his household goddess, Vesta—always the same question spun in his mind. How should he best respond to the high priest's demand that he condemn the Nazarene teacher to death? What would be the safest ruling? So much was at stake.

Pilate still chafed from earlier Jewish complaints to Emperor Tiberius about his actions, and he was determined to keep a low profile in the province. He could ill afford to be caught in the middle of a local feud or for the excitable Jews to carry further grievances to Rome. According to Tribune Ocella, there was no clear indication that the Nazarene preached revolt against imperial rule. But despite this lack of evidence, Pilate was keen to placate the influential Jewish leaders who seemed determined to use Roman power to rid themselves of an inconvenient opponent. And the tribune's report of a suspected messianic plot was deeply disturbing. There was no denying that the Galilean Jesus had been hailed as a king on his recent arrival in the city—what if he was to be the focus of an uprising? As usual, Pilate had consulted an augur who sought to interpret Jupiter's will by studying the patterns of flying birds and the entrails of animals, but no satisfactory guidance was forthcoming from that source either.

By the time the group of priests, elders, and scribes had arrived at the palace with their prisoner, Pilate had been out of bed for two hours, although the sun was still barely over the horizon. The delegation would not enter the gentile-held building for fear of being defiled during the feast week, so Pilate had granted them an audience on the raised pavement outside the palace.[64] He had deeply hoped to hear sufficient cause for a judgment of *majestus*, which would justify execution for treason. But the accusations lacked convincing evidence, amounting to an unsubstantiated claim that the teacher challenged the payment of tribute to Augustus Caesar, and charges that he perverted the Jewish nation, declaring himself to be a messiah, king, and—even worse, apparently—son of god.

Pilate had no interest in these concerns, and he had impatiently and optimistically instructed the complainants to take the man away and judge him according to their law. But the priests had adamantly rejected this suggestion, making their ultimate intention crystal clear by pointing out that they no longer had the legal power to put anyone to death. Now it was finally time for Pilate to interview the Galilean directly, and he was determined to assess what threat this man might pose, not only to the stability of imperial rule in the region but to the security of the prefect himself.

His drumming fingers paused as a clanking sound approached along the corridor. Then a shackled figure was led shuffling into the chamber. The prisoner stood patiently, waiting in silence, and the prefect's pale blue eyes met a surprisingly steady, almost unsettling gaze. Moments passed. The prefect stared intently, his eyes narrowing as he tried to pierce the composure of the man standing before him. Then he dived into the most pressing concern.

"Jesus from Galilee, you have heard the accusations brought against you. I ask you now: are you indeed 'King of the Jews?'"

The gentle answer was not helpful.

"So you say."[65]

Pilate frowned, took a deep breath, and tried again.

"What about the many things you have heard your fellow Jews testify against you? Have you any response to these claims?"

The prisoner offered no reply. Pilate was impressed but also disconcerted by his impassive dignity. There was none of the usual passionate declaration of innocence or tearful begging for mercy. Instead, this man seemed unmoved by his possible fate, standing like a rock in the midst of the tumult that raged around him. Pilate made yet another attempt.

"Tell me, where are you from?"

Again—no answer. The interview was proving to be disappointingly unfruitful, and the prefect's tone became edged with frustration.

"Do you choose not to speak to me? Do you not know that I have the power to release you or to have you crucified?"

If Pilate thought this might shatter his captive's equanimity, he was mistaken.

"You would have no power at all against me," Jesus responded serenely, "unless it was given to you from above."

Pilate found the ambiguous response discomfiting.

"I ask again," he insisted urgently, leaning forward with an elbow on one armrest, "do you teach that you are the rightful king of the Jews?"

This time, the answer came in the form of a question.

"Do you say this yourself, or did others tell you about me?"

Pilate answered impatiently, "Am I a Jew? Your nation and the chief priests delivered you to me. Why is this? Tell me, what have you done?"

"You say I am a king. But my kingdom is not of this world. For if my kingdom were of this world, then my servants would fight, that I would not be delivered up. But my kingdom is not from here."

This reply did not help Pilate at all. Could a claim to be king of *another* world be regarded as a threat to the empire? The prefect's bemused frown deepened as he listened carefully to his prisoner's next words.

"For this reason have I come into the world," Jesus stated evenly, "that I should testify to the truth. And everyone who is of the truth will listen to my voice."

Pilate sighed heavily and sat back, shaking his head in exasperation. Truth! That was a word he heard all too often. Every man vehemently claimed to possess the truth. But how could this be, when each individual had their own version of it? The present situation was a perfect example: some Jews believed that Jesus was truly a prophet from God, which meant that any action against him could precipitate a violent protest, but to the teacher's opponents, he was truly a blaspheming insurrectionist who must die, or *they* would create havoc. The situation called for astute diplomacy.

Ornate drapes bellied out as a cool breeze blew through the open window. Dropping his square chin onto one hand, the Prefect of Judea, bearer of the imperial authority and might of Rome, contemplated the silent figure before him who was so completely at his mercy. It seemed that no further guidance would be forthcoming.

"Truth!" he blurted out, expecting no answer. "What is truth?"

25

I Find No Fault with This Man

THE SUN WAS STILL low over the horizon when Rachel stepped hesitantly through the maze of dusty streets, slowly ascending the Tyropoeon valley toward the Upper City with the Temple Mount towering on her right. But this time, unlike her previous excursion that still haunted her dreams, her walk was not directed toward the home of Benjamin. She faltered. Where indeed was she heading?

She had wakened early, oppressed by a strange restlessness that compelled her from her house without a clear sense of purpose. Now she felt caught between fearful trepidation and the relentless urge to proceed. Her heart raced and her mouth was dry. Again and again, she halted and tried to turn back to the safety of her home, but a powerful force continued to drive her onward. To where, she did not know. But her feet somehow knew the goal, and she reluctantly submitted to being drawn forward like a weary fish on an unyielding line of fate.

The streets were already becoming busy, and as currents of people swirled around her, Rachel stopped again, this time in anticipation. Sensing that her mysterious destination was nearby, she raised her head, searching anxiously for clues. Then her gaze rested upon a squat grey building near the three towers of Herod's Palace. And her feet once again paced along the stone paving, bringing her closer and closer to the Roman military barracks. Why was she here in this unfamiliar place? Was she supposed to meet someone? Her heart beat furiously, but her feet did not slow down as she prayed instinctively.

El Shaddai, be present with me. El Elyon, guide and protect me.

The long barrack block extended ahead of her with small windows identifying individual squad rooms. As raucous peacock calls mingled with the whicker of horses, Rachel slowed down, intimidated by the purposeful tramping of soldiers around her. Then she became aware of the covered basket on her arm, which made her look like a woman bringing supplies to a military father or husband. She prayed that whatever errand she might be on, it would soon be over.

Pulling her headscarf across her face, she kept her eyes on the ground and followed her feet, which seemed to be on a mission of their own. Then the light dimmed and she was in a passageway, pressing against the wall as if to melt into the rough plaster. Droning voices reached her ears, and through a doorway just ahead, she could see three men seated at a long wooden table: a uniformed commander, a scribe writing on a wax tablet, and an older man with a long scar across his cheek who seemed to be giving instructions, leaning in and drawing a finger across the tabletop in explanation. As Rachel's eyes gradually adjusted, her gaze penetrated the gloom behind the three figures, and she could make out two Roman soldiers partially concealed in a dark, curtained annex at the rear of the room. The danger of the situation almost overpowered her, and she struggled mentally against the leadenness of her feet, her mind screaming at her to retreat and flee.

Then one of the soldiers in the annex turned his head slightly, and Rachel inhaled sharply. The floor beneath her seemed to teeter. It was Daniel! Daniel with a man she did not recognize, both in Roman uniform. The two silently pulled out glinting daggers, their hands moving in slow motion as in a nightmare. They looked at each other in readiness and a sure knowledge arose in Rachel's mind—they were waiting for a signal! A signal that was late in coming. As she watched in horror, they both adjusted their stance slightly, leaning forwardly tensely as if poised for action. Then Daniel nodded slightly and raised his right hand, his fist flexing against the hilt of the knife . . .

Thou shalt not kill.

The sonorous words flooded Rachel's mind, and Daniel froze. She was sure that he, too, had heard them! His head whipped round and his face blanched as he recognized Rachel in the dark passage. She felt a powerful kick in her womb as the voice sounded again in her mind.

Thou shalt not kill.

Moments seemed to stretch out unnaturally as the three Romans continued to talk, oblivious to the drama of life and death unfolding around them. Rachel slowly shook her head from side to side, fixing Daniel's eyes with a silent but imploring gaze. Holding her breath, she prayed urgently.

El Shaddai, preserve us! Please spare Daniel. El Elyon, help us!

In the darkened annex, Daniel's left hand reached out as gradually as a creeping shadow and held back the knife hand of his partner.

Then Rachel was gone.

An ethereal morning mist hung over the dewy gardens of Herod's Palace, eddying around the still-flaming open braziers and wafting through the buzz of activity in front of the raised pavement and judgment seat. The shocking news was spreading rapidly—the Temple leaders had arrested Jesus and brought him before Pilate on charges of sedition! As a result, the small gathering of the teacher's accusers and followers was being steadily swollen by pilgrims eager to hear the prefect's verdict.

The mood was uncertain and explosive. Some loudly denounced the teacher for leading Jews astray, some argued just as heatedly that he was a good teacher, while others insisted he was the promised Messiah who would lead Israel to freedom. As the verbal confrontations grew louder, Roman soldiers stood at tense attention on the raised platform, continuously scanning the men below for signs of hidden weapons.

On the edge of the animated crowd, a small knot of Jesus's closest followers huddled in dread, scarves and shawls pulled over their heads. Tears poured down the faces of Jesus's mother, Mary from Magdala, and other women who had traveled with Jesus and supported him. The men in the group tried to offer comfort, but Simon Zealotes and Judas Iscariot were not among them, having positioned themselves close to the platform with other selected conspirators. The two disciples kept their arms wrapped tightly across their concealed swords as they exchanged tense glances. All hinged on Pilate's action. Would he offer to release Jesus as they had been informed?

A hum of excitement swelled as Pilate appeared on the pavement, somber in his formal dress, followed by two guards who led a chained figure between them. With a stern frown, the prefect lowered himself into the seat of judgment and raised his hand. Voices gradually dropped, and Pilate directed his gaze to the group of accusing priests and elders near the platform.

"You have brought this man to me," he intoned solemnly, indicating to Jesus, "as one who perverts the people. I have interviewed him and considered all evidence provided. And I have reached my verdict. This is my finding . . ."

A deep hush fell on the crowd.

"I find no fault with this man and—"

A roar of rejection burst from the Temple priests and Pharisees, and Jesus's supporters threw up their arms, crying out with ecstatic relief. Soldiers stepped forward with hands on their swords as Pilate raised his voice above the uproar.

"I say again that I find no basis for a charge against this man concerning those things of which you accuse him! I have found no capital crime in him, and neither has Herod Antipas, your own leader who has authority over Galilee and who I have consulted. I will therefore chastise this man and release him!"

But Jesus's determined opponents had no intention of allowing this vital opportunity to slip through their grasp. Caiaphas stepped forward and lifted a demanding arm as his voice rang out strongly above the tumult.

"We have told you that this man stirs up the people, teaching throughout all Judea, beginning from Galilee even to this place! If he were not an evildoer, we would not have delivered him up to you!"

Then Pilate employed the tactic he so hoped would resolve his dilemma. He raised his hand again, waited for the furor to subside, and spoke.

"You have heard my finding. But I also declare a concession during your feast time! To all who stand here, I offer to release one Jewish prisoner according to custom."

Jesus's mother groaned and clutched at John in desperate yearning. Could it be that her son would be spared after all? She closed her eyes, praying fervently for mercy. A buzz of speculation sizzled through the growing throng. Release a prisoner? Release who?

"I planned to set free the man known as Barabbas!" Pilate announced.

There were shouts and loud groans of shocked disapproval. Inhabitants of Jerusalem knew Barabbas and his so-called freedom fighters to be opportunistic thugs who terrorized the city, randomly attacking Jews as well as Romans. Pilate's spirits lifted as he noted the clear lack of support for his proposal—he had chosen well. Now the success of his plan hinged on the popularity of the Galilean teacher.

"However," he called out loudly, "I can instead release to you—Jesus of Nazareth!"

Judas and Simon tried to restrain exultant grins as they edged closer to the platform. Their strategy was unfolding precisely as it should. They nudged their close compatriots who felt surreptitiously for weapons beneath their cloaks as they raised their voices, shouting, "Yes! Release Jesus!"

The call was taken up by others, but an equally vociferous cry was raised by the Temple leaders, whose only concern was that the Galilean pretender should not be released.

"Release Barabbas!"

"No! Release Jesus! Jesus!"

"Release Barabbas!"

As the conflicting demands escalated in volume, Pilate stood up and cried out passionately, "I ask you all—who do you wish me to release to you? Barabbas or Jesus who is called Christ? Do you wish me to release the King of the Jews?"

Jesus's followers clamored urgently for his freedom: "Yes! Release Jesus of Nazareth!"

But the cry of opposition intensified: "No! Not this man! Release Barabbas! Barabbas!"

Judas's head swiveled wildly as he scanned the crowd in anxious dismay. Jesus's supporters, both paid and unpaid, should have been in the majority by now, and the call for his release should have been dominant. But to Judas's growing alarm, even some of their allies were now taking up the call for Barabbas!

"Release Jesus!" he shouted desperately, panicking as his croaking cry was swamped by the vehement howls of competition. Then he froze in horror as a sinister whisper drifted past him, coming from no identifiable source.

"*Releeeasssse Barabbassss,*" the sibilant voice hissed. "*Releeeassse Barabbassss.*"

The call for Barabbas's release took on even greater power, and Pilate tried once more.

"What then shall I do with Jesus who is called Christ?"

"*Cruuuccciffffy him . . .*" The hoarse, inhuman whisper circulated among the crowd, and faces became distorted with hatred.

"Crucify him!" came the chilling, concerted roar.

"Crucify him! Crucify him!" yelled the chief priests and Temple officers, punching their fists into the air.

"Why? What evil has he done?" cried Pilate, his voice almost lost among the screams that mingled with spine-chilling peacock wails. "Why do you wish me to crucify your king?"

But the chief priests screamed back, "We have no king but Caesar!"

Then Caiaphas stretched himself to his full height and pointed an accusing finger at Pilate. Shouts gradually died down and all eyes watched intently as the high priest played his trump card.

"If you release Jesus *HaNotzri*," his voice thundered, "you are no friend of Caesar's! For everyone who makes himself a king speaks against Caesar!"

The flicker of Pilate's eyes was barely noticeable. But the threat had struck home. The term *Amicus Caesaris*, "Caesar's friend," was reserved for those who enjoyed the emperor's favor. Losing this title was a hazardous result that could jeopardize one's political position and lead to ostracism from Roman life or even worse. It was over. In a matter of minutes, the order for the release of Barabbas was given, Jesus was condemned, Pilate had left the platform, and the teacher was gone. Taken away to be scourged and crucified.

With hands still on their hidden weapons, Judas and Simon slowly turned their unbelieving, ashen faces to each other. What had just happened? Jesus was gone! And any opportunity for a rescue mission was gone with him! Judas slumped in devastated bewilderment against a pillar. He was aghast, his shattered mind reeling as he tried to comprehend this outcome. How could their plan have miscarried so badly? Why had they failed? What had he done! As Jesus's opponents stalked away in stately triumph, and his disciples sobbed and groaned in anguish, Judas slowly subsided to become an inert bundle on the cold flagstones.

26

For This Reason I Came

LUCIUS'S RED CLOAK FLAPPED like the wings of a furious dragon, billowing out in the tugging wind as he marched rapidly back to the Antonia fortress. Behind him, the two accompanying soldiers exchanged a querying glance and suppressed their puffing. They were used to their tribune's forceful manner, but they had never before seen him this taciturn or this driven.

A vision remained seared into Lucius's memory, and he scanned his surroundings, feverishly searching in vain for a sight to overwrite it. Again, the crumpled figure convulsed as vicious flails stripped flesh from his back and thighs, exposing sinew and bone. Again, gouts of blood and red tissue spattered the ground. Again, the face of the torturer twisted into a grotesque mask of loathing as he poured his energy into each swing of his powerful arm. Again, the watching mob crowed in triumph at every driving stroke.

Lucius had overseen many scourgings but none as appallingly inhuman as this. And he had been further unnerved by an ominous hissing that seemed to hover in the air, assailing his ears and shaking his composure. Eventually, he had to halt the brutal process. His instruction was to have the man crucified not flogged to death. And then came the most ghastly moment, which still left Lucius quaking inwardly with horror: the panting Galilean had turned his bloody head and held the tribune's eyes with a penetrating gaze. And the words that rang then in the tribune's mind still echoed relentlessly in his memory:

For this reason I came . . . For this reason I came . . . For this . . .

"Pick up the pace there!" Lucius bellowed to the men behind him, trying to drown out the appalling words.

Joseph's teachings also surged like pounding, tossing waves in the tribune's mind, threatening to overturn his fundamental beliefs. God was a bridegroom and shepherd, like this teacher, Jesus. God loved his people and his work was not yet done. God would provide a final atonement to replace repeated blood sacrifices . . . Again, the *flagrum* ripped away flesh, again the torturer licked spittle from his taut, white lips, again Jesus's dark eyes rested on him: "*For this reason I came.*" Lucius shook his head, grimacing in distress as the image of the crucified Jesus now flared up in his mind and he remembered the pensive look on Joseph's face as he quoted the ancient prophecy:

> When they look on him whom they have pierced, they shall mourn
> for him.

Lucius groaned softly in anguish. Something was wrong. Something was terribly wrong. He could not analyze or comprehend these developments, but a bitter chill had spread like a deathly plague throughout his body, and he was desperate to escape. His mind was made up. He would appeal to Caesar on the grounds of ill health and return to Rome. He would marry Alessandra and pursue his career far away from mystifying, arcane Judaism and this baleful city. Return to the sensible order of state religious rituals and the protection of his household god, Janus. But for some reason, Lucius's memory of the familiar two-face statuette in its shrine failed to bring the usual comfort: the clay god merely stared mutely in both directions.

Shepherd and bridegroom. Final atonement. Replacement of blood sacrifices. What if . . . ? What if . . . ?

"Pick up the pace, I say!"

Daniel thrust urgently through the milling people, struggling to suppress his growing dread. He had no idea what had happened to the insurrection plot. What did it mean that he and Caleb had heard no trumpet signal? Had the plans changed without them knowing? What was Pilate's verdict? What had happened to Jesus? Daniel tried to slow his rapid breathing, reminding himself yet again that they had not failed in their mission: there had been no trumpet call. Rachel's sudden appearance at the barracks had been a shock, but it was surely irrelevant. And the commandment against killing that had risen in his mind must have been merely an old memory. Daniel clung anxiously to one important fact: there had been no trumpet call. He and Caleb had followed orders, but no signal had come. That was the only reason he had held back their strike.

After the three Romans had left the room, he and Caleb had marched from the barracks as steadily as possible in their state of confusion. Daniel's first instinct was to race directly to Herod's Palace to find Judas and Simon Zealotes. But Caleb had insisted they adhere to the previously agreed strategy: if anything did not go according to plan, the conspirators were to leave the city and await further orders. So the two had scrambled hastily into their tunics and cloaks, buried the Roman uniforms under a pile of rocks, and split up to make their way to safety.

But Daniel now found himself being increasingly jostled in the narrow street. A crowd had developed around some event that was making very slow progress. Looking for a way to escape the crush, he pressed along the edge of the throng toward a side alley. He could hear crying and wailing. Then he discovered the cause of the commotion.

In a space within the crowd, three men were stumbling forward under the weight of crucifixion crosspieces tied across their bent shoulders. Panting anxiously, Daniel shoved further along the rough wall, oblivious to the tearing of his skin in his urgency to see the faces of the men. Yes, two of them were familiar to him as brutal accomplices of the thug Barabbas. But he did not recognize the third man who suddenly collapsed onto the ground, heaving and gasping for breath. His face was swollen and bloody, but Daniel gave a shuddering sigh of relief—it was not Jesus. Then a woman fell to her knees and crawled toward the fallen man, her body wracked by tearing sobs as two men gently tried to draw her back. Daniel felt winded and nauseous as he recognized them as Jesus's disciples, John and Simon called Peter. The third prisoner must be Jesus after all! Panic welled up inside Daniel and his gaze flashed in all directions, searching frantically for a path of flight. Then he froze in nightmarish terror as one of the Roman guards pointed to him.

"You!" came the imperious call.

Daniel's legs felt limp and the blood drained from his face. Then he heard a quavering voice on his right.

"M . . . Me, sssir?"

Daniel peered sideways in sweating trepidation. A dark-skinned man beside him pointed to himself with wide-eyed fright.

"Yes you, fellow! You look strong enough. Help this man carry his cross. We don't have all day!"

Daniel pressed against the wall, faint with fear as his nervous neighbor lurched forward to assist the fallen prisoner. Jesus struggled painfully to his knees, groaned deeply, and turned his head to look into Daniel's eyes. Daniel gasped in shock. Jesus knew! He knew about Judas's arrangement with the Temple priests. He knew about Daniel's involvement in the rebellion plot. He knew it all! Tears ran down Daniel's cheeks as words pulsed like blood in his mind:

> *For this reason . . . I came . . . For this reason . . . I came.*

Then Daniel knew with perfect clarity that Simon Zealotes and Judas were wrong: Jesus was not merely another political claimant. And Rabbi Hilkiah was also wrong: Jesus was not a teacher of falsehoods. As Daniel looked upon Jesus's sobbing followers, he finally understood that these men and women were somehow closest to the truth about this unique figure.

Jesus labored slowly to his feet and staggered forward, supported by his reluctant assistant. Gripped by pity and dread, Daniel edged closer to the disciples he recognized, determined to remain beside them. Although Jesus's life was approaching its end, Daniel was filled with the certainty that for reasons he could not yet comprehend, his own was just beginning.

27

It Is Done

THUNDER VIBRATED THROUGH THE small room and a brilliant scar of lightning briefly illuminated the lone face peering anxiously out of the window. When Rachel fled the military barracks, she had to force herself not to run as she pushed through streets that crackled with rumors about the arrest of the Galilean teacher. She had no idea what might have unfolded around Daniel, but she passionately hoped he had held back the glinting blades and escaped without being observed.

El Elyon, spare Daniel. I pray, Lord, keep him from all harm. El Shaddai, be with us now.

Rachel bowed her head and let tears flow unchecked down her face and onto her tunic. Even though she had reached home safely, everything still seemed so uncertain and fraught with danger. If only she could take comfort in the presence of her Abba. If only she could again hear his deep, sure voice and feel protected and loved. But he would not even acknowledge her existence. And neither would anyone else. She was a sinful, adulterous woman, deserving only of death. Rachel felt paralyzed by a gripping sense of foreboding that was intensified by the threatening clouds that sucked the light out of the room. Her life was falling apart and her future seemed bereft of hope. To whom could she turn? Could she even approach God in her disgraced state? In quiet desperation, she mumbled words from an ancient psalm: *"My God, My God, why have You forsaken me?"*

Her shoulders shook and she submitted to an overpowering sense of abandonment, collapsing onto the earthen floor as waves of shuddering sobs wracked her body. She could weep as loudly as she wished. No concerned neighbor would tap at her door to offer solace. No arms would reach around her to ease the pain. Not now. Not ever. For one weak, misguided act, she was forever lost.

Then a vivid image arose: warm dark eyes gazed intently into hers and a sun-browned arm reached out to her. The joyous sense of forgiveness that she had received from Jesus had been gradually eroded by a growing sense of dread, but her sobbing now subsided as she sat back, losing herself in the memory of his comforting presence. Once more, she heard his compassionate voice: "*Neither do I condemn you.*"

She clutched at the words in desperate eagerness. Perhaps, despite what she had done, there was still reason to be optimistic. Others might never forgive her disgrace, but the iron clamp around her heart eased with the hope that she was not a condemned soul and that Jesus could somehow redeem her in God's eyes. Mary from Magdala had been tenderly sympathetic after the terrifying charge of adultery, and she had urged Rachel to return with them to Galilee. An uplifting resolution slowly took shape in Rachel's mind: she would accept the invitation and start a new life. She would strive to be a better person and find purpose in raising a child to walk with God. Her lips moved slightly as a psalm flowed freely through her:

> Create in me a clean heart, O God,
> and renew a steadfast spirit within me.
> Do not cast me away from Your Presence,
> and do not take Your Holy Spirit from me.
> Restore to me the joy of Your salvation,
> and uphold me by Your generous Spirit—

But then another image exploded in Rachel's consciousness, violently shattering her optimism. Jesus was dying! She saw his swollen face etched with exhaustion and pain—blood dripped from the reddened points of cruel thorns on his brow, and his bruised mouth gasped for air. Rachel scrambled to her feet in panic and despair, clutching at the wall for support as another psalm tumbled unbidden from her lips:

> My God, My God, why have You forsaken me?
> Why are You so far from helping me,
> And from the words of my groaning?
> All those who see me ridicule me;
> They shoot out the lip, they shake the head, saying,
> "He trusted in the Lord, let Him rescue him;
> Let Him deliver him, since He delights in him!"

Rachel sagged heavily, dazed by an appalling vision of suffering as the words of the psalmist continued to spill out through her sobs, rising from unknown depths.

> *I am poured out like water,*
> *And all my bones are out of joint;*
> *My heart is like wax;*
> *It has melted within me.*
> *My strength is dried up like a potsherd,*
> *And my tongue clings to my jaws.*
> *They pierced my hands and my feet;*[66]
> *I can count all my bones.*

As Rachel struggled helplessly against the nightmarish images, a strange tingling sensation traveled slowly along her arms and up the back of her neck, and the pounding of her heart slowed down. For the first time, she realized that despite its dreadful words, this prophecy offered a reassuring conclusion. Her voice grew stronger as she completed the ancient psalm:

> *All the ends of the world*
> *Shall remember and turn to the Lord,*
> *And all the families of the nations*
> *Shall worship before You.*
> *It will be recounted of the Lord to the next generation,*
> *They will come and declare His righteousness to a people who will be born,*
> *That He has done this.*

Somehow, although Rachel could not make clear sense of it, the horrendous suffering and desolation described in the psalm were associated with the triumph of all nations finally being restored to God. Her spirits started to lift, matched by a ray of light that speared the murky clouds to shed its brightness in the gloom of the little house. Inhaling deeply, she shakily repeated the profoundly prophetic words.

"*He has done this.*"

Then thunder vibrated the frail walls again, and darkness moved in.

Darkness moved over the hill known as *Golgotha*, "place of a skull." On the top of a Roman cross, a description of Jesus's crime was written in Greek, Latin, and Hebrew: "King of the Jews."

Jesus's mother leaned heavily upon John. Her crumpled face was no longer capable of tears, her heart was no longer capable of prayer, but her feverish, adoring eyes never left her son. The teacher's followers sobbed in acute grief and misery. Despite Jesus's repeated warnings, they were not prepared for this. No one could ever be prepared for this obscene horror. Their cherished, compassionate, inspiring, courageous, loving teacher was now stretched naked and broken on a cross, suffering unspeakable agony.

Callously ignoring the devastated weeping, Jesus's opponents jeered mockingly, laughing and wagging their heads in contemptuous ridicule.

"Hahaha! He saved others, but it seems he can't save himself!"

"Yes! You who promised to destroy the temple and build it in three days, save yourself and come down from the cross!"

"He trusts in God, right? So let God deliver him now, if He wants him! For didn't he say, 'I am the Son of God'?"

"I say if he really is the King of Israel, let him come down from the cross so we can all believe in him!"

Jesus groaned in anguish. Searing cramps raced up his calves from his shattered feet. His chest heaved—he could not breathe. Agonizing flashes of jagged pain blazed along his arms as he tried desperately to raise himself and open his chest. He grimaced and sobbed as his shoulder tore from its socket. He frantically took a shallow gulp of air, but now he could not exhale. His dry throat was closing and his heart pounded as if it would burst.

But far, far worse than the physical torment was the crushing weight of perversion and sin that bore down upon him. It was as if collective millennia of human iniquity and depravity were being loaded upon him, suffocating him as much as the collapse of his straining lungs. The darkness overhead was but a pale shadow of the intense blackness that flooded his soul.

"*Eloi, Eloi, lama sabachthani?*" he cried out, quoting from the well-known psalm: *My God, my God, why have you forsaken me?*

Someone who stood by misinterpreted the Galilean accent and said, "He is calling the prophet Eliya. Let us see whether Eliya will come to save him!"

Jesus's life force was draining away. His half-closed eyes rested upon his distraught mother collapsed in the arms of the grey-faced John, and he forced out words in shallow pants. "Woman . . ." he heaved, "behold . . . your son . . . John . . . behold . . . your . . . mother."

At Jesus's words of loving concern, John's last reserves of strength crumbled and he wept brokenly, allowing tears to course through his unkempt beard as he tenderly held Mary close to his chest. From that hour, he would be her son and keep her safe in his home.

Jesus's strength was failing.

"I . . . thirst," he croaked.

Someone took a sponge of vinegar on a hyssop stalk and held it gently to his bloody mouth. Suddenly pushing up his body in agony, Jesus gulped for air and cried out with a loud voice.

"Father, into your hands I commit my spirit!"[67]

Then his head sagged weakly, and he spoke his last three words on the cross, echoing the closing line of an ancient psalm and indicating that he had accomplished his earthly work for his Father.

"It is done."[68]

28

I Am with You Always

THUNDER REVERBERATED LOUDLY ACROSS the city, and Hilkiah looked up nervously as the floor trembled. The darkened sky seemed like a portent of evil. Three students chatted brightly among themselves, seated around his stone bench, but the rabbi found it difficult to concentrate, his thoughts continually wandering back to Rachel.

How could she have done this? Her shameful conduct left him feeling bereft and hollow. How could she behave in this way, after all his diligent training? Was there no end to the depravity of the human heart? Of course he could no longer have the disgraced woman under his roof, but her absence seemed to steal the very light and warmth from his home. Acutely aware of his age and increasing fragility, the rabbi hugged his worn prayer shawl around him as meager protection against the chill of the stone bench. How would he manage without Rachel? And what was Shabbat without a woman to light the candles and recite the blessing? How could she do this to him? His reverie was interrupted by an eager voice. Hilkiah reluctantly turned his head to focus on the ardent faces, feeling the bitter loss not only of Rachel but also Daniel and Benjamin who no longer sat at his feet.

"Rabbi, we have been discussing God's Servant who is described in Isaiah's prophecy. This verse from the scroll tells us that he will appear as an ordinary man and will be rejected:

He has no form or comeliness;
And when we see him,
There is no beauty that we should desire him.
He is despised and rejected by men,

A man of sorrows and acquainted with grief.

Although this Servant will not seem to be anyone special, some teachers claim that his suffering and grief will bring redemption to Israel. Could this be true, Rabbi?"

Hilkiah sighed deeply and nodded. Isaiah's Suffering Servant figure was indeed associated with God's plan of restoration and atonement. Looking up at the roof, he closed his eyes and said solemnly, "Hear Isaiah's prophecy about God's Servant, who will bear the iniquities of our nation." As the young men listened respectfully, the rabbi recited Isaiah's prophecy, losing himself in the cadence of the prediction that was written in the prophetic perfect tense, as if the event was already accomplished:

> *Surely he has borne our griefs*
> *And carried our sorrows;*
> *Yet we esteemed him stricken,*
> *Smitten by God, and afflicted.*
> *He was pierced for our transgressions,*[69]
> *He was bruised for our iniquities;*
> *The chastisement for our peace was upon him,*
> *And by his stripes we are healed.*[70]
> *All we like sheep have gone astray;*
> *We have turned, every one, to his own way;*
> *And the Lord has laid on him the iniquity of us all.*
> *He was oppressed and he was afflicted,*
> *Yet he opened not His mouth;*
> *He was led as a lamb to the slaughter . . .*

Hilkiah's voice slowly faded as the enormity of the prophecy settled heavily on his heart. Who could carry such a burden?

"What a terrible prophecy!" exclaimed a student. "Why would God wish to lead a man to the slaughter like this?"

"Yes," agreed another. "What is the point of this dreadful prediction, Rabbi?"

Hilkiah wearily pushed himself up from the bench and took a few steps to stare absently at the blurred square of window. "Be assured, young Shemuel," he murmured, "this prophecy does end on a positive note. The Servant will indeed suffer, but through his submission to God's will, the seed of God will be justified." The rabbi's wavering voice proclaimed the ancient promise:

When You make his soul an offering for sin,
He shall see his seed, he shall prolong his days,
And the pleasure of the Lord shall prosper in his hand.
He shall see the labor of his soul, and be satisfied.
By his knowledge My righteous Servant shall justify many,
For he shall bear their iniquities.
Therefore I will divide him a portion with the great,
And he shall divide the spoil with the strong,
Because he poured out his soul unto death,
And he was numbered with the transgressors,
And he bore the sin of many,
And made intercession for the transgressors.

"But Rabbi, how can this be? How can one man bear the sins of us all and justify us before God?"

The students frowned as they mulled over the implications of the verses. Who could possibly intercede for everyone's transgressions? Hilkiah's usual enthusiasm was lacking, but he turned to provide the ready answer.

"The explanation lies in our concept of corporate identity, young Hiram, through which one man can represent many."

"Do you mean," came the keen interjection, "like when *Kohen HaG-adol* represents all Israel by wearing a breastplate with the names of our twelve tribes inscribed upon it?"

"This is correct, Shemuel. Similarly, 'Israel' can refer to the son of Isaac, the tribe of Israel, or our entire nation. This collective identity also applies to Isaiah's prophecy: the Servant is the individual appointed by God to liberate His people, but at the same time he represents all Israel before God.[71] In this way, the Servant's suffering will also be our suffering, and the resulting atonement will cover our sin."

"So who is this servant, Rabbi? He surely can't be the warrior-king Messiah?"

Hilkiah gnawed his lips in uncharacteristic uncertainty. "This is a much-neglected text, Shemuel, and its meaning is not clear. However, we must wait patiently for the Arm of God to reveal His power."

The young men debated excitedly, keen to believe that God's Servant would come in their lifetime and that his suffering would atone for Israel's iniquity and rescue them from God's wrath. But oppressed by a dark sense of despondency, Hilkiah could not feel the same confidence or hope. Three sets of eyes turned to regard the rabbi as he spoke softly, blinking back tears.

"We hold fast to God's promise: '*Behold, I am with you and will keep you wherever you go.*' But we must also not forget Jeremiah's warning: '*Listen! The cry of the daughter of my people from a far country: The harvest is past, the summer is ended, and we are not saved.*'"

"Brothers and sisters, do not despair! The Lord warned us that we would have to remain strong. Somehow, we must find direction together."

But even as he spoke, John struggled to believe his words. Overwhelmed by a sickening sense of loss, the apostle slid down onto the wooden bench, searching hopelessly within himself for the confidence he so longed to provide the traumatized men and women around him. And without much success, he tried to smile encouragingly at the red-bearded newcomer who had not left his side since their Lord's horrendous execution two days ago.

On this first day of the new week, the day after the *Pesach* Sabbath, pilgrims were celebrating the joyous feast of Firstfruits, bringing spring offerings to God as the pledge of the greater harvest. John again heard Jesus's promise:

> If I am lifted up, I will draw all people to myself. If a seed of wheat
> falls into the earth and dies, it bears much fruit.

But if this was a reference to their teacher's appalling crucifixion, it still made no sense to John. Jesus's death was the end of all their hopes, so how could it provide the promise of a future harvest for God?

In broken-hearted pity, John contemplated his fellow disciples who huddled inside the locked room, murmuring fearfully and muffling their weeping. The apostle Judas was nowhere to be seen, and a rumor was circulating that he had taken his own life. A recent shock had also unsettled them even further—the body of their beloved teacher was not in the tomb! John and Peter had confirmed the implausible report of the women who had gone early that morning to anoint his body. Joseph of Arimathea, who had spent much time in discussion with Jesus, had arranged for him to be reverently interred, but now the precious body was missing.[72] Gone! Who would have interfered with his corpse? And why? The monstrous act of desecration left them feeling even more vulnerable and under attack.

In one corner, Jesus's mother wept inconsolably. Her heart was an aching bruise and she felt bilious. What had been the point of it all? Why had her child ever been born? The angel had assured her that the miraculous baby would be Son of the Most High, but God must have known his life would end this way. He had known it all the time. He had watched while she joyfully nurtured the gurgling baby, lovingly guided the toddler, and diligently taught Scripture to the ardent young boy, but He had foreseen that every step led relentlessly to the horrendous moment when she cradled her precious son's shattered body.

Why? Why? Why? The question jangled painfully in Mary's mind. Her son had served the Lord faithfully, never wavering in his commitment. And *this* was his reward! God had watched while they tortured and scourged Jesus and hung him up in naked humiliation and broken agony. Bitter tears ran down her face. It would have been better had he never been formed or even been stillborn! Anything rather than suffer this excruciating death. Although Jesus had often warned them about the trials ahead, she had never comprehended that his life would end in such agony. How could this possibly be God's will? A spasm of pain shook her body and she grimaced in acute distress. Mary from Magdala leaned closer and gently touched her arm.

"Imma?" she asked anxiously. "What can I do to help? You must eat sometime. Can I bring you food?"

But the older Mary merely shook her head dumbly, shocked at the wild, despairing thoughts that accompanied her anguish. Then she became aware of a sudden hush. The murmuring and crying had ceased. Turning slowly, she saw the disciples pushing backward against each other, retreating hastily toward the walls. And in the cleared center of the room stood a familiar figure with the tender smile they all adored.

Jesus's mother groaned in a pained confusion of doubt and hope. Leaning forward weakly with one yearning arm outstretched, she whispered brokenly, "Jesus . . . Can it be you?"

Then the Magdalene's awed voice sounded in the shocked silence. "Yes . . . Yes! It is the Lord!"

Jesus held out his arms to show the nail marks, and his vibrant, beloved voice thrilled through each person, touching their very soul. "I say to you all: take heart. For I have overcome the world!"

Many trembling hands were now reaching out toward the teacher in disbelieving elation as Jesus's strong voice filled the room.

"All authority in heaven and on earth has been given to me. Therefore go and make disciples of all nations, teaching them to obey everything I have commanded you. And surely I am with you always, to the
very end of the age."

Tears of jubilation ran down glowing faces that reflected how each
heart had been set singing. The words of the risen Jesus filled them all
with unshakable certainty and confidence: they were loved, they were not
alone, and their lives were forever changed.[73]

Epilogue

RAISING HIS GNARLED HAND against the glare of the sun, John stood gazing out through cypress branches across the small island of Patmos. Houses were strewn among the vineyards, sprawling across the hot stony slopes and down to the pebbled shore. From his elevated position, John could see far across the deep blue of the placid Aegean that stretched to the horizon, dotted with uninhabited outcrops of rock.

The aged apostle was in a pensive mood, yearning for home. Would his exile ever be brought to an end? Would the emperor who succeeded Domitian be any more tolerant of the gospel message? But John also knew that he was far more fortunate than other followers of the Lord. Unlike the many who had fallen decades ago, he could at least continue preaching the good news to anyone on the island who would listen.

The faces of martyred friends appeared in John's mind, raising a deep sadness: Stephen had fallen first, stoned to death by the Sanhedrin; the Lord's skeptical brother James had come to believe in him after his miraculous resurrection and helped to lead the Jerusalem church, only to be killed later by hostile religious leaders;[74] John's own beloved brother James was murdered on the orders of Herod Agrippa; the ardent Simon Peter and the converted persecutor Paul who had encountered the risen Jesus on his journey to Damascus—all long dead. John drew comfort from the knowledge that they were safe in the hands of God.

Then John remembered the red-bearded Daniel who had joined them directly after the crucifixion. John smiled fondly as he recalled how the young scholar's face had lit up when Mary Magdalene brought in the woman called Rachel. It had seemed fitting that the two were soon married, and only a few years later Barnabas reported that they were both working in the church at Antioch, raising two children while providing powerful eyewitness testimony to the resurrected Lord.

John sighed and let his thoughts wander. Today was the Lord's Day, the day of Jesus's miraculous rising, and memories of his teachings swirled in the apostle's mind as he gazed out across the ocean. On the shore of Galilee, the risen Lord had given them bread and fish to eat, and he had provided opportunities for Simon Peter to redeem himself for denying their master after his arrest. Three times, Jesus asked him: "Simon bar-Jonah, do you love me?" And each time, Peter answered: "Yes, Lord, you know that I do."

Then Jesus had held the disciple firmly by the shoulders and given him direct instructions: "Follow me. And feed my sheep."

Hoping for further information, Peter had pointed to John and asked, "Lord, what about this man?"

But Jesus's answer had been strangely ambiguous: "If I desire that he remain until I come, what is that to you? You must follow me."

What could these words mean? The apostles had often discussed this strange saying among themselves, and some had interpreted it as a promise that John would never die.[75] In his writings, John pointed out that Jesus had not said that at all, but he had puzzled over the words for decades. Why had he survived so much longer than Jesus's other followers? And in what way was he supposed to see the Lord come?

Sighing from sorrow and weariness, the apostle stretched his back. Then he raised his arms, closed his eyes to the bright sunlight, and settled into a deeply contemplative state of prayer. Until to his surprise, he heard a loud voice like a trumpet behind him:

What you see, write in a scroll.

Hardly knowing whether he was awake or dreaming, John slowly turned in trepidation. Before him was a dazzling vision of seven golden lampstands and a figure with eyes of fire and brilliant white hair. His face shone like the sun, instantly reminding John of the time that he, James, and Peter had seen Jesus become a glorious object of light. A two-edged sword projected from the figure's mouth, and the shocked John fell at his feet like a dead man. He felt a hand rest upon him as the powerful voice like many waters spoke to him:

Do not be afraid. I am the first and the last, and the Living One. I was dead, and behold, I am alive forever and ever. I have the keys of Death and of Hades. Write therefore the things which are, and the things which will happen hereafter.

How long John was rapt in the astounding vision, he could not tell.[76] But when it was over, he staggered into his simple home, grasped reed pen, ink, and papyrus, and prepared to write as Jesus had instructed him in the vision. Perhaps this was why he had been kept alive for so long!

As he shakily dipped his pen, John recalled the older vision in the scroll of Daniel, in which one like a Son of Man came with clouds of heaven to receive an everlasting dominion. An angel had then instructed that the prophecy be sealed, but John's recent vision revealed that Jesus had earned the right to break this seal. A multitude arrayed in white sang a praise song to the slain Lamb, which John now inscribed:

> *You are worthy to take the book and to open its seals: for you were killed, and bought us for God with your blood out of every tribe, language, people, and nation!*

An elder had spoken to John in his vision, and the apostle murmured his message as he inscribed it, remembering the promise of the prophet Isaiah that God would remove the tears of His people:

> *These are they who came out of the great suffering. They will never be hungry or thirsty, for the Lamb who is in the middle of the throne shepherds them and leads them to springs of life-giving waters. And God will wipe away every tear from their eyes.*

Pen flew over papyrus as John hurriedly scrawled words about those who had been beheaded for their testimony to Jesus. With thumping heart, he described awful calamities falling upon the earth: hail, fire, blood, plagues, and death. Yet still, mankind did not repent or turn from their worship of idols of gold and silver, or from their violence and immorality. Then angels called out to one like a son of man upon a cloud, echoing a prophecy of Joel:

> *Send in your sickle and reap; for the hour to reap has come; for the harvest of the earth is ripe!*[77]

A winepress was trodden outside the city, and blood poured out. As John closed his eyes, he could again see the great white horse, on which sat a crowned man with eyes of fire, clothed in a garment stained with blood from treading the winepress of the wrath of Almighty God. This glorified figure of Jesus issued a stern warning:

Those whom I love, I rebuke and discipline. So be earnest and repent!

Words flowed from John's pen, describing how finally the old serpent and deceiver was cast down. All humanity then stood before the white throne of judgment, but those whose names were inscribed in the Book of Life were spared the second death. Again, the apostle heard the voice of many waters and mighty thunder calling out an invitation that reminded John of Jesus's parable about the wedding feast for the king's son:

Hallelujah! For the Lord our God, the Almighty, reigns! Blessed are those who are invited to the wedding supper of the Lamb!

As he continued to write furiously, John relived his vision of the new heaven and new earth arriving as promised in ancient scripture. And the new holy city of Jerusalem descended out of heaven from God, prepared like a bride for Jesus. But there was no Temple because Jesus, who had said he was greater than the Temple, now replaced this structure and provided the meeting place between God and His people. At the beginning of creation, God had separated light from darkness, water from land, and the heavens from the earth, but now there was no longer any darkness, there was no sea—a symbol of chaos—and heaven and earth were united through the person of Jesus.

On the gates of the new city were inscribed the twelve tribes of Israel, and on its foundations were the names of Jesus's twelve apostles. John sat back in awe as a realization struck him: the New Jerusalem would combine the ancient history of God's chosen people and Jesus's work on earth! It was immediately clear to the apostle that his recent vision depicted the fulfillment through Jesus of God's repeated promise that He would finally redeem humanity and His entire creation. Filled with uplifting optimism, John preserved for posterity the words of the glorified Jesus:

Behold, I am making all things new! I will give freely to him who is thirsty from the spring of the water of life.

Wiping away tears of elation, the apostle inscribed the words he had heard emanate from the celestial throne:

God's dwelling is with His people.

Into John's mind flashed the certain knowledge that Jesus's death, resurrection, and return would provide a physical enactment of the seven feasts of God,[78] from his *Pesach* sacrifice and his rising on the day of First-fruits, through to his trumpeted return, the final redemption, and the ingathering of humanity to tabernacle with God. John inhaled slowly, astounded by the grandeur of God's vast cosmic plan for His creation.[79] Through the work of His Son, there would finally be no more suffering. Joy welled up in the apostle's spirit. Yes, trials still lay ahead, but his hand trembled as he recorded Jesus's glorious promise that anyone who overcomes will be made a pillar in God's house. And he took heart as he inscribed Jesus's reassuring promise in the wondrous vision:

> *Behold, I come soon. My reward is with me, to repay to each man according to his work. I am the Alpha and the Omega, the First and the Last, the Beginning and the End.*[80] *I, Jesus, have sent my angel to testify these things to you for the assemblies. I am the root and the offspring of David, the Bright and Morning Star. The Spirit and the bride say, 'Come!' He who hears, let him say, 'Come!'*

John laid down his reed pen, rose stiffly, and walked outside in a daze. The setting sun was radiating a crown of bright golden beams into the blue sky, and it cast a long shadow onto pale rock as the apostle raised his arms in worship, suffused by a blissful peace that was beyond comprehension.[81] Tears coursed unhindered down his face as he reverently whispered words that would ring out through the ages.

"Yes, come, our Lord Jesus! *Maranatha!*"[82]

Endnotes

1. "God brought into contempt the land of Zebulun and the land of Naphtali . . . His name will be called Wonderful, Counselor, Mighty God, Eternal Father, Prince of Peace" (Isa 9:1–6).

    The lands allocated to the descendants of Jacob's sons Zebulun and Naphtali incorporated the towns of Nazareth and Capernaum. Isaiah prophesied the coming of a child who would bring light to these regions.

    This prophecy, which is found in the oldest Isaiah text (in the Dead Sea Scrolls) contains titles that are highly significant for Christianity. In the same way that Jesus is both the divine Son of God and equal with the Father, this promised child would be both Prince of Peace and Eternal Father. And Jesus promised to be a counselor in the form of the Holy Spirit: "I will ask the Father, and he will give you another *parakleton* to help you and be with you forever—the Spirit of truth . . . I will not leave you as orphans; I will come to you" (John 14:16–18). The Greek word *parakleton* means advocate or counselor.

    It is often suggested that Isaiah must have been applying these messianic titles to the future king Hezekiah of Judah. However, according to the Jewish Talmud, some rabbis disagreed that Hezekiah could have been the Messiah: "This was said *in opposition* to Rabbi Hillel, who maintained that there will be no Messiah for Israel, since they have already enjoyed him during the reign of Hezekiah" (Babylonian Talmud, Sanhedrin 98b). An extra-biblical Jewish text from the first or second century AD explicitly depicted Hezekiah as a different figure from the Messiah (see 2 Baruch 63). Isaiah's words might be an example of a prophecy that applied partly to that period and partly to the future, as Jewish scholar Joseph Klausner commented: "I, along with most modern scholars, consider this whole prophecy messianic. The prophet *wished and longed* that Hezekiah would be a 'wonderful counsellor' and a 'prince of peace'; but Hezekiah was such a person only in a limited way. Hence the wish and longing of the prophet to see his ideal *completely* realized are his Messianic expectations" (*Messianic Idea*, 64–65, original emphasis).

    In the Hebrew text of Isaiah, the promised child is said to be born of an *almah* (Isa 7:14), which means young maiden rather than virgin (*betulah*). However, a young unmarried Jewish girl of that period would be expected to be a virgin, and Isaiah called the birth a "sign" (Hebrew: *ot*), which was the term for a miraculous act of God. The pre-Christian Greek version of the Old Testament (the Septuagint) directly translated *almah* as *parthenos*, meaning virgin.

2. "The Spirit of the Lord shall rest upon Him."

    The prophecy is found in Isaiah: "The Spirit of the Lord shall rest upon Him
    . . . And in that day there shall be a Root of Jesse, who shall stand as a banner
    to the people; For the Gentiles shall seek Him, and His resting place shall be
    glorious" (Isa 11:2–10). Rabbinic teaching regards this as a prophetic reference
    to the promised Messiah: "In that day there will be a root of Jesse, which will
    stand for an ensign of the peoples, unto him will the nations seek, that is, seek the
    king Messiah, David's son, who will remain hidden unto the time of redemption"
    (Midrash Psalm 21.1–3). Also: "The Messiah was blessed with six virtues, as it is
    written: 'And the spirit of the Lord shall rest upon him, the spirit of wisdom and
    understanding, the spirit of counsel and might, the spirit of knowledge and of the
    fear of the Lord'" (Babylonian Talmud, Sanhedrin 93b).

3. "His cousin Jesus."

    Jesus's mother was described as a relative of John the Baptist's mother (Luke
    1:36), although it is not clear exactly how they were related.

4. "The Son of Man has no place to lay his head" (Matt 8:20; Luke 9:58).

    Jesus often referred to himself as "Son of Man," which seems to have been a sig-
    nificant innovation. In the Old Testament, the phrase simply meant a human be-
    ing, and there is no evidence that this was used as a specific title in pre-Christian
    Judaism or that there was any expectation of a coming savior-figure called the
    "Son of Man." A text known as the Similitudes of Enoch did depict a heavenly
    Son of Man, but Professor of Hebrew Scripture James VanderKam points out that
    "there remains widespread agreement that at least a few significant sections were
    added to the Similitudes during their textual history" ("Righteous One," 176).
    According to biblical scholar F. F. Bruce, "There does not appear to have been any
    existing concept of 'the Son of Man' which Jesus could have taken over and used
    either to identify himself or to denote a being distinct from himself. The expres-
    sion as Jesus used it was evidently original to himself" ("Son of Man Sayings," 60).

5. "The Angel of the Lord appeared to Jacob and said, 'I am the God of Bethel, where
    you anointed the pillar.'"

    In this astounding claim in Genesis 31:13, the Angel of the Lord explicitly
    identifies himself as the God of Israel.

6. "God appeared in human form to Abraham at Mamre."

    Genesis records that three men visited Abraham at Mamre (Gen 18:1). However,
    when the men went toward Sodom, Abraham remained standing before the Lord
    (Gen 18:22) and only two angels arrived at Sodom (Gen 19:1), which suggests that
    one of the figures was an appearance of God. A rabbinic text explicitly states that
    Abraham encountered God at Mamre: "The Holy One blessed be He, said to the
    angels, Go to him; and the Lord followed them and tarried near Abraham until the
    angels were gone (Gen 18:22) . . . According to Rabbi Simon, the later words have
    out of reverence been modified by the scribes, for in truth it was the Lord's presence
    which stood and waited for Abraham" (Midrash Psalm 18:29).

7. "Who was this mysterious being?"

    The Angel of the Lord is unique in scripture, in that he is differentiated from
    God and yet directly assumes His role. Instead of using the typical words of a
    messenger ("Thus says YHWH"), this figure consistently speaks with a voice of

personal, divine authority.

For example, when God instructed Abraham to sacrifice his son Isaac, the Angel of the Lord prevented this by calling out from heaven, and he then said, "Now I know that you fear God, since you have not withheld your son, your only son, from Me" (Gen 22:12b). The implication is that Abraham owed obedience directly to the Angel as if he were God Himself. In Genesis 22:17, God promised to multiply the descendants of Abraham, and the Angel of the Lord later claimed this same power when he promised to multiply the descendants of Abraham through his concubine Hagar; after this interaction, Hagar believed she had encountered God (Gen 16:10–13).

Samuel Meier, a professor of Near Eastern languages and cultures, remarks that the Old Testament Angel of the Lord acts in highly unusual ways: "The angel of YHVH in these perplexing biblical narratives does not behave like any other messenger known in the divine or human realm. Although the term 'messenger' is present, the narrative itself omits the indispensable features of messenger activity, and presents instead the activities which one associates with Yahweh and other gods of the ancient Near East" ("Angel I," 88).

It is interesting that the first-century Jewish scholar Philo identified the Angel of the Lord as God taking on a form visible to human apprehension: "So that when he says, 'I am the God who was seen by thee in the place of God' [Gen 31:13], we must understand this, that he on that occasion took the place of an angel, as far as appearance went, without changing his own real nature" (*On Dreams* 1.238–39, translated by Charles Young).

Jewish biblical scholar Alan Segal points out that pre-Christian monotheistic Judaism did include belief in an angelic manifestation in heaven that was equivalent to God (*Two Powers*, x). But this concept came to be condemned as heretical in the face of Christian claims, and thereafter Jewish writers became uneasy about the ambiguous Angel of the Lord, sometimes altering the associated scripture. For example, the first-century Jewish historian Josephus described only God interrupting Isaac's sacrifice, without mentioning the Angel (*Antiquities* 1.13.4), and in contradiction to scripture and the rabbinic interpretation of Genesis 18 (see note 6 above), he claimed that all three figures who met Abraham at Mamre explicitly declared themselves to be angels (*Antiquities* 1.11.2). The rabbinic commentary Genesis Rabbah also changed scripture by describing four angels appearing to Hagar in Genesis 16 instead of only the Angel of the Lord, and it omitted the verse in which the Angel identified himself as the God of Bethel (Gen 31:13).

Theologian James Dunn considers that the Angel of the Lord was "a way of describing the presence and saving power of Yahweh" (*Christology in the Making*, 150–51). And biblical scholar Geerhardus Vos makes this comment: "We must assume that behind the twofold representation there lies a real manifoldness in the inner life of the Deity. If the Angel were Himself partaker of the Godhead, then He could refer to God as his sender, and at the same time speak as God" (*Biblical Theology*, 73). This brings to mind Jesus's claim that "anyone who has seen me has seen the Father" (John 14:9b) as well as Paul's teaching that the Son is the visible image of the invisible Father (Col 1:15), which is also implied in Hebrews 1:3. Many theologians therefore regard the Angel of the Lord as the pre-incarnate Christ—God's messenger sent into the world and also God himself appearing in human form. This would explain Jesus's words: "If you believed

Moses, you would believe me, for he wrote about me" (John 5:46).

8.   "The Lord our God, the Lord is one!" (Deut 6:4).

Interestingly, this central declaration of Judaic monotheism does not describe the One God as *yachid*, which means numerically one, but as *echad*. This word indicates unity in multiplicity, as when it describes evening and morning forming one day (Gen 1:5), and a man and wife becoming one flesh (Gen 2:24). Theologian Richard Bauckham suggests that the complex Judaic monotheism at the time of Jesus was therefore not a simple "unitariness" but allowed for distinctions within the divine identity (*Jesus and the God of Israel*, 17). This might have helped Jesus's followers to accept that he could also be the presence of God.

9.   "The Assyrians conquered Israel . . . The Babylonians later defeated Judah."

Archaeology confirms some of the biblical events around the conquering of Israel and Judah. For example, scripture records the Assyrian King Sennacherib's campaign against Judah in the time of King Hezekiah (2 Kgs 18:13–15; 2 Chron 32:9–10), and the Sennacherib Annals contain these supporting lines: "As for Hezekiah the Judahite, who did not submit to my yoke: forty-six of his strong, walled cities . . . I besieged and took them . . . Himself, like a caged bird I shut up in Jerusalem, his royal city" (Taylor Prism, col. 3, translated by Daniel D. Luckenbill). Second Chronicles 32:9 names Lachish as one of the besieged cities, and a relief from Sennacherib's palace at Nineveh reads, "Sennacherib King of the Universe, King of Assyria, sits on a throne and the spoils of Lachish are paraded before him." The scriptural record that Sennacherib's son Esarhaddon reigned after his murder (2 Kgs 19:37; Isa 37:38) is also confirmed by the Prism of Sennacherib.

The Babylonian Chronicles support the biblical report in the book of Jeremiah that King Nebuchadnezzar II of Babylon defeated Egypt at the Battle of Carchemish and conquered the city of Hamath. And they also confirm that when the Judean King Jehoiachin would not pay tribute, Nebuchadnezzar took him captive to Babylon and replaced him with his uncle (2 Kgs 24:8–17). Scripture recorded that Nebuchadnezzar fought against Lachish and Azekah (Jer 34:7), and a pottery shard unearthed at the site of Lachish contains this chilling letter to an officer in the city: "May [my lord] be apprised that we are watching for the fire signals of Lachish according to all the signs which my lord has given, because we cannot see Azeqah." (See Ahituv, *Echoes from the Past*, 70).

According to the Old Testament, the Persian King Cyrus allowed exiled Jews to return to Jerusalem and rebuild the temple (2 Chron 36:23; Ezra 1). This is consistent with the sixth-century Cyrus Cylinder, which records Cyrus's policy of allowing captives to return home to reconstruct their religious buildings.

Professor of archaeology Aren Maeir comments that "from the early eighth century onwards . . . there is relatively good agreement between the biblical accounts on the one hand and the archaeological evidence and extra-biblical texts on the other" ("Israel and Judah," 3523).

10. "The northern group had finally built their own temple to God on Mount Gerizim."

Mount Gerizim is still the center of the Samaritan religion, with most followers living nearby. Archaeologists have found a large stone structure of unhewn limestone slabs on the mountain, approximately twenty meters square and eight meters high, which is thought to be the altar built by the Samaritans in the fifth or sixth century BC.

11. "Not only do they love to sell us into slavery . . . [they] offered to dedicate their Gerizim temple to the pagan god Jupiter."

The Jewish historian Josephus wrote: "The Samaritans were in a flourishing condition, and much distressed the Jews, cutting off parts of their land, and carrying off slaves" (*Antiquities* 12.4.1). He also described how the Samaritans aligned themselves with Hellenic culture in the second century BC to avoid persecution by the Seleucid King Antiochus: "When the Samaritans saw the Jews under these sufferings, they no longer confessed that they were of their kindred, nor that the temple on Mount Gerizim belonged to Almighty God . . . So they sent ambassadors to Antiochus, and an epistle, whose contents are these: 'To king Antiochus . . . we therefore beseech thee . . . to give us no disturbance, nor to lay to our charge what the Jews are accused for, since we are aliens from their nation, and from their customs; but let our temple, which at present hath no name at all be named the Temple of Jupiter Hellenius'" (*Antiquities* 12.5.5).

After bitter controversy over the legitimacy of the Gerizim Temple and where the Temple tax should be paid, the Samaritan temple was destroyed by Judean Jews in the second century BC, fueling the long-standing hatred between the two groups.

12. "The harvest festival of Shavuot or Pentecost."

The word "Pentecost" is based on the Greek *pentékonta* (fifty) because this feast was celebrated fifty days after the Firstfruits Festival of Passover. The historian Josephus confirms that first-century Jews did use this Greek name for the feast: "That feast, which was observed after seven weeks, and which the Jews called Pentecost, (i.e. the 50th day), was at hand" (*War of the Jews* 2.3.1).

13. "Terrified that the throng meant to cast him down from a neighboring clifftop."

Luke 4:29 records this incident at the Nazareth synagogue. According to the Jewish Talmud, a condemned man was to be pushed from a cliff that was the height of two men; if he survived, he was then stoned to death (Mishnah, Sanhedrin 6.4).

14. "The palatial Antonia fortress."

The Apostle Paul was taken up some stairs from the Temple Mount into a castle (or barracks), from where he addressed the people below (Acts 21). This would have been the Antonia fortress, and the first-century Josephus provided eyewitness details of this structure: "Now as to the tower of Antonia, it was situated at the corner of two cloisters of the court of the temple, of that on the west, and that on the north; it was erected upon a rock of fifty cubits in height, and was on a great precipice . . . On the corner where it joined to the two cloisters of the temple, it had passages down to them both, through which the guard (for there always lay in this tower a Roman legion) went several ways among the cloisters, with their arms, on the Jewish festivals, in order to watch the people, that they might not there attempt to make any innovations" (*War of the Jews* 5.5).

15. "Palestine had fallen into a widespread state of turmoil and violence."

After the death of King Herod the Great, various men tried to forcefully declare themselves king, and according to Josephus, many of them created havoc among the Jewish people: "And now Judea was full of robberies; and as the several companies of the seditious lighted upon any one to head them, he was created a king immediately, in order to do mischief to the public. They were in some small measure indeed, and in small matters, hurtful to the Romans; but the murders they committed upon their own people lasted a long while" (*Antiquities* 17.10.8).

16. "The very inner Holy of Holies, hidden behind a thick curtain, in which you finally found—nothing."

The Holy of Holies in King Solomon's Temple contained the Ark of the Covenant, which was lost before the exiles returned from Babylon to rebuild the Second Temple. It seems significant that the Temple curtain that barred mankind from God's Presence was woven from blue, red, and purple threads (Exod 26:1). If blue represents heaven and red is the color of humanity (*adamah*: earth; *adom*: red), then purple, as the combination of both colors, would symbolize Jesus's human-divine (and royal) nature. The Temple veil that tore at Jesus's death was therefore said to represent his body that was broken to restore humanity to God (Matt 27:51; Luke 23:45; Heb 10:20). This symbolism is strengthened by the fact that images of cherubim were woven into the Temple curtain (Exod 26:31), and two cherubim barred humanity from God's presence after the rebellion of Adam and Eve in the Garden of Eden (Gen 3:24).

17. "He and Andrew had returned to Capernaum."

The brothers Andrew and Simon were originally from Bethsaida (John 1:44), but it seems they had taken up residence roughly six miles away in Capernaum (Mark 1:21–29; Luke 4:31–38) where Jesus was also living at the time (Matt 4:13).

18. "An appalling sense of guilt."

I have experienced this supernatural sense of unworthiness, which is a devastating comprehension of how you appear to God without His grace. All self-satisfaction and excuses evaporate, and you are assailed by a profoundly humbling awareness of your fundamental self-centeredness and sinfulness in God's eyes. But this *un*worthiness is not the same as being worth*less*, and sincere repentance is followed by a deep sense of God's forgiveness and love.

19. "There is no one but You who can pardon sin."

This quote is from the rabbinic Midrash Psalm 17:3, and the belief is confirmed by many scholars of Judaism. According to Daniel Johansson, "No firm evidence can be found which demonstrates that other figures than God forgave sins. Various strands of early Judaism conceived of human and angelic agents who interceded on behalf of others, expiated sin and mediated forgiveness from God, but they all seem to have shared the view that forgiveness is divine prerogative" ("Who Can Forgive Sins?" 351).

There have been claims that the Dead Sea scroll CD 14:18–19 describes a messiah who forgives sin. However, scroll scholars García Martínez and Tigchelaar refute this and translate the text as: "Until there arises the messiah of Aaron and Israel. And their iniquity will be atoned through meal and sin-offerings" (*Dead Sea Scrolls*, 575).

Some scholars have translated the Prayer of Nabonidus in scroll 4Q242 to read, "An exorcist pardoned my sins." However, the scroll is in five separate fragments, and Wise et al. combine them in this form: "[I prayed to the Most High,] and He forgave my sins. An exorcist a Jew, in fact, a mem[ber of the community of exiles came to me and said . . ." (*Dead Sea Scrolls*, 342). Frank Cross offers a similar translation ("Fragments of the Prayer of Nabonidus," 260–64). In all other Dead Sea Scroll texts, only God is said to grant forgiveness.

Jesus therefore seems to have been unique in professing to have the power to forgive sin.

20. "This is he of whom it is written: 'I will send my messenger ahead of you, who will prepare your way before you.'" See Matt 3:3; 11:10; Mark 1:2–3.

This refers to Old Testament prophecies: "The voice of one who calls out, 'Prepare the way of Yahweh in the wilderness! Make a level highway in the desert for our God!'" (Isa 40:3), and "Behold, I send My messenger, and he will prepare the way before Me" (Mal 3:1a). In the Gospels, this preparation for the arrival of God is directly associated with Jesus.

21. "Here is a glutton and a drunkard."

This accusation against Jesus (Matt 11:19; Luke 7:34) was a severe and dangerous allegation because it was the specific description in Mosaic law of a rebellious son who should be stoned to death: "And they shall say to the elders of his city, 'This son of ours is stubborn and rebellious; he will not obey our voice; he is a glutton and a drunkard.' Then all the men of his city shall stone him to death with stones; so you shall put away the evil from among you, and all Israel shall hear and fear" (Deut 21:20–21).

22. "A glittering mass of silver, gold, and snowy marble."

The historian Josephus provided valuable eyewitness testimony to the Jerusalem Temple before its destruction by the Romans in AD 70: "The outward face of the temple in its front wanted nothing that was likely to surprise either men's minds or their eyes; for it was covered all over with plates of gold of great weight, and, at the first rising of the sun, reflected back a very fiery splendor, and made those who forced themselves to look upon it to turn their eyes away, just as they would have done at the sun's own rays. But this temple appeared to strangers, when they were coming to it at a distance, like a mountain covered with snow; for as to those parts of it that were not gilt, they were exceeding white" (*War of the Jews* 5.5).

23. "John the Baptist was dead."

In the first century, Josephus recorded the death of John the Baptist at the hands of Herod Antipas: "Now some of the Jews thought that the destruction of Herod's army came from God, and that very justly, as a punishment of what he did against John that was called the Baptist: for Herod slew him who was a good man, and commanded the Jews to exercise virtue, both as to righteousness towards one another, and piety towards God, and so to come to baptism . . . Herod, who feared lest the great influence John had over the people might put it into his power and inclination to raise a rebellion (for they seemed ready to do anything he should advise), thought it best, by putting him to death, to prevent any mischief he might cause . . . Accordingly he was sent a prisoner, out of Herod's suspicious temper, to Machaerus, the castle I before mentioned, and was there put to death" (*Antiquities* 18.5.2).

The Gospels link the murder of John the Baptist to Herod Antipas's birthday celebration (Mark 6:21). Such observances do seem to have been a practice of the period because Josephus wrote about Herod Agrippa: "When Agrippa was solemnizing his birthday . . . he gave festival entertainments to all his subjects" (*Antiquities* 19.7.1).

24. "As a Judean from the town of Kerioth."

John 6:7 describes Judas as being the son of Simon Iscariot. This name is thought to possibly mean man (*ish*) of Kerioth, a Judean town that is mentioned in Joshua 15:25.

25. "Simon Zealotes—the zealous one."

In Matthew 10:4 and Mark 3:18, this disciple Simon is called *Kananaios* (or *Kananites* in some manuscripts). This derives from the Hebrew *kanai*, meaning zealous, although it was sometimes incorrectly rendered as meaning from the town of Cana.

26. "Bridegroom. Shepherd. Bringer of rest."

These roles claimed by Jesus were directly associated with God in the Old Testament. And unlike any prophet or teacher, Jesus shared other attributes with God.

- Controlling natural elements: God parted the waters of the Red Sea and the Jordan River, and Jesus calmed a stormy lake.

- Providing miraculous food: God provided manna for years in the desert, and Jesus multiplied loaves and fishes.

- Providing refuge: Psalms promises that "the Lord also will be a refuge for the oppressed, a refuge in times of trouble" (Ps 9:9), and Jesus wept when Jerusalem rejected his offer to gather them under his wings of protection (Luke 13:34; Matt 23:37).

- Being a banner to the people: Moses called God "The Lord-is-my-Banner" (Exod 17:15), and Isaiah wrote about the prophesied Messiah: "In that day there shall be a Root of Jesse, who shall stand as a banner to the people" (Isa 11:10a).

27. "Take my yoke upon you . . . and you will find rest for your souls" (Matt 11:29).

The yoke was a strongly Jewish image. For example, a rabbinic text instructs that "one should first accept upon himself the yoke of the Kingdom of Heaven and then take upon himself the yoke of [God's] commandments" (Mishnah, Berakhot 2:2). However, Jesus instructed people to accept his own yoke and obey his commandments. It also seems significant that the concept of "rest" was included in Isaiah's prophecy about the messianic cornerstone (Isa 28:12–16).

28. "Not one yod or tittle shall pass from the law" (Matt 5:18).

A *yod* (called a jot or iota in some translations) is the smallest Hebrew letter, shaped like an apostrophe, and a tittle is an even smaller mark. The Gospels record many other Aramaic/Hebrew terms such as *ephphatha* (be opened; Mark 7:34), *talitha koum* (little girl, I say to you, rise; Mark 5:41), *corban* (temple offering; Mark 7:11) and *raca* (fool; Matt 5:22). This usage indicates the Palestinian origin of the Greek Gospels, together with other strongly Semitic elements such as idioms, syntax, Hebrew parallelism, and wordplay like sons (*banim*) compared to stones (*abanim*) in Luke 3:8 and Matthew 3:9.

29. "Your fathers ate manna in the wilderness" (John 6:49).

It is considered likely that *manna* means "what is it?" from the Hebrew *mah*: "what."

30. "See, I lay a stone in Zion . . . a rock of offense to both the houses of Israel."

These prophetic words are from Isaiah 28:16 and 8:14, which the Talmud applied to the expected Messiah. "The son of David cannot appear ere the two ruling houses in Israel shall have come to an end . . . for it is written, And he shall be for a Sanctuary, for a stone of stumbling and for a rock of offense to both houses of Israel" (Babylonian Talmud, Sanhedrin 38a). Jesus associated himself directly with this significant messianic imagery (Mark 12:10).

31. "The kohen and his shofar there at the Royal Stoa."

A stone, which seems to have fallen from the southwest corner of the Temple Mount onto the street during the destruction of the Temple in AD 70, is inscribed with the Hebrew words *l'bet hatqia*, meaning "to the place of trumpeting." The stone suggests that this corner was the place designated for the ritual blowing of the horn.

32. "Rejoice that your names are written in heaven" (Luke 10:20).

The names of God's people are written in heaven and in the Book of Life (Phil 4:3; Heb 12:23), and John's Revelation states that only those whose names are written in the Lamb's Book of Life will enter the New Jerusalem (Rev 21:27). By contrast, the names of those who reject God are written in the dust of the ground (Jer 17:13).

33. Old Testament psalms and the Dead Sea Scrolls often used the double "Amen, Amen" to confirm another person's statement, but Jesus used the phrase to ratify his own words, as in John 5:19, often translated as "truly, truly."

34. "How dare he call God his Father?"

Jesus spoke to his disciples about "your Father" but referred to God as "my Father," which was extremely rare in Judaism. So far this usage has only been found in Qumran scroll 4Q372 in a prayer by Joseph to "my Father and my God."

35. "The Pharisee Gamaliel stood and turned to face the council."

The Apostle Paul studied under this highly respected teacher (Acts 22:3). Gamaliel's speech is recorded in Acts 5:34–39 as part of the debate regarding action against Jesus's followers soon after his crucifixion, but his argument also seems relevant at this point in the narrative.

36. "That injunction applies to the practice of sorcery or idol worship."

Babylonian Talmud, Sanhedrin 67, contains the instruction to execute those involved in sorcery or idol worship.

An extract from the Munich Babylonian Talmud is also interesting in this regard: "It was taught: On the Eve of Passover they hung Yeshu. And the herald went out before him for 40 days [saying], 'Yeshu the Notzri will go out to be stoned for sorcery and misleading and enticing Israel to idolatry. Anyone who knows [anything] in his defense must come and declare concerning him.' But no-one came to his defense so they hung him on the Eve of Passover" (Sanhedrin 43a).

37. "Our powers under Roman rule are severely curtailed" (see John 18:31).

The Sanhedrin council did exercise some civic powers, but it is generally thought that it was not able to impose the death penalty at the time of Jesus. When Herod's son Archelaus was removed from power in AD 6, his territories of Idumea, Judea, and Samaria fell under the rule of a Roman governor who alone had the power of capital punishment; according to the historian Josephus, "Archelaus's part of Judea was reduced into a province, and Coponius, one of the equestrian order among the Romans, was sent as a procurator, having the power of [life and] death put into his hands by Caesar" (*War of the Jews* 2.8.1). Josephus also recorded that Ananus was removed from his position as Jewish high priest when he assembled the Sanhedrin without the consent of the Roman procurator and instigated the stoning of Jesus's brother James (*Antiquities* 20.9.1).

It seems that around AD 70 the Romans did still theoretically recognize the right of Temple leaders to demand the death of Gentiles who crossed the partition on the Temple Mount, because Josephus quoted the emperor's son Titus as saying, "Have not you, vile wretches that you are, by our permission, put up this partition-wall before your sanctuary? . . . Have not we given you leave to kill such as go beyond it, though he were a Roman?" (*War of the Jews* 6.2.4). However, there is no evidence that during the time of Jesus any Gentiles did cross this boundary or that this Jewish power of execution was exercised.

38.   "Judas the Galilean who urged us to resist Roman taxation."

The historian Josephus wrote, "Under [Coponius's] administration it was that a certain Galilean, whose name was Judas, prevailed with his countrymen to revolt, and said they were cowards if they would endure to pay a tax to the Romans and would after God submit to mortal men as their lords" (*War of the Jews* 2.8.1).

39.   "Unless you believe that I am" (John 8:24).

The Greek phrase used here is "*ego eimi,*" which literally means "I am" rather than "I am he." In the Hebrew Bible, God identified Himself with the Hebrew phrase *eh-yeh*, translated in the pre-Christian Greek version (the Septuagint) as *ego eimi*: "Thus you shall say to the children of Israel, 'I AM (*ego eimi*) has sent me to you'" (Exod 3:14b). Jesus might therefore have been making an implicit claim to divinity when he used this phrase.

God's words in Greek OT	Jesus's words in NT
"Indeed before the day was, I am (*ego eimi*)" (Isa 43:13a).	"Most certainly, I tell you, before Abraham came into existence, I am" (John 8:58). The crowd wanted to stone Jesus for this statement.
"Do not fear, for I am with you" (Gen 26:24b).	"I am. Do not be afraid" (Mark 6:50b).
"Behold, I am with you and will keep you wherever you go" (Gen 28:15a).	"Behold, I am with you always, even to the end of the age." (Matt 28:20b).

40.   "Believe my works that you have seen with your own eyes" (John 10:38).

Jesus's appeal to the evidence of his miraculous works echoes God's condemnation of the unbelieving Israelites in the desert: "How long will these people reject Me? And how long will they not believe Me, with all the signs which I have performed among them?" (Num 14:11).

41. "The good news must be preached to all nations" (Mark 13:10).

    The concept of "good news" has an Old Testament background: "You who bring good news to Zion . . . say to the towns of Judah, 'Here is your God!'" (Isa 40:9 NIV). "Good news" (*euangelion* in Greek) is gōd-spell in Old English, which is the basis for the term "gospel."

42. "Those who exalt themselves will be humbled" (Matt 23:12; Luke 14:11).

    Jesus's words echo the solemn Old Testament warning about God's judgment in the last days: "The lofty looks of man shall be humbled, the haughtiness of men shall be bowed down, and the Lord alone shall be exalted in that day" (Isa 2:11).

43. "God's Chosen One will be our king and our shepherd."

    As a precursor of the Messiah, David was also a shepherd and king. Interestingly, Jesus and David were both of the house of Judah and were both persecuted by a Saul of the tribe of Benjamin.

44. "See, your king comes to you, righteous and victorious, lowly and riding on a donkey."

    This prophecy from Zechariah 9:9 is regarded as messianic in rabbinic Judaism: "If they [Israel] are meritorious, [Messiah will come] with the clouds of heaven; if not, lowly and riding upon an ass" (Babylonian Talmud, Sanhedrin 98a). According to the Jewish scholar Joseph Klausner, "The Jews wait for one 'lowly and riding upon an ass' who is to come, and the Christians affirm that the Messiah has already come as one 'lowly and riding upon an ass'" (*Messianic Idea*, 203–4).

    The patriarch Jacob also predicted the coming of a significant figure that was associated with a donkey and was connected to the choice vine that represented God's chosen people: "The scepter shall not depart from Judah, nor a lawgiver from between his feet, until Shiloh comes; And to Him shall be the obedience of the people. Binding his donkey to the vine, and his donkey's colt to the choice vine" (Gen 49:10–11a). Shiloh was used as a name for the Messiah, and this figure in Jacob's prediction is regarded as messianic in a Dead Sea scroll and a rabbinic text:

    - "The scepter shall not depart from the tribe of Judah . . . until the messiah of righteousness comes, the branch of David" (scroll 4Q252 col. 5.1–3).

    - "If one sees a choice vine, he may look forward to seeing the Messiah, since it says, Binding his foal unto the vine and his ass's colt unto the choice vine" (Babylonian Talmud, Berakhot 57a).

    - "Rabbi Johanan said: For the sake of the Messiah. What is his name?—The School of Rabbi Shila said: His name is Shiloh, for it is written, until Shiloh come" (Babylonian Talmud, Sanhedrin 98b).

45. "I am coming and I will dwell in your midst" (Zech 2:10–11a).

    The New Testament links God's promise to Jesus's incarnation: "And the Word became flesh and dwelt among us" (John 1:14a) and also to Jesus's second coming: "Look! God's dwelling place is with His people, and he will dwell with them" (Rev 21:3b).

46. "It was the tenth day of Nisan, and Jewish families were carefully selecting unblemished male lambs in preparation for the ritual Pesach sacrifice" (see Exod 12:3–6).

    According to John's Gospel, Jesus arrived at Lazarus's house in Bethany six days before the beginning of the Passover week; a dinner was given in his honor, then a crowd heard about him and came to the house, possibly on the following day; on the day after that, Jesus entered Jerusalem (John 12:1–12). It is therefore likely that Jesus's triumphal entry took place four days before Passover, on the tenth of Nisan, identifying him as the chosen, flawless lamb of sacrifice. It is also interesting that Israel crossed the Jordan into the Promised Land on the tenth of Nisan (Josh 4:19).

47. "As a hen gathers her chicks under her wings" (Matt 23:37; Luke 13:34).

Wings were an Old Testament image of God's protection (Ps 57:1; 36:7; 63:7; 91:4). Jesus's cry of loving pity for Jerusalem seems to echo God's words: "Oh, that My people would listen to Me, that Israel would walk in My ways!" (Ps 81:13).

48. "Myriad images of nightmarish terror."

The Jewish historian Josephus, who fought in the Roman-Jewish war, described the appalling brutality of this siege and the destruction of Jerusalem in AD 70 by Titus, the army commander and son of Emperor Vespasian (*War of the Jews*, books 5–7). The Temple was completely destroyed: "Caesar gave orders that they should now demolish the entire city and temple . . . It was so thoroughly laid even with the ground by those that dug it up to the foundation, that there was left nothing to make those that came thither believe it had ever been inhabited" (*War of the Jews* 7.1.1). The only part of Herod's Temple Mount complex that remains today is a section of the western foundation, sometimes referred to as the Wailing Wall.

49. "There before me was one like a son of man, coming with the clouds of heaven. He approached the Ancient of Days and was led into his presence" (Dan 7:13–14).

Rabbinic Judaism interpreted this vision as messianic: "One verse reads of the king Messiah that One like the sun (*sic*) of man came to the Ancient of Days, and they brought him near before Him" (Midrash Psalm 21:5). Rabbi Akiba is said to have interpreted the thrones described in Daniel 7:9 as being set for God and the Messiah (Babylonian Talmud, Chagigah 14a). Clouds of heaven represented God's Holy Presence (Exod 13:21; 40:34–35; Num 9:15; 14:14), and they are also associated with Jesus's return (Rev 1:7).

50. "His followers now included even learned scribes" (see Matt 8:19).

Scribes and tax collectors who followed Jesus would have been able to make notes about his work and teachings. This would have helped to stabilize the early traditions, together with the heavy emphasis on rote memorization in first-century oral cultures.

51. "The Jews had already complained to Emperor Tiberius about Pilate's conduct as Prefect of Judea."

The incidents of the standards and the shields are recorded by the Jewish Philo in his letter to Emperor Gaius and by Josephus (*Antiquities* 8; *War of the Jews* 2), although it is not clear whether the affair of the shields happened before or after Jesus's death. Pilate's prefecture came to an end when a messianic Samaritan group gathered at Mount Gerizim, and Pilate executed the ring-leaders to prevent a possible insurrection. In response to bitter complaints, he was summoned to Rome to answer for his action, but by the time he arrived, Emperor Tiberius was dead. After that, there is no mention of Pilate in history.

52. "They shall make a remedy for the heel in the days of the King Messiah."

This messianic belief is recorded in the Jerusalem Targum on Genesis 3:15.

53. "This is a strange concept for us, too."

Judaism does encourage humility and generosity toward one's enemies (Prov 25:21–22; 24:17), but Jesus's teaching that one should actively love one's persecutors seems to have been an innovation.

54. "A man who was healed at the pool of Bethesda."

In John's Gospel, Jesus healed a man at the pool of Bethesda (*beth-hesda*: place of mercy), which was said to have curative powers. Excavations in Jerusalem have uncovered two connected pools with an intervening wall, which are believed to have formed this healing pool. Archaeologist Simon Gibson points out features of this double structure that are consistent with the gospel narrative: there is evidence of covered colonnades that would have been in five sections around and between the two pools, as mentioned in John 5:2; the broad landings would have facilitated the moving of disabled people; there is a sluice gate between the pools with a drainage exit, which could have caused the bubbling that some manuscripts of John's Gospel described as the result of an angel stirring the waters. Gibson also comments that layers of bright red soil might explain early Christian comments about the bloody color of the water in this healing pool. See Gibson, "Excavations at the Bethesda Pool," 22–26.

55. "The correct pronunciations for lamb, wool, wine, and donkey."

This confusion of pronunciation is described in the Babylonian Talmud: "They said to him, 'Foolish Galilean, what do you mean?' Galileans did not pronounce the guttural letters properly so it was unclear whether he sought a donkey [*hamor*] to ride, or wine [*hamar*] to drink, wool [*amar*] to wear, or a lamb [*imar*] to slaughter" (Erubin 53b). The text Megillah 24b also stated that priests from the northern cities of Haifa and Beit She'an were not allowed to recite the Priestly Benediction because their poor pronunciation of the guttural letters distorted the meaning of the prayers. When Peter was in the courtyard of Caiaphas's Palace, his distinctive accent identified him as a Galilean (Matt 26:73).

56. "Six covenants."

God's six covenants were established through Adam (Gen 2:15), Noah (Gen 9:11), Abraham (Gen 15:18), Moses (Deut 11:22–23), the nation of Israel (Deut 30:15–16), and David (2 Sam 7:16).

57. "When they look on him whom they have pierced, they shall mourn for him."

This prophetic verse is from Zechariah 12:10 (RSV), and the Hebrew Masoretic Text of the Bible also describes this figure as being "thrust through." The Jewish Talmud and Tosefta both regard this as a messianic prophecy, but they choose to apply the piercing to two messianic figures that are still expected to come. The book of Daniel also contains a prediction about an anointed prince who will be "cut off, but not for himself" (Dan 9:26b KJV). The Jewish scholar Joseph Klausner stated that "almost all of Daniel is Messianic in spirit; but Chapters 2, 6–9, and 12 are Messianic in essence" (*Messianic Idea*, 228). These ancient texts therefore contained powerful images that seem to have foreshadowed Jesus's crucifixion and atoning death.

58. "The Messiah will first be sent to us, and God will later institute Olam Habbah: the perfect World to Come."

It is a common rabbinic belief that there will be an interval between the coming of the Messiah and the establishment of the final, perfected creation. These two stages are similar to the period between a Jewish betrothal ritual and married life, which in turn are strongly reminiscent of Jesus's work: he first paid the betrothal price through his death (1 Cor 6:20; 7:23), then went to prepare a place for redeemed humanity in heaven (John 14:2–3), and he will return to receive the New Jerusalem as a bride (Rev 21:1–5). The Apostle Paul also wrote that the Holy Spirit was provided to believers as a pledge or down payment, similar to the role of a dowry (2 Cor 1:22; 5:5; Eph 1:13–14).

59. "Disciples who spoke only Greek."

It is not surprising that the gospel manuscripts were written in Greek. The Greek version of the Hebrew Bible (the Septuagint) was widely used in Palestine long before the turn of the era, and Jesus's disciples Philip and Andrew spoke Greek, as did some members of the early Jerusalem Church (John 12:20–21; Acts 6:1). Biblical scholar Martin Hengel concludes from literary evidence that Greek-speaking Jews comprised between ten and twenty percent of the Jerusalem population at the time of Jesus, and he believes it highly probable that the Greek message about Jesus was formulated by his first followers in that city (*Hellenization*, 10–11, 18).

60. "In what way could his death bring an increased harvest to God? This was not part of messianic expectation."

It is sometimes claimed that Jesus's followers only believed he had risen from death because there was a popular expectation of a messianic figure that would die and rise. However, agnostic scholar Bart Ehrman makes this categorical statement about Judaic expectations: "In no surviving Jewish text—whether in the Hebrew Bible or later, up to the time of Christianity—is the Messiah said to die and be raised" (*Jesus, Apocalyptic Prophet*, 218). Martin Hengel agrees: "In the light of all our present knowledge, the suffering and dying Messiah was not yet a familiar traditional figure in the Judaism of the first century AD" (*Atonement*, 40).

There have been sensational claims that a dying messiah is described in the Dead Sea Scrolls, but many scholars refute this. Scroll translator Geza Vermes comments, "The recently and groundlessly advanced theory that 'the Prince of the Congregation, Branch of David' of 4Q285 is a suffering and executed Messiah is contradicted both by the immediate context and the broader exegetical framework" (*Dead Sea Scrolls*, 12). Vermes concludes, "Neither the suffering of the Messiah, nor his death and resurrection, appear to have been part of the faith of first-century Judaism" (*Jesus the Jew*, 38).

61. "Jesus will celebrate the Pesach supper in the city with us twelve."

The three Synoptic Gospels explicitly identify Jesus's last meal as the Passover meal (Mark 14:12–18; Matt 26:17–21; Luke 22:7–9), while John mentions that the priests would not enter Pilate's praetorium the following morning because the defilement would prevent them from eating the Passover (John 18:28). However, two facts suggest that the Last Supper was indeed the Passover supper.

First, the entire seven-day festival was referred to as the Passover: "In the first month, on the fourteenth day of the month, you shall have the Passover, a feast of seven days" (Ezek 45:21). The Jewish historian Josephus confirmed that the entire week's Feast of Unleavened Bread was called the Passover (*Antiquities*

14.2.1; 17.9.3). Second, according to Jewish biblical scholar Alfred Edersheim, a Jew who was defiled by entering a gentile home would still have been able to eat the Passover lamb that night because the ritual defilement only lasted until sunset. However, the defilement would have barred him from eating the *Chagigah* offering, which was consumed during the daytime on the next day of Passover and which was also designated by the term *Pesach* (*Life and Times of Jesus the Messiah*, 865–66).

John's Gospel does record that the day of Jesus's trial was "the preparation of the Passover" (John 19:14). However, this was not preparation for the first Passover supper but rather the Friday preparation for the start of the Passover Sabbath at nightfall: "It was the Preparation Day, so that the bodies wouldn't remain on the cross on the Sabbath (for that Sabbath was a special one)" (John 19:31). The other three gospels confirm that Jesus died on Friday, the Preparation day for the Sabbath (Luke 23:54; Mark 15:42, Matt 27:62–66).

62. "He will offer to release one prisoner."

All four gospels record Pilate's offer to release a prisoner, but there is a lack of clarity about the basis for this action. Mark and Matthew regard this as being Pilate's custom (Mark 15:6; Matt 27:15). In John, Pilate identifies this as a Jewish custom, saying, "You have a custom, that I should release someone to you at the Passover" (John 18:39). Luke simply states that Pilate "had to release one prisoner to them at the feast" (Luke 23:17), without providing a reason. There is no evidence of a tradition in which Roman governors of Judea released a prisoner during the Passover celebration. As Pilate had only been governor for a few years, it is possible that he devised this offer of release as a strategy to resolve his tricky political dilemma.

63. "Blinking through bloody sweat."

Excretion of blood through the skin, known as hematidrosis, occurs when blood capillaries rupture into the sweat glands, usually under extreme stress. In *The Crucifixion of Jesus*, forensic pathologist Frederick Zugibe describes the physical and emotional causes of this phenomenon, cites recorded incidents, and supports its authenticity in Jesus's case.

64. "Pilate had granted them an audience on the raised pavement outside the palace."

Roman governors of Judea were usually stationed in the coastal city of Caesarea, but they would often reside in Jerusalem to monitor the unstable feast times. Philo noted that Pilate stayed in Herod's Palace during feasts ("Embassy to Gaius" 306). And Josephus recorded that when the procurator Florus was in Jerusalem, he stayed at Herod's Palace, which had a place of judgment in front of it: "Now at this time Florus took up his quarters at the palace; and on the next day he had his tribunal set before it, and sat upon it, when the high priests, and the men of power, and those of the greatest eminence in the city, came all before that tribunal" (*War of the Jews* 2.14.8).

65. "So you say."

Jesus's response to Pilate's question about being King of the Jews is recorded in Greek as "*Sy legeis*," or "You say" (Luke 23:3; Mark 15:2). This seems be a form of affirmative response because when Judas asked Jesus if he would be the betrayer, Jesus answered, "*Sy eipas*": "You have said" (Matt 26:25).

66. "They pierced my hands and my feet."

   Psalm 22 provides a powerful description of terrible thirst, piercing, and bones being pulled out of joint, all strongly suggestive of the agonies suffered during crucifixion. The Hebrew words for "pierced" and "lion" are very similar, and some manuscripts of the Hebrew Masoretic Text use the phrase "like a lion my hands and my feet" instead of "they pierced my hands and my feet." However, the pre-Christian Greek Septuagint uses "dug/pierced" in this line, and the oldest manuscript of Psalm 22 (Dead Sea Scroll 5/6 HevPsalms) seems to use the word "pierced" (see Abegg et al., *Dead Sea Scrolls Bible*, 519).

67. "A sponge of vinegar on a hyssop stalk . . . Father, into your hands I commit my spirit!" (See John 19:29 and Luke 23:46.)

   Jesus's words echo an ancient psalm: "Into your hands I commit my spirit" (Ps 31:5a). Jesus's death on the cross also seems to be remarkably foreshadowed in an Old Testament purification ritual. Defiled persons such as lepers were not allowed in the Israelites' camp where God dwelt (Num 5:2–3), but there was a cleansing rite for those who were healed. This ritual involved hyssop, cedar wood, red yarn, and two birds: one bird was sacrificed and its blood sprinkled seven times on the defiled person, and the other bird was released (Lev 14:2–7). By comparison, a hyssop stalk was held up to Jesus's mouth, he bled seven times (when he sweated blood, at his scourging, from the crown of thorns, at three points on the cross, and when his side was pierced), he was sacrificed on a wooden cross that was red with his blood, but his spirit was released into the hands of his Father.

68. "It is done."

   Jesus's last words are recorded in Greek as *tetelestai*: "It is done/finished" (John 19:30), which echoes the closing verse of Psalm 22:31: "He has done this." The prophet Isaiah used a similar phrase to describe God's redemptive work: "Sing, O heavens, for the Lord has done it! . . . The Lord has redeemed Jacob, and glorified Himself in Israel" (Isa 44:23).

   Dietrich Bonhoeffer suggested that ancient Davidic psalms should be regarded as transmitting in a timeless way the words of the eternal Christ. According to Bonhoeffer, David was the ancestor of the incarnate Christ, and therefore, "the future Messiah spoke through him. The prayers of David were prayed also by Christ. Or better, Christ himself prayed them through the forerunner David" (*Psalms*, 18).

69. "He was wounded for our transgressions" (Isa 53:5).

   Different translations use "wounded" or "pierced" here, but Jewish scholar Joseph Klausner pointed out that the Hebrew Masoretic Text translates the same word used in this verse as "pierced" in Isaiah 51:9 (*Messianic Idea*, 165 n. 25).

70. "Surely he has borne our griefs and carried our sorrows; Yet we esteemed him stricken, smitten by God, and afflicted . . . And by his stripes we are healed" (Isa 53:4–5).

   This remarkable text predicted a coming Servant of God who would be a light to the Gentiles; he would suffer in order to accomplish God's will; his vicarious suffering and death would bring healing, and he would intercede for the forgiveness of others' sins. All these actions point directly to the work of Jesus. It is also significant to note that the "arm of the Lord" symbolized God's direct work of salvation (Isa 51:9–10), and Isaiah 53 used this significant image to describe God's Servant.

At the time of Jesus, the dominant messianic expectation was of a warrior-king, and there is no indication that the Messiah was expected to die (see note 60). However, Isaiah's prophecy of a suffering figure came to be regarded as messianic within Judaism, and the only debate has been whether this Servant figure is an individual (as in Isa 52:13) or the nation of Israel (as in Isa 43:10). But it is important to note that rabbinic tradition did interpret these verses as referring primarily to an individual Messiah. For example, in the Talmud, we read: "Rabbi Jochanan said: For the sake of the Messiah. What is his [the Messiah's] name? . . . The Rabbis said: His name is 'the leper scholar,' as it is written, Surely he hath borne our griefs, and carried our sorrows: yet we did esteem him a leper, smitten of God, and afflicted" (Babylonian Talmud, Sanhedrin 98b). Modern Jewish prayers for the Day of Atonement also recognize an individual Messiah in Isaiah's prophecy: "He hath borne the yoke of our iniquities, and our transgression, and is wounded because of our transgression. He beareth our sins on his shoulder, that we may find pardon for our iniquities. We shall be healed by his wound, at the time that the Eternal will create him (the Messiah) as a new creature." See *Mahzor la-Yom Kippur*, 282–84 (original brackets), which can be read at https://archive.org/details/maohzorlayomkippoounknuoft.

According to Judaic scholar Joel Rembaum, the dominant rabbinic interpretation was that the Servant figure in Isaiah 53 was an individual Messiah, and Judaism only developed an exclusive emphasis on the collective-Israel interpretation to refute Christian claims about Jesus's atoning work ("Jewish Exegetical Tradition," 291–93). Talmud specialist Daniel Boyarin agrees with this assessment (*Jewish Gospels*, 152).

71. "The Servant is the individual that . . . represents all Israel before God."

The concept of corporate identity was a common feature of Judaic thought. As Stephen Dempster points out, "oscillation between a group and an individual within the group as its representative is certainly common in the Tanakh" (*Dominion and Dynasty*, 69 n. 26). The fourteenth-century Rabbi Shlomoh Astruc argued that this collective identity could be applied to the prophecies of Isaiah: "When [Isaiah] speaks of the people, the King Messiah is included in it, and when he speaks of the King Messiah, the people is comprehended with him" (Driver and Neubauer, *Fifty-third Chapter of Isaiah*, 129).

Biblical scholar Martin Hengel comments that individual and collective interpretations of Isaiah's Servant are therefore both possible "because a messianic figure is always at the same time a representative of the whole people. This still holds even in early Christianity" (*History of Isaiah 53*," 81). Stuhlmacher agrees: "In Judaism the individual figure of the Servant-Messiah is the prince appointed by God, a prince who rules over the people of God and simultaneously represents them before God. So also with Jesus. He is the Son of God who leads the people of God; yet that people also constitutes his body" ("Isaiah 53," 147).

72. "Joseph of Arimathea had arranged for him to be reverently interred."

There is no reason to doubt that Jesus's body was laid in a tomb. All four gospels report that the Sanhedrin member Joseph of Arimathea supervised Jesus's entombment, and it is highly unlikely that the later church would have invented this detail at a time of increasing hostility with Judaism. It is often claimed that Jesus's body would not have been properly buried because he was executed by the Romans. However, the first-century Jewish historian Josephus reported that customary burials did take place after crucifixion: "The Jews used to take so much care of the burial of men, that they took down those that were condemned and crucified, and buried them before the going down of the sun" (*War of the Jews* 4.5.2). The bones of a crucified man have also been found gathered together after burial and placed in a traditional ossuary (a chest for bones, used from the first century BC to the first century AD). The man's legs had been broken to speed up death, and an iron spike that was driven through both heels is still embedded in the bone. See Tzaferis, "Crucifixion: The Archaeological Evidence."

73. "Their lives were forever changed."

The disciples would later be further inspired by the pouring out of the Holy Spirit at Pentecost. Jewish theologian Pinchas Lapide made this observation about the dramatic change in Jesus's followers: "When these peasants, shepherds, and fishermen, who betrayed and denied their master and failed him so miserably, suddenly could be changed overnight into a confident mission society, convinced of salvation and able to work with much more success after Easter than before, then no vision or hallucination is sufficient to explain such a revolutionary transformation." Their radical change of heart led Lapide to this conclusion: "I accept the resurrection of Easter Sunday not as an invention of the community of disciples, but as a historical event" (*Resurrection*, 125, 131).

Theologian N. T. Wright undertook an extensive investigation into afterlife beliefs recorded in the Old Testament, post-biblical Judaism, and pagan texts, and he concluded that the claim of Jesus's physical resurrection would have been as controversial in his time as in ours: "Nothing in Jewish beliefs about the Jewish god, and certainly nothing in non-Jewish beliefs about non-Jewish gods, would suggest to devotees that they should predicate resurrection of their object of worship. Some sort of new life beyond the grave, quite possibly: resurrection, certainly not" (*Resurrection*, 25). In other words, the disciples' belief in Jesus's resurrection cannot easily be explained by anything other than his actual rising from death.

74. "The Lord's skeptical brother James was killed by hostile religious leaders."

The first century Jewish historian Josephus recorded the death of Jesus's brother James in Jerusalem. This took place in AD 62 when the Roman governor had died and his replacement took some time to arrive: "Festus was now dead, and Albinus was but upon the road; so [high priest Ananus] assembled the sanhedrim of judges, and brought before them the brother of Jesus—the one called Christ—whose name was James, and some others; and when he had formed an accusation against them as breakers of the law, he delivered them to be stoned" (*Antiquities* 20.9.1).

Josephus had written earlier about Jesus in *Antiquities* 18, which meant that two books later, he could identify James as the brother of this man. The underlined sections in this other text are almost certainly later Christian interpolations, but scholars widely believe that the bulk of the passage was written by Josephus: "Now there was about this time Jesus, a wise man, if it be lawful to call him a man; for he was a doer of wonderful works, a teacher of such men as receive the truth with pleasure. He drew over to him both many of the Jews and many of the Gentiles. He was [the] Christ. And when Pilate, at the suggestion of the principal men amongst us, had condemned him to the cross, those that loved him at the first did not forsake him; for he appeared to them alive again the third day; as the divine prophets had foretold these and ten thousand other wonderful things concerning him. And the tribe of Christians, so named from him, are not extinct at this day" (*Antiquities* 18.3.3).

75. "Some had interpreted it as a promise that John would never die."

Jesus's words about John ("If I desire that he remain until I come . . .") are found in John 21:22–23.

76. "John was rapt in the astounding vision."

It is significant that John's revelation and Paul's vision on the road to Damascus both shared central features with Ezekiel's vision of God, in which the prophet saw a bright likeness of a man and fell to the ground (Ezek 1). Paul experienced a blinding vision of the glorified Christ, so it is no surprise that he could speak of Jesus as being in the form of God (Phil 2:6). And like Ezekiel, John was carried up by God's Spirit to see the glory of God in Jerusalem (Ezek 8:3–4; Rev 21:10–11), also symbolically ate a scroll that tasted like honey (Ezek 3:3; Rev 10:10), and was sent to prophesy for God—but while Ezekiel was sent to Israel (Ezek 3:4), John was sent to "many peoples, nations, languages, and kings" (Rev 10:11).

77. "Send in your sickle and reap; for the hour to reap has come; for the harvest of the earth is ripe!"

These words from Revelation 14:15 echo the prophetic words of Joel in the Old Testament: "Put in the sickle, for the harvest is ripe. Come, go down; for the winepress is full, the vats overflow—for their wickedness is great" (Joel 3:13).

78. "A physical enactment of the seven feasts of God."

Jesus's death, resurrection, and promised return provide a powerful embodiment of the symbolism in the ancient annual festivals of Judaism. See "Christological Significance of the Seven Judaic Feasts" at the front of the book.

The Passover is particularly interesting in that even today Jewish families set a place for the prophet Elijah in the hope that he will come to proclaim the arrival of the Messiah during that significant feast. The modern Passover supper also includes an intriguing ceremony that seems directly relevant to Christianity. Unleavened dough is pierced to prevent rising, and three cooked *matzot* breads are placed in separate compartments of a specially designed bag that forms a triunity—three in one. At one stage of the ritual meal, the middle bread is taken out and broken, one half is put back (to be eaten as the "bread of affliction"), and the other half is wrapped in a cloth and hidden in the house. This is later brought back to provide the last food of the night. The *matzot* are said to possibly represent Abraham, Isaac, and Jacob, or the priests, Levites, and Israelites, but the unity of the three has strong Trinitarian implications. There is also no explanation for why one of these pierced breads is broken, wrapped, hidden, and brought back a second time to complete the sacramental meal. But it is powerfully reminiscent of Jesus's broken, pierced body being buried in a linen cloth, his claim: "This bread is my flesh" (John 6:51), and the expectation of his return.

79. "The grandeur of God's vast cosmic plan for His creation."

Through the work of Jesus, humanity and creation will finally be brought to a state that far exceeds the existence in Eden. The first Adam defied God's will, but Jesus's obedience as the last Adam has enabled him to enter God's presence as a representative of humanity. As Otfried Hofius explains, "Christ has not simply come alongside the sinner in order to take away something—namely, guilt and sin; he has rather become identical with the sinner, in order through the surrender of his life to lead sinners into union with God and thus to open them to fellowship with God for the first time. Christ thus dies not only 'in place of' the sinner; he dies 'for' him in such a way that his death is as such the sinner's death and his resurrection is as such the sinner's 'coming to God.' Therefore no restitution takes place here, but rather new creation . . . a *new* being that the sinner never before possessed" ("Fourth Servant," 174–75; original emphasis).

The Apostle Paul taught that Jesus's redeeming work will affect the entire creation (Col 1:19–20). In the words of C. S. Lewis, "Our species, rising after its long descent, will drag all Nature up with it because in our species the Lord of nature is now included . . . For God is not merely mending, not simply restoring a status quo. Redeemed humanity is to be something more glorious than unfallen humanity would have been" (*Miracles*, 198). This is the exhilarating, liberating, reassuring, and inspiring message of Christianity.

80. "I am the Alpha and the Omega, the First and the Last, the Beginning and the End" (Rev 22:13).

In the Old Testament, God is called "First and Last" (Isa 44:6), and in John's revelation vision, this name is bestowed upon the glorified Jesus. The first and last Greek letters, alpha and omega, correspond to the Hebrew aleph and tau, and the letter aleph is spelled using aleph, lamed, and peh. These letters are all highly symbolic:

- The pictograph for aleph is an ox head, which represents authority and power. Its symbol is a unity of three letters: two yods (which represent hand or God) connected by a vav, which means "hook" or "peg." In esoteric Judaism, the upper yod is said to represent the hidden aspects of God and the lower yod represents God as revealed to humanity.

- Lamed is associated with spiritual learning, and its pictograph is a shepherd's staff.

- Peh represents the power of the spoken word and is associated with holiness and prayer.

- Tau means mark or seal, and its pictograph is two crossed sticks. It symbolizes truth and perfection, and it is an emblem of infinity.

It might also be significant that Jesus's full Aramaic name, Yehoshua, is similar to the Tetragrammaton of God's name, YHWH, with the insertion of the Hebrew letter shin: a fiery crown that unites three branches of flame.

81. "A blissful peace that was beyond comprehension."

As an atheist, John C. Wright had his own experience of this supernatural peace. He admits that he found himself troubled by the implications of his logical analysis: "Each time I followed the argument fearlessly where it led, it kept leading me, one remorseless rational step at a time, to a position the Church had been maintaining for more than a thousand years. That haunted me . . . But it was impossible, logically impossible, that I should ever believe in such nonsense as to believe in the supernatural. It would be a miracle to get me to believe in miracles. So I prayed. 'Dear God, I know (because I can prove it with the certainty that a geometer can prove opposite angles are equal) that you do not exist. Nonetheless, as a scholar, I am forced to entertain the hypothetical possibility that I am mistaken. So just in case I am mistaken, please reveal yourself to me in some fashion that will prove your case . . . If you do not exist, this prayer is merely words in the air, and I lose nothing but a bit of my dignity. Thanking you in advance for your kind cooperation in this matter, John Wright.'"

John quips that God must have a sense of humor because he had a heart attack two days later. He describes his profound experience while awaiting surgery in hospital: "A sense of peace and confidence, a peace that passes all understanding, like a field of energy entered my body. I grew aware of a spiritual dimension of reality of which I had hitherto been unaware. It was like a man born blind suddenly receiving sight. The Truth to which my lifetime as a philosopher had been devoted turned out to be a living thing. It turned and looked at me. Something from beyond the reach of time and space, more fundamental than reality, reached across the universe and broke into my soul and changed me . . . I became aware of the origin of all thought, the underlying oneness of the universe, the nature of time: the paradox of determinism and free will was resolved for me. I saw and experienced part of the workings of a mind infinitely superior to mine, a mind able to count every atom in the universe, filled with paternal love and jovial good humor." John joined the church in 2008.

These extracts are reproduced with his kind permission, and his full account is available at https://strangenotions.com/wright-conversion/.

82. "Maranatha!"

The Aramaic *Maran* means "Our Lord," and the Apostle Paul used the phrase *Maranatha*, which means "Our Lord [Jesus] come" (1 Cor 16:22). As Paul's churches were largely Greek-speaking, this Aramaic tradition strongly indicates that the expectation of Jesus's return as divine Lord originated in Palestine.

To our human thinking, it might seem that Jesus's promise in Revelation that he will "come soon" has not been fulfilled. However, "a thousand years in Your sight are like yesterday when it is past" (Ps 90:4a), so that "one day is with the Lord as a thousand years, and a thousand years as one day" (2 Pet 3:8). We must be patient and continue to call out in faith: "*Maranatha!*"

Bibliography

Abegg Martin Jr., et al. *The Dead Sea Scrolls Bible: The Oldest Known Bible Translated for the First Time into English*. New York: HarperCollins, 1999.

Bauckham, Richard. *Jesus and the God of Israel*. Grand Rapids, MI: Eerdmans, 2009.

Bonhoeffer, Dietrich. *Psalms: The Prayer Book of the Bible*. Minneapolis: Augsburg Fortress, 1974.

Boyarin, Daniel. *The Jewish Gospels: The Story of the Jewish Christ*. New York: New Press, 2012.

Bruce, F. F. "The Background to the Son of Man Sayings." In *Christ The Lord: Studies in Christology presented to Donald Guthrie*, edited by H. H. Rowdon, 50–70. Leicester: InterVarsity, 1982.

Cross, Frank Moore. "Fragments of the Prayer of Nabonidus." *Israel Exploration Journal* 34 (1984) 260–64.

Dempster, Stephen G. *Dominion and Dynasty: A Biblical Theology of the Hebrew Bible*. New Studies in Bible Theology 15. Downers Grove, IL: InterVarsity, 2003.

Dunn, James D. G. *Christology in the Making: A New Testament Inquiry into the Origins of the Doctrine of the Incarnation*. 2nd ed. Grand Rapids, MI: Eerdmans, 1996.

Edersheim, Alfred. *The Life and Times of Jesus the Messiah*. Peabody, MA: Hendrickson, 2009.

Ehrman, Bart. *Jesus, Apocalyptic Prophet of the New Millennium*. New York: Oxford University Press, 1999.

Gibson, Simon. "The Excavations at the Bethesda Pool in Jerusalem: Preliminary Report on a Project of Stratigraphic and Structural Analysis (1999–2009)." *Proche-Orient Chrétien Numéro Spécial* (2011) 17–44.

Hengel, Martin. *The Atonement: The Origins of the Doctrine in the New Testament*. Translated by John Bowden. London: SCM, 1981.

———. "The Effective History of Isaiah 53 in the Pre-Christian Period." Translated by Daniel P. Bailey. In *The Suffering Servant: Isaiah 53 in Jewish and Christian Sources*, edited by Bernd Janowski, and Peter Stuhlmacher, 75–146. Grand Rapids, MI: Eerdmans, 2004.

———. *The "Hellenization" of Judaea in the First Century after Christ*. Translated by John Bowden. London: SCM, 1989.

García Martínez, Florentino, and Eibert J. C. Tigchelaar, eds. *The Dead Sea Scrolls Study Edition*. Leiden: Brill, 1999.

Hofius, Otfried. "The Fourth Servant in the New Testament Letters." Translated by Daniel P. Bailey. In *The Suffering Servant: Isaiah 53 in Jewish and Christian Sources*, edited by Bernd Janowski, and Peter Stuhlmacher, 163–88. Grand Rapids, MI: Eerdmans, 2004.

Johansson, Daniel. "'Who Can Forgive Sins but God Alone?' Human and Angelic Agents, and Divine Forgiveness in Early Judaism." *JSNT* 33 (2011) 351–74.

Klausner, Joseph. *The Messianic Idea in Israel: From its Beginning to the Completion of the Mishnah*. Translated by W. F. Stinespring. New York: Macmillan, 1955.

Kosior, Wojciech. "The Angel in the Hebrew Bible from the Statistic and Hermeneutic Perspectives: Some Remarks on the Interpolation Theory." *The Polish Journal of Biblical Research* 12 (2013) 55–69.

Lewis, C. S. *Miracles*. 1947. Reprint, London: Harper Collins, 2002.

Maeir, Aren M. 2013. "Israel and Judah." In *The Encyclopedia of Ancient History*, 3523–27.

Meier, Samuel A. "Angel I, Angel of Yahweh, Destroyer, Mediator I." In *DDD*, 81–90.

Rembaum, Joel E. "The Development of a Jewish Exegetical Tradition Regarding Isaiah 53." *Harvard Theological Review* 75 (1982) 289–311.

Segal, Alan. *Two Powers in Heaven: Early Rabbinic Reports about Christianity and Gnosticism*. 2nd ed. Leiden: Brill, 2002.

VanderKam, James. "Righteous One, Messiah, Chosen One, and Son of Man in 1 Enoch 37–71." In *The Messiah: Developments in Earliest Judaism and Christianity; The First Princeton Symposium on Judaism and Christian Origins*, edited by James H. Charlesworth, et al., 169–91. Minneapolis: Fortress, 1992.

Vermes, Geza. *The Complete Dead Sea Scrolls in English*. London: Penguin, 2004.

Vos, Geerhardus. Biblical Theology: Old and New Testaments. Carlisle, PA: Banner of Truth Trust, 2012.

Wise, Michael, et al., trans. *The Dead Sea Scrolls: A New Translation*. New York: HarperCollins, 2005.